I0664423

First Steps

The Richard Jackson Saga, Volume 16

Ed Nelson

Published by Eastern Shore Publishing, 2024.

Table of Contents

Other books by Ed Nelson

The Richard Jackson Saga

Book 1 The Beginning

Book 2 Schooldays

Book 3 Hollywood

Book 4 In the Movies

Book 5 Star to Deckhand

Book 6 Surfing Dude

Book 7 Third Time is a Charm

Book 8 Oxford University

Book 9 Cold War

Book 10 Taking Care of Business

Book 11 Interesting Times

Book 12 Escape from Siberia

Book 13 Regicide

Book 14 What's Under, Down Under?

Book 15 The Lunar Kingdom

Book 16 First Steps

In the Richard Jackson World

Mary, Mary

Stand-Alone Story

Ever and Always

Cast in Time Series

Book 1: Baron

Book 2: Baron of the Middle Counties

Book 3: Count

Book 4: Earl

Book 5: Earl of the Marches

Dedication

This book is dedicated to my wife Carol for her support and help as my first reader and editor.

Thanks to my editors, Old Rotorhead, Ernest Bywater, Lonely Dad, and Antti.

In Memory of Ernest Bywater 1954-2022

A great Australian and a good friend.

This fictional journey started with the Bellefontaine Ohio School class of 1962.

Professionally edited by Janet E. Rupert

Quotation

That's the way it happened, give or take a lie or two.

James Garner as Wyatt Earp describing the gunfight at the OK Corral in the movie *Sunset*.

Copyright © 2022

E. E. Nelson
All rights reserved
Eastern Shore Publishing
2331 West Del Webb Blvd.
Sun City Center, FL 33673

This story is a work of fiction. Names, characters, organizations, places, events, and incidents are either products of the author's imagination or are used fictitiously. Any resemblance to actual persons, living or dead, or actual events is purely coincidental.

ISBN 979-8-89434-020-3
Library of Congress Control Number: 20229113

Chapter 1

I had received a hand-delivered message that one of my teams had a possible lead on creating anti-gravity. Sending it by hand was the only safe way on the moon.

We had codes upon codes at this point, but we had groups like the secretive NSA working full-time to break our codes. There is no doubt that they could do this. Most people had never heard of this agency. The only reason I knew of them was an off-the-cuff comment made by a president.

I wasn't even going to say which president. I didn't think the NSA was aware I even knew they existed, which is fine. The UK and China have agencies like that, but I don't know their names. All I can do is act as though they exist and act appropriately.

Such a change from Hollywood actor to head of state. Don't they know it is not polite to read another person's mail?

That reminded me I had to check up on our program to intercept all messages sent through Earth satellites and a computer center on the moon to decrypt them. Yeah, I'm becoming a hypocrite.

Back to the anti-gravity, I made a quick trip to Earth to check up on May-ling. That was my announced reason.

Upon landing on Earth at the launch center, I was approached by a supervisor I knew well.

"This way, Your Majesty. We have a conference room arranged for a briefing."

"Thank you."

Waiting in the room were two people I had met before. They were from Jackson Research. They were older, in their early thirties.

"Thank you for meeting with us, Your Majesty."

"Forget the titles, and I'm Rick."

They both relaxed their stiff posture at that. I suppose they had never met a king before.

"I'm Tom, the division manager, and this is John from the team that made the discovery. Rick, you sent a sample of exotic ore found in the asteroid belt. We had several teams working on them. John's team came up with some curious results. John, would you share those with Rick?"

"Your, uh, Rick, We refined some of the sample and then made a thin coating out of it. We wanted to see how it would adhere to other substances. A one-meter square of steel was coated with the refined metal, which still has to be named.

"We hadn't tried to control its thickness at this point. Once the melted metal solidified, we ran several tests to see if the materials were bonded or if the ore would peel off easily. It didn't want to separate at all.

"We needed to bring the ore back to red hot before we could begin to scrape it off. Even that was a long and tedious process. A technician was assigned to heat the metal and use a chisel to remove the ore coating.

"The technician went on his lunch break. He left a piece of test equipment on the workbench. He didn't realize that the electric cord was in contact with the coated steel plate. Since the plate was hot, it melted the electric cord.

"When the technician returned from lunch, the steel plate was now floating in the air. It had risen about six inches. The only thing restraining it was the electric wire which was now fused to the plate.

"To say this caused a ruckus is putting it mildly."

As he told me this, he opened a folder with black and white pictures of the steel plate in the air.

"Our team gathered and brainstormed on what to do next. We feared losing the anti-gravity effect forever if we changed anything. We gathered as much information as possible before trying anything as extreme as turning anything off and on."

I broke in, "That was well thought out. What did you find?"

"We measured everything as precisely as we could. We now measured the coating thickness, which was an uneven paint job. It averaged out as five mils, about what is used on automobiles.

"Next was the electric current. It was DC, nothing irregular about it. We sent a request to the steel provider for the metallurgical breakdown of the steel used to form the plate.

"Times, temperature, humidity, and even the phase of your moon were recorded."

"You know it is not actually my moon, just a portion of it."

"Oh, I thought it was all yours now."

"It may come to that, but not yet. What other findings did you make?"

"We then started loading weights on the plate. It made no difference up to one thousand pounds. That was as high as we could go with what we had available.

"Next, we hot spliced a longer wire to the equipment cord. As soon as it was plugged in and the direct wire disconnected, the plate rose to the limit of the cord.

"We then attached a rheostat to the circuit. When we varied the current, the plate would rise and lower according to the input. We found that a sharp increase in wattage caused the plate to move faster. We found that we could stabilize the plate's height by keeping the wattage at 1500 watts. This was all done with the weights still in place."

"What were your next steps?"

"It had been a long day, and we were mentally exhausted, so we locked the room and left it guarded by security."

Tom said, "We also set up CCTV to record the plate and the doorway all night so we could tell if anyone tried to enter the room without authorization."

"Good thinking."

John continued, "After reviewing all the data and concluding that we had collected everything we could, our next step was to see if we could turn it completely off. That was almost a disaster."

"What happened?"

"As I was reaching to unplug the electrical cord, Anne, one of our teammates, yelled, "Stop!"

I was glad I did. She pointed out I was about to drop a thousand pounds of loose weights in the middle of the room."

We unloaded the weights, thanking Anne many times along the way. I lowered the steel plate to within half an inch of the table. We were now recording everything on CCTV to show you the results. I left them under lock and key at the Research Center as I assume security on this project is very high."

"As high and tight as it can be made. I need a list of everyone in the know currently. No one is to be added to the list without my say."

"Okay, but we will have to bring others into it eventually."

"I understand, but we need to be careful. Just so you know, I intend to run a background check on everyone in the know. If they have a financial problem, it will be taken care of, and we will help them with anything we can. Desperation will make people do things they would never consider otherwise."

I'm glad I read all those spy novels.

"What about someone with a gambling problem or something like that?"

"I'm certain they will enjoy their new job on the moon. Not imprisonment, but no opportunity to get in trouble. How many people are we talking about anyway?"

"There are six of us."

"The odds are then that no one will have any problems that cause concern. We have to see where this goes, but all of you will be well rewarded."

"We just got sidetracked."

"What happened when you turned the current off?"

"The plate came down with a thunk! It would have been a mess if those weights had been on it, and we might have been killed."

"We must make certain that Anne gets a special reward."

"Is a trip to the moon possible? That is all she talks about."

"I think I can make that happen. Now you're killing me. Were you able to turn it back on, and did it work?"

John started to draw his answer out as a tease, but the look I gave changed his mind.

Almost as one word, it came out.

"I plugged it back in, and the plate returned to its position."

"It looks like we have anti-gravity. I have to give some thought as to what to do next. By the way, who was the technician who melted the electric cord to the ore?"

"Frank Evans."

"The name of the ore is evantonium."

Chapter 2

I had just stepped out of the conference room when a thought hit me. I turned around before the others had even stood up. "We seem to have anti-gravity. What about gravity?"

From the blank looks I received, they didn't understand.

"We can make things lighter. Can we make them heavier?"

Tom replied, "We have been so focused on anti-gravity that we haven't given higher gravity a thought. I don't see how that would be possible."

"Have you tried anything simple like reversing the polarity of the current?"

"No."

"Try that and see what happens. I suggest putting a small scale on the plate and a one-pound weight when you try it. Also, I think it is time to upgrade the safety of the testing. Separate rooms for the observers and the testbed. We dodged a bullet, thanks to Anne. Let's not tempt fate again."

"A new test suite is in the process of being set up as we speak."

Another thought came to my mind.

"Do you think we could talk your crew into running all their tests on the moon in the near future? I'm certain that it is the only way to keep it secret. I would pay for everything, including moving families if needed."

"Can I discuss it with my group?"

"Tom, I want everyone's positive buy-in. As I said earlier, it isn't imprisonment, but I would like to limit the spying opportunities until we have working models."

"I will call a team meeting as soon as John and I get back to California."

I asked John, "How would you feel about working on the moon?"

"I would have to discuss it with my wife. What would we do about schooling our two kids? They are in the first and fourth grades."

"We already have a school set up, so that won't be a problem. Also, there is a fully staffed hospital on site."

I chuckled as I added, "We don't have much in the way of outdoor activities yet. But we do have a large play area inside the base. As an additional incentive, I will double everyone's salary. My new kingdom hasn't instituted an income tax yet. There are no promises for the future, but any taxes wouldn't be retroactive."

Tom broke in, "Count me in."

John spoke up right behind him, "Me, too."

"It looks like Anne's trip to the moon has become a tour group."

Once more, we shook hands, and I departed. My next stop was to the Forbidden City to see my wife.

On the short flight to Beijing, I thought about the ramifications of controlling gravity. The possibilities were mind-boggling. I didn't write anything down. Maybe I was paranoid, but this had to be handled carefully.

Once at the palace, I went immediately to May-ling's suite. I called it hers because I spent little time there. This was a sad state of events, but the reality was that we lived two different lives. I had no idea how this would work out in the long run.

I did know that I would make it work out. I loved her, and she is the mother of my child.

She was waiting for me. We had two hours of personal time before any meetings. We used them wisely.

After our first frantic hour, we brought each other up to date on what we had done. Mostly administrative matters. When it came time for me to tell her about our advances in controlling gravity, I wrote a note asking if the room might be bugged.

She nodded yes.

We both needed a shower at that point, so I could whisper under the running water what had been discovered. She asked if she could share it at this time. I asked her not to until we knew for certain that it worked. We had just taken our first steps.

She was okay with that. It made me feel good. It was us against the world. Not just the world but the whole solar system!

When we were dressed for our meetings, her baby bump was noticeable. I loved to feel her belly, knowing a new life was growing there. Our new life.

A son would be wonderful, someone to teach how to be a man or play baseball. A daughter was a scary thought. I made a vow that I wouldn't be wrapped around her finger. Right.

I pity the fool who would try to date my little girl.

May-ling's maternity clothes were decorated with good luck charms in gold thread. She told me pictures were taken for the state media every time she appeared in a new outfit.

The Chinese people followed her pregnancy avidly. The rest of the world even showed some interest. A division of Mary's company was coming out with a line of maternity clothes based on May-ling's.

Mary's new company had a different name, The Modern Woman, and had no direct link to her young lady's clothing line. A connection might imply encouragement where it wasn't needed!

Security guards escorted us when we left the suite, and May-ling had two secretaries vying for her attention on different issues.

Our first meeting was on the state of the new province of Siberia. I was there as a courtesy.

Things were advancing well.

The summer harvest was ready to start in their short growing season. Rye was doing particularly well, to the point that it could be exported. Other crops were making the Siberians self-sufficient. These were barley, wheat, buckwheat, and millet. Vegetables like peas, cabbage, turnips, carrots, onions, and garlic made for a decent diet.

The tsars and the following communist governments had mismanaged agriculture badly. Now using crop rotation and tractor-drawn equipment, the land was productive. These tractors were the most expensive part of developing Siberia.

Butter production was one thing the Russians got right until their internal politics messed it up. This was now being revived and promised to be a great success.

There was some fur trapping going on, but it wasn't encouraged. The empress had decided the government would be neutral on the issue.

Evidence had been found that copper, zinc, manganese, nickel, chromium, molybdenum, cobalt, rare earths, and silicon were all present. Efforts were underway to mine the various ores. It would take several years before the results were known.

I couldn't help but think about how anti-gravity would affect the mining industry. The ability to send supplies and ship out ores from the most remote areas would be priceless.

The Chinese viewed Siberia as a new frontier that gave them hope for a better life. If used wisely, it would. The Siberian wealth was enormous. Even better was the relief valve provided for population growth.

While the information was interesting, what I found fascinating was the maneuvering and turf fights among the department heads. They were all trying to get a bigger share of funding for their groups, irrespective of their actual needs.

Presiding over the meeting, the empress allowed it to continue for a while. She then told them each what their department's portion would be.

This shut them up but raised another question in my mind. She had her numbers down pat. How did she decide on them? It was obvious that these had been decided upon before this meeting. Was there an earlier meeting?

Meetings upon meetings were giving me a headache. Was this my fate?

After the meeting, May-ling and I adjourned to the empress's dining room for lunch. I asked her how the budget numbers had been decided. It seemed she had an independent team keeping track of the logistics needed to develop Siberia to China's advantage.

At least I was doing something right with my teams working on the issues I faced.

I asked her if the pace ever let up, and she told me it didn't. If anything, the pace was always increasing.

At the moment, she was trying to decide if Tibet should be given its freedom. The communists had invaded Tibet in the early 1950s, based on claims going back to 1720.

She saw it as nothing but a drain on China's resources for the foreseeable future. She was inclined to let them go with a strong treaty binding them together.

I again thought about what anti-gravity would do for transportation through the Himalayas. Without any information, I was on the side of the Tibetans. They weren't historical Chinese and wanted to preserve their way of life.

I had no idea what that way of life was but had never heard anything horrible, so I was inclined to let them live it. I knew I would never try yak butter if I had my way.

I tried to joke about that, but my wife and her grandmother didn't see anything funny. They thought it was wonderful in tea.

Chapter 3

I received a phone call from my sister Mary. This was very unusual, to say the least. First, with our ten-year age differences, we had little to chit-chat about over long distance. The fact it was a long distance was even stranger.

She had to stay far beyond her normal bedtime to make this call. Mum had always been strict about bedtimes when we were young. I remember cleaning my room, getting it inspection ready every day for weeks, to be able to stay up half an hour later to watch *Sargeant Bilko*.

Mum would inspect my work, and the day wouldn't count unless it passed. It took me six weeks to complete the deal.

To my knowledge, she hadn't lightened up at all, so whatever Mary was calling about was important, at least to Mary.

"Hi, short stuff, what's up?"

"I want to invite you and May-ling to Stockholm, Sweden, on December 10 for the Nobel Prize awards. I was notified today that I'm the winner in physics."

"Congratulations! May-ling and I will be there. That, of course, depends on when the baby arrives. It is due about that time."

"I'm so glad, Rick."

"That's not why you called, though, is it?"

"What do you mean?"

"What did you have to do for Mum to stay up this late past bedtime?"

"Oh poo, you are no fun. I have to wash dishes after dinner every day for two weeks."

"Wow, it must be important. You know it will cost you."

"What! You won't do something for free for your baby sister?"

"I know what my baby sister is like when she goes for Boardwalk and Park Place, so no!"

"Please, Ricky, will you help me?"

There had never been a question that I wouldn't help her. I just wanted to have some fun with the little wretch.

"What do you need help with? No blank checks. I did that for you once and ended up wearing a tutu at your kindergarten show and tell."

"But you were so cute. All the girls liked you."

Just what I wanted, a bunch of six-year-old fans.

"Give it up, Mary. What do you need?"

"Do you remember that container full of clothes that had to be abandoned out in space?"

"Yeah, last seen, it was headed out towards Mars."

"I would like you to retrieve it."

"What for?"

"You know we were sending those clothes to the moon with the idea of returning them to Earth and auctioning them off as having been to the moon. The money would have fed a lot of puppies."

"I bet those puppies are fat."

"Meany! There are always more puppies that need feeding."

I wonder how that happens. Rather than feeding them, Daddy should be snipped.

"What would you do with the clothes now?"

"We would auction them off. The auction would be for retro clothes that were lost in space."

"They were only lost a few months ago."

"Silly, they are from last season, so they are now retro."

"My mistake."

"The fact they were lost in space will make them worth a lot more. We ran the idea past a focus group of young ladies. They would pay ten times the tag price for one of them."

"That's not bad. Your stuff isn't the cheapest out there."

"We don't use the word cheap; there are less expensive brands, but ours are the best designed, made by expert seamstresses using the finest fabrics to the highest standards."

"You've been hanging around the advertising group for too long."

"They are fun people. They have taught me how to improve my negotiation skills by upselling my product."

Nope, never going to play Monopoly with her again.

"Since we now have the hyper-speed rockets, we can catch the clothes. I doubt if they will be out past Mars yet. It is going to cost you."

"How much?"

"Don't name it, but you remember that project I asked you to think about?"

"Yes, I do. I have some thoughts, but it would take some trial and error to test them out."

"JE Research has several working prototype models. I would like you to look at them and see if you can establish how they work. It was a serendipitous discovery. It works, but we don't know why."

"Oh, I would love to be part of that."

"Who knows, you might receive a second Nobel for that."

"That would be so cool. I would have two, and Patty wouldn't have any! She was jealous when I called her about winning mine. She talks to her grandfather about how she can win a Peace Prize."

"I never associated the word peace with you two."

Mary giggled a bit. "She is thinking about starting a war between two countries and then settling it with peace talks. Her grandfather knows how to start wars."

What will JFK say when I call him about a ten-year-old girl starting a war?

We made plans to go to JE Research when May-ling and I are in California next week.

After hanging up, I couldn't wait to tell May-ling about my kookie sister and her plan to auction off the lost-in-space clothes.

I was surprised when I was informed that my sister wasn't a kook. She was a marketing genius. I knew she was a genius in mathematics and physics, but marketing?

May-ling also told me, "Rick, you have to let me choose several outfits from the cargo container so we can save them for our daughter when she is old enough."

I stuttered for a moment, "We are having a girl?"

"If not this time, one of our four children should be a girl. I had our family trees checked out, and the odds are that if not the first, at least the second will be a female."

"Oh," was my weak reply.

"Those outfits will be worth a fortune, and any young lady who wears them will be considered of high social standing."

"I would think that being the daughter of a king and prospective empress would do that."

"Fashion is better. A poorly dressed princess is to be pitied. Our daughter won't be poorly dressed."

"Yes, dear."

I had learned a few things about married life already.

She continued, "It will be best if you have Mary write a letter of authenticity for them. Some TV shows I have watched say that will help the dresses go up in value."

I replied, "If nothing else, by the time our daughter is grown enough to wear them, they will be back in style."

"The style may come around once more, but these will be the ultimate in retro."

At this point, I regretted that cargo of clothes. I wished it had fallen into the Sun. But then my daughter might end up considered a fashion-challenged princess. What a horrible fate. How our daughter could be considered fashion-challenged, I couldn't fathom. We were the wealthiest people in the world. But I was a mere male.

After that conversation, I called the mission control center at the launch site and told them to set up a flight to retrieve the missing dresses.

Since I was the boss, no one argued, but you could tell they wondered what the heck I had been smoking. To confuse them even further, I made it a 1A priority flight. This was the same priority given to human rescue.

I told them I wanted the flight plan on my desk first thing in the morning.

The boss usually gets what the boss wants. The flight plan was waiting for me the next morning. It would be a nine-day flight to catch up with the capsule, a day to transfer its contents, and ten days back.

The longer time to get back was because the capsule would be moving further away from the Earth all the time.

I thought about having a thermite grenade placed on the capsule after emptying it. That way, no one could have the bright idea of trying to retrieve it later. Safety considerations led me to change my mind. I hope I don't regret that decision in the future.

I sent a telegram to Mary telling her all had been arranged. I wasn't going to stay up until the middle of the night to call her. My mum had probably taught May-ling how to handle people staying up past bedtime.

I shared everything at dinner with May-ling, the empress, and several ambassadors to China. All the ladies present thought Mary was brilliant. The guys had a blank look. None of the men were foolish enough to express an opinion.

The next day May-ling and I began our journey to the United States. I hadn't seen my family in a while, and the anti-gravity project was the most important thing on my plate.

That didn't mean I got off without any paperwork on the flight. Running a kingdom was tough, especially when even your toilet paper was imported.

Chapter 4

Until I became the king of Luna and the Solar Reaches, I could easily fly into the United States. Just file a flight plan and go. Now I had to let the State Department know when I would be arriving and why. Nothing had been said about being denied permission to enter, but I understood my U.S. citizenship was now in question.

King of Luna and the Solar Reaches is too much to say all the time, so I'm going to use King of Luna. Even the late-night show King of Lunatics would be better.

This time it was for a family visit and an update on my U.S. holdings. Holdings instead of businesses. If I bought another house there, would it be my demesne? The medieval term made me think of knights jousting. I wondered if we could do that on the moon. Nah.

We flew into Ontario International Airport, where a representative of the U.S. State Department was waiting to welcome me. From his age and how he was dressed, you could tell that my arrival was not considered much consequence.

When he realized that May-ling was accompanying me, he went pale. Apparently, the arrival of the Crown Princess of China was a big deal. Way over his pay grade.

It was the State Department's problem since I had notified them that my wife would be accompanying me. If anything, this was a good thing as no press was waiting for us.

An airport van took us to my waiting Cessna. I flew us to the forest ranger base, where we were picked up by a waiting limo.

At Jackson House, the whole family was there. Hugs were given all around. It was so good to see everyone again. May-ling had previously met everyone before, so she was welcomed without great fanfare. Well, that is except for my parents, who were soon to be grandparents. They both were excited.

She was informed that a nursery room was being furnished. They just needed to know if the child was a boy or a girl.

It was strange that for so many years, my mum had told me she wasn't ready to be a grandmum yet. Now she couldn't wait. Dad had a large grin, and I think he would be handing out many a cigar.

Mum, Dad, and May-ling disappeared to check out the new room. As they were leaving the room, I heard, "Of course, there will be a registered nurse on duty at all times and a doctor on call."

No, they wouldn't be doting grandparents at all.

After my parents absconded with May-ling, I could catch up with my brothers and sister. I was lucky we had arrived in the early afternoon, so Mary was out of whatever school she was attending today.

It was hard to think of her attending the fourth grade and Stanford University simultaneously.

Denny was his usual self. It seemed he had chosen his lifestyle. Free and easy. His photography studios were making him a ton of money. They were now a national chain. His work was now making personal appearances at grand openings.

He continued his passion for real-life photography and won prizes for capturing the human condition. His other passion was women, all of them. Still, he is my brother, and nothing was evil in him. He was like the proverbial four-horned billy goat, two on top and two below.

I asked Eddie what he had been up to.

"The usual. I've been road racing a lot. I tried NASCAR but got tired of driving in big circles all the time. Paul Newman got me interested in the course at Watkins Glen, and I love it."

"How is your sponsorship?"

"We're set for this season, but if I need help, I will give you a call. That reminds me, could we set up a cross-country rally on the moon?"

"Hmm, I don't know if it would be feasible or if it would get a bunch of people killed. Let me have some people check it out. It could be fun."

"Thanks, Bro."

"Bro?"

"New term for brother. Think it started in the ghettos."

"Oh, street slang, not to be used by us kings."

As I said that, I put my nose in the air. All three of them found small cushions to throw at me. It was good to be home.

"Mary, how is school going for you?"

"Things aren't very good right now."

"How? Are the teachers loading you with too much work?"

"Oh no, that part is easy. I'm ahead of most of my teachers. I've got a request in to test out of all my current classes."

"Does that include your fourth-grade lunches?"

She giggled at that, "No, you can't test out of lunch. You have to eat your way out."

"Silly me. Then what is not going okay?"

"My sorority is becoming boring."

"I thought you guys were on double-secret probation or something like that for being party animals."

"We were, but that is over."

"Congratulations."

"No, it is terrible, and it is all my fault."

"What did you do?"

"Because my dress company is famous and you married the Crown Princess of China and then became King of the Moon, all the social climbers have been joining. Then I had to win that stupid Nobel, and now the brains all want in."

"So, your sorority is becoming respectable."

"Not only that, some of the best party animals have already moved out of our house because it is now boring."

She practically wailed when she told me, "By the time I'm old enough to be a real party animal, we will be an old lady's knitting society."

"The horror! Why don't you have a bunch of the members run naked across the quad? That will get things going."

How was I to know I had just invented streaking?

"That's a great idea! Thanks, Ricky, you are my best brother! That will get us in trouble and put us back on double-secret probation, and all the dull people will leave."

"Party time!" she yelled.

I don't think they can extradite kings.

My brothers both smirked at me. Almost in unison, they said, "I'm going to tell Mum."

It was good to be home until they told on me.

Mum, Dad, and May-ling rejoined us, and we were served coffee and tea. Mum even made certain to have yak butter available. May-ling had some, and I tried to talk my siblings into trying it. It turned out Mum had already forced some on them, and there was no way they were going to repeat the experience.

As we had our drinks, mine black coffee, talk turned to the container of clothes that was now lost in space. That wasn't really true, as we had always known its trajectory out of the solar system. I even had a vision of the far future in which an alien race would find them and a new fashion craze would start.

Life was good between sips of coffee and a bite of upside-down pineapple cake.

The women all had ideas of what to do with the dresses. Most would be sold at charity auctions. The retrieval was being made public, so the news was spreading worldwide.

It would be another week before the clothes were back on Earth, but already there were many requests. The Smithsonian and the London Museum of Natural History had asked for something.

One of the dresses had been designed by a young French lady on Mary's design staff. We decided to donate her design to the Louvre. In doing so, the designer could open her own high couture house.

The women agreed that several outfits had to be set aside for future granddaughters. None of them wanted any fashion-challenged offspring.

It got so bad that I was asked if I could "lose" a shipment of boys' clothes.

I looked at Dad, and he shrugged his shoulders. He wasn't about to get involved.

"I'm not about to commit fashion fraud! However, I suspect we could send a capsule full of clothes on a long-term test to see how fabrics hold up in space."

I was learning that some battles shouldn't be fought. This was one of them.

Denny and Eddie both sneered at me. Let them. Their turn would come.

A phone rang in the background, and a few moments later, a maid whom I had never met came in and informed the group as a whole that the President of the United States was on the line for King Richard of the Lunar Kingdom and the Solar Reaches.

She managed to get that out all in one breath without fainting. She must be new to the house, or it would have been, "Hey Ricky, the prez is on the line. Should I tell him to call back?"

We weren't really that loose in our talk and actions, but it was fun to think of.

I picked up the phone next to the coffee table. Its ringer had been shut off so it wouldn't interfere with our conversations.

"Richard Jackson here."

Hold one moment for the president.

"King Richard, I just discovered you are visiting your parents."

"May-ling and I will be here for a few days."

"Could I entice you and May-ling to visit Jackie and me in the White House this trip?"

"Any reason besides the photo op, Mr. President?"

"Nothing underhanded, I assure you, Rick. We don't have a trade agreement with your kingdom, and I would like to start the process. Also, a photo op would help. My popularity has taken the normal dip before mid-term elections, so this could give me a boost."

"Always glad to help an honest politician."

"Hey, I always stay bought!"

"That's what I like about you. Not the staying bought but the directness."

"Now, if we could only get Bobbie and Teddy to understand that."

"Good luck."

Chapter 5

After discussing the White House visit with May-ling, we agreed to attend a State Dinner in a week. I hadn't figured out how it turned from an informal phone call to a State Dinner, but JFK would get his photo op. He certainly was a politician's politician.

May-ling, Mary, and I were taken by limo to the JE Research campus the next day. It was done quietly. No motorcycles escorting us with sirens blaring. The first time it happened to me, it was thrilling. Now it was a pain.

Several unmarked cars were around us, but they didn't stand out. I had no problem with that. After all, it is for my wife's and unborn child's safety.

Upon arrival, we were received with no ceremony. That was at my request. While the ceremony was as much for the people I was visiting as showing respect, they took up time. As someone famous once said, "Ask me for anything but time!"

We were taken directly to the anti-gravity test area. I was glad to see that they had several security checkpoints that had to be passed on the way in. The final checkpoint was limited to those who were already on the project.

There was a well-set-up conference room, which to me meant they had coffee, tea, and donuts. There were even sodas or hot chocolate for Mary. There was no yak butter for May-ling's tea, but I was too much of a gentleman to bring it up.

I did slip a note to Tom that May-ling liked yak butter in her tea. I'm certain there would be some available if she ever returned this way. Since we were near Chinatown in LA, there would be some available.

We were brought up to date on their current findings. My suggestion of reversing polarity had been tried. It was an off the top of my head thought. It worked!

Once polarity was reversed, the gravity field increased. A scale had been set on the metal plate coated with evantonium. A calibrated one-pound weight was set on it. They found they could change the current amplitude in the same values as the negative scale and correspondingly increase the weight shown on the scale.

They then built a simple control panel to change currents and polarity to any setting they liked. To this point, they could increase the weight of the one-pound test piece to tons. These settings could be enough to destroy the test rig. They didn't try that again.

"What are your next steps, Tom?"

"We want to try it with AC as everything has been with DC so far. Also, we would like to vary the cycles to see if there is a better rate for the process."

"Do you have anything set up to run?"

"Yes, the transformer that increases or decreases gravity is ready to run."

We all adjourned to the test area. As requested, we weren't in the actual room where the test was run. Our room was more like a bunker at the launch site. We would see the test on CCTV.

The test run was flawless. Tom operated the control panel, which varied current and polarity. He could move the apparent gravity up and down at will. Safety stops were built into the transformer to stop anything from sinking into the earth or lifting the roof off.

We were all in awe of what we were seeing; that is, all but Mary, who was muttering to herself.

"Mr. Einstein, you have a lot to answer for." Or something like that.

She had a notebook and was making notes like crazy. All of a sudden, she shouted, "Eureka!"

I asked her what her breakthrough was.

She said, "Nothing. I have always wanted to yell that."

My look to her must have been sour as all get out.

"Ricky, I do think I understand what is happening here and can even develop the math to explain it. I wanted to have a little fun at the same time."

They had better shut that sorority down before she was of age.

"Can you explain it simply?"

"Yes, the electricity is being shunted from the evantonium to another dimension. It turns out that gravity is a much stronger force than we thought. Most of it is exerted through one of the dimensions posited by the Closed Unoriented Bosonic String Theory. These are twenty-six dimensions of the traceless Jordan algebra J3(O)o of 3×3 Octonionic matrices."

So much for simplicity.

"Does sending this force through a different dimension put us in any danger?"

"Oh, no. If it did, the universe would have already collapsed or blown up."

Good to know.

While we were discussing this, the test was completed, and the chamber was set up to use alternating current rather than direct.

It didn't take very long at all. Tom turned on the first level of AC to see how gravity would react.

It reacted violently. The explosion compressed the room we were in. Later, they measured it and found that the walls had moved by six inches on the explosion side.

We were all thrown to the floor. Fortunately, I somehow landed under May-ling to cushion her fall.

Our room was over one hundred linear feet from the test room. Everything between us at the test site was destroyed.

We were shaken but not stirred to quote Mr. Bond. There was some minor bruising, but all would have died if I hadn't insisted on the safety precautions.

Mary had a comment when the dust literally settled.

"Take that, Mr. Edison! That will teach you to electrocute puppies!"

Interestingly, she knew about the fight between Tesla and Edison over AC and DC currents. That was not a pleasant story.

We returned to our original conference room. There was a very brief lesson learned. It boiled down to, "Don't run AC through evantonium."

Mary told us she thought she knew why that was so but would have to work on the math to prove it.

Jokingly, I told her, "Once you have that worked out, you will be up for a second Nobel Prize. I suggest you start working on faster-than-light travel for your third."

"I think I know how to do that, but we don't have the necessary new element to create the fields."

Barbie dolls, sororities, and Nobel Prizes—that is my sister.

We all agreed that we had enough excitement for one day, so we agreed to meet tomorrow to discuss possible uses of our gravity work.

At home, May-Ling and I adjourned for a nap, and other indoor sports considered normal after extreme danger.

For dinner, we were going to one of Mum's charity events. Mum wanted to remind the donor world that she could bring heavy firepower if needed. Namely a king and crown princess.

One nice thing about the evening was that we were fed quite well. Mum hated the rubber chicken circuit and went to extremes to provide wonderful meals.

We didn't have to go out as the event was at Jackson House. We sat down as a mere fifty for dinner. Every seat had its own serving footman. I didn't peek into the kitchen setup, but it must have been like a scene from Hell. Hell's Kitchen.

Hell, or not, my steak tenderloin was cooked exactly as I liked it. It wasn't strange that I wasn't allowed to drink all the wines in each course because I was underage in the U.S. If Mum or Dad poured me a glass in California, it was allowed, but not the wait staff.

I wouldn't have any anyway because May-ling wouldn't drink during her pregnancy. Chinese doctors had advocated this for centuries. U.S. doctors were coming around to this way of thinking.

Since we were sitting next to Anna Romanov, the table conversation was brilliant and fun. A shopping expedition was set for tomorrow. May-ling told me she would be accompanying them.

My reply was, "Yes, dear."

This statement set off all the women within hearing distance in whoops of laughter.

May-ling and I had circulated through the crowd during the cocktail hour with our Cokes in hand. We had done our round of polite talk for Mum and were able to escape, er withdraw, right after dessert.

The next morning, I returned to JE Research while May-ling got ready to go shopping. Mary wouldn't be attending today as she had lunch with her school friends and a Stanford physics department meeting. I think the school was still trying to figure out how to get their hands in her pocket over fusion.

Wait until they hear about gravity fields. They will have a cow.

I was looking forward to today because we were bringing the discovery into the real world.

Chapter 6

My trip to JE Research was much quicker today because I had a helicopter service pick me up and take me there. The drive around LA was long and a waste of time. I am licensed to fly helicopters but have not checked out on this large passenger model.

I'm seriously considering buying one for each of my Jackson Houses and keeping them on standby. They are so much more convenient.

I allowed a bit of ceremony today. The people had earned it, and I had picked up an hour by flying.

The ceremony was an all-hands affair in the main presentation area. It was more like a movie theater with a stage and all. I was introduced by the research head and gave a five-minute impromptu speech. I was getting a lot of practice at it these days.

Adjacent to the conference room, a large breakout area was set up with morning refreshments. I had to wonder about that. I agreed to this session at the last minute, yet they had all this ready.

I had to ask if this had been laid on for every day of my visit and gone to waste or if they were miracle workers. It turned out neither; there were many scientific presentations, and this was the normal daily fare.

I did the meet and greet with coffee in hand with the two hundred or so employees present. Most of them were pleasant introductions. A few turned into hard sells of personal projects. The research head who accompanied me took note of each project mentioned. I made no commitments about them.

I murmured, "That sounds interesting," to each of them. I suspect they would be in for an uncomfortable meeting later today.

This session went on for an hour or so. After people met me, they would depart for their work area. That is except for one young lady who kept flirting with me. I didn't respond to any of her lures which included bending over in a low-cut dress, but she kept trying.

I finally got tired and asked her if she shouldn't be at her workstation. This cold question seemed to bring her to her senses as she fled the room. I wondered if she would be employed here at this time tomorrow. I had no feelings about that either way.

The research head wanted to say something, but he held it back. We both ended up acting as though the incident never occurred.

With that torture over, I proceeded to the day's main event, a discussion on the possibilities of our varying gravity device.

It had been easy calling it anti-gravity, which semantically spoke of making things lighter. After a five-minute discussion on what to call it, we settled on gravity control. I won't relate to how silly some of the suggestions got. If nothing else, it made the mood a lot lighter.

It was amazing how word of that young lady's embarrassing and failed attempts had spread. I revised my thoughts about being employed tomorrow to thinking she was being escorted out the door right now.

I thought about relating the story of the stewardess who was naked in my bed on a flight but decided that it shouldn't make the public rounds. Besides, I was now a married man. I didn't need scandal attached to my name.

We then got down to serious business. On one of the new whiteboards, uses would be written down.

The first and most obvious was one earth gravity for the moon colony. Beside the possibility was another column for unanswered problems.

With the colony, the biggest yet-to-be-answered question was how large an area could be "controlled"? This meant how much current would need to be applied. Simply put, would we need to dedicate outlets in every room, or could one large connection handle the issue?

There was a possibility that we would have to have many separate areas painted with the ore solution and electrified. A series of experiments were planned to answer this question.

The second possibility discussed was installing it on all of our spacecraft to make travel more comfortable. I was most interested in this one as I hated the toilets in those things. I realized this even held somewhat for those on the moon.

The experiments already proposed would answer the useability on our spacecraft.

The third major thought was using gravity control to lift objects into orbit. The unanswered question here was what would be used for propulsion? Was there a balance that would allow a platform to "float" to orbit, then take off to outer space, or would we need to reduce weight to Earth neutral and then provide rocket assist?

After the top three came a long list covering everything from trains, planes, and ships. All could be replaced.

The armies and the air forces of the world would love the device. The navies, not so much. An air force could have an entire airfield lifted and moved like the current aircraft carriers. The airfields could be made into virtual fortresses with underground facilities.

The army could move as much artillery into position as they desired. Why have paratroops when a landing platform with several companies and a unit of tanks could come down anywhere?

Marines would never assault a beachhead again. The face of warfare would be changed dramatically.

As I had previously thought, remote areas could be served easily. The world was changing.

This led me to think of the changes already in progress. The fusion reactors were built and put in place worldwide. The infrastructure was being placed underground as much as possible.

Over five million people were employed in the effort worldwide last time I was updated. The United States and most of western Europe had ninety percent of their wiring underground at this point.

While the electricity was being put into underground troughs, deals had been made to run new telephone lines, so they also were out of sight. The troughs were designed to run new wiring without digging everything up.

Asia and Africa were the big challenges. They had the labor, but they didn't need electricity yet! A peasant village in India didn't have TV, radios, or telephones in every home. One phone might serve the whole village. The power source, in many cases, was pedal-powered generators.

There was no handy solution for this except time. In time their economies would improve, and their needs would develop.

Australia was doing well in the populated areas. The Outback probably would remain the Outback for the foreseeable future.

Along these lines, one of my teams was tracking the labor force of each continent. The United States was our most advanced situation. Soon they would have more workers than needed as the infrastructure was put in place. This was offset by older workers retiring and not being replaced, as those entering the workplace were more educated and could handle more complex jobs.

I was under no illusion that it would work for everyone. I hoped there would be few enough of these so that the local social safety nets could handle these cases.

If not, I was prepared to offer further support to local governments but didn't want to get into a direct payment situation. My team estimated this approach would work for almost ten years until crunch time.

Crunch time is when countries like Pakistan and India have more workers than needed with few safety nets. All we could do was keep looking for new work for them.

I discussed this with May-ling as we updated each other on our projects. She pointed out that Africa would be far behind the rest of the world. Why didn't we start hiring third-world labor and moving them to Africa?

This would delay even more the third-world excess labor problem. In Africa, where things weren't about to move as fast, we didn't need to bring in heavy equipment. For example, using small bulldozers would get the job done but would be slower and require more manpower, yet not slow down the overall development of Africa.

Brilliant!

I was yanked out of my reverie back to the world of gravity control.

"Rick, the room size test has started and looks promising. It appears that we would need the equivalent of one light socket for every two thousand square feet."

I ordered, "Once these have been confirmed, shut everything down here and remove all evidence of what we have been doing. Move everything to the moon. We have an area already prepared behind the fusion machines' manufacturing area, so security is already in place.

"Also, assemble a testbed large enough to hold a fusion generator for power and two hyperjet engines. Put housing for passengers on board."

He didn't question my order. It was a good thing because I didn't think why I might need it quickly.

"Also, the exploration people have been told to make evantonium a priority. We need to lock down a good supply, both for our needs and to maintain control of the process."

Was I being greedy or prudent?

Chapter 7

"May-ling, am I being greedy or prudent in keeping the secret of anti-gravity from the world?"

I asked her this quietly in our suite at Jackson House that evening.

"I think you are prudent, dear. You will use it to improve the lives of your kingdom. Others would immediately see and use the military applications. It would be a race, and the first to implement weapons would turn on the others."

"I think you are being pessimistic in your outlook. Surely they wouldn't attack others unprovoked."

"They would. I don't want you even to share it with my grandmother, the empress."

"Who would she attack?"

"India has been in China's sights for over a thousand years. She wouldn't hesitate."

"That would be bad for India but worse for China."

"Rick, why do you say that?"

"Bad for India because they would be a conquered country, bad for China because they conquered India and now would have to rule it."

"China knows how to rule its citizens."

"That's the problem. They won't be Chinese citizens, not for many generations. China would have an ongoing insurgency within its new borders. The insurgency could spread throughout China as the various warlords, or as they are now known as princes, see their chance to have total power."

"You have a point, but I don't think that would stop the empress and her advisors. They would use the Tamerlane solution and have all that rebel and everyone in that city put to death and the city razed to the ground."

"The empress would do that?"

"Yes, you have only ever seen her good side."

"I had thought better of her."

"Don't trust her any more than any of the other countries in the world."

"Oh, it's not that bad."

"Who would come to your aid, if needed?"

"The United States and the United Kingdom, at least."

"The only reason they support you being king is that the Rods from God give you supreme military power. Also, you are no other threat as you couldn't begin, much less win, a ground war. Your threat is defensive, not offensive, so they will leave you alone if you leave them alone.

"Rick, you are so naïve at times. Do you realize that your true power is your economic power? With your gold-backed economy, you could destroy theirs quickly. Yes, they could seize the Australian goldfields, but they don't know how much gold is in the asteroid belt.

"If you didn't have this power, they would depose you and seize everything in a heartbeat."

"So, what should I do?"

"Continue, my wonderful husband. Be your helping self but keep your advantages until your position is entrenched."

"You are saying continue as I have been doing?"

"Yes, help improve the living standards of all on Earth. Explore and find the riches of the solar system before others do."

"That won't be hard to do, as we are the only ones capable of exploring the system right now."

"It won't take them long to catch up. They all are working on it both night and day."

This open conversation with my wife gave me a lot to think about. First and foremost were her comments about her grandmother. Next was about all the others waiting to take me down.

The more I thought about it, the more I realized how blind I had been. The historical reality says this is the way it is, and it will always be that way. If we were all kings, it would be a game of thrones.

Knowing this, what to do? History says that the only way to win is to become more powerful than others and destroy those who challenged you.

In a way, I had already done that with the Soviet Union. They had actively tried to destroy my family and me. It didn't bother me to set things off in that state. They started it; I didn't try to end it, but I set off a chain of events. It was more like the Soviet Union was ready to fall, and it was just the luck of the draw that my actions knocked the dominos over.

It took me a long time to get to sleep that night.

The next day May-ling and I, along with our entourage, flew to Washington, DC. We were staying at Mum and Dad's house in Georgetown.

The day after that, we had an early meeting at the Department of Commerce to start the framework of a trade agreement between the United States and my kingdom.

They needed it more than we did, as we were recognized by and traded with every major country worldwide. You would think that this would have made them easier to deal with.

The Commerce Secretary, Mr. Hodges, acted as though we had better give up everything in their favor or face a trade embargo. He was getting close to being rude in his demands when I stood up.

"There will be no trade agreement with the United States. We will deal with other countries."

"What makes you think they will deal with you?"

"We pay in gold."

"The G-Twenty have agreed to suspend trade unless you agree with our terms."

"Then your nations will be barred from space."

"You and your so-called kingdom will be barred from Earth. See how long you can hold out."

As May-ling and I left the room, I was handed a newspaper. I had been preempted. The headline blared, "Walking on the moon out of trade agreements." The first paragraph told how we had made unreasonable demands and now would bar all nations from space unless we got our way. It wasn't one of Dad's papers.

I made a phone call to JE Research as soon as we returned to the residence. It was probably bugged, so we had to move fast.

"Tom?"

"Yes, Rick, what can I do for you?"

"Has the testbed with the fusion hookup and jets been assembled yet?"

Yes, it is ready to go. It is a mash-up of a hyper-jet engine and a Greyhound bus. The cabin is pressurized, so you can take it to one of our space stations if needed. It may be ugly, but it will work."

"How do you know?"

"We've been up to L1 and back. Anne will be your pilot."

"So, she gets her trip to the moon sooner than she thought. Have the—what are we calling it anyway?"

"The short bus."

"I don't want to know why. How soon can you have it in Rock Creek Park, Washington DC, near the Old Mill?"

"Going suborbital in about an hour."

"Do it."

Next, I called the 707 pilots and told them we would return to California. Be prepared to take off when we got there in about an hour.

This was a misleading phone call. It was a dirty trick on the pilot and crew, but it would mislead the listener if my phone were bugged.

The following call was to Jim Williamson, my CEO for Jackson Enterprises.

"Jim, Rick here."

"Hi, Rick, what's up."

"Go to Delta immediately."

"Say again."

"Go to Delta immediately."

"Right."

He then hung up. Two things happened there. I told him I wasn't being coerced by giving the same message twice.

The second was plan Delta. We had a series of plans in place for unspecified but serious events. They ranged from Alpha, business as usual, to Omega, destroying all records and hiding ASAP. Delta meant to implement the plan to source our needs on the moon from non-tracible sources.

We had a series of warehouses scattered around the world. Any products needed would be shipped to those warehouses. From there, the plan had been to ship them to the Chinese launch site.

Now with gravity control or GC, we could pick the items up at the warehouse. The trick would be to avoid radar detection. That was one of the considerations in selecting the warehouse locations.

All were outside populated areas, and the geography was such that we could fly in and out to a spot where we could go to orbit with little chance of detection.

We had an office without connections to the main JE headquarters, which would place orders. It had a separate hidden budget. The people working there had no idea that I was their employer. They were told it was an international mining concern with remote locations.

My last call was to the White House. I had no problem getting through. It was as though the phone call was expected.

"Mr. President, this is King Richard of Luna. I'm sorry that May-ling and I will not be able to make the photo-op today. We have urgent business back in California and are about to depart."

"Rick, I'm sorry things haven't worked out. We can't allow a threat over our heads to go unchallenged."

"When have you been threatened?"

"The sheer existence of the weapons is threat enough. We have to ask you to demilitarize and surrender control of your bases to a consortium of the major nations. Even your mother-in-law is part of the consortium."

"So, the song is correct."

"What?"

"Never mind. I will let you know my decision after we return to California."

"Safe travels."

I made one other call to Dad's office. I left a message asking a reporter to go to the private part of Washington National and observe what occurred.

Chapter 8

Mum and Dad's house was pretty fancy. It had an underground parking garage. I could see that advantage as Georgetown has narrow streets and little parking. It must have cost a small fortune to have the garage dug out under the two-hundred-year-old house.

While riding the elevator down to the garage, I thought about how lucky the timing of the GC discovery had been. We had set up warehouses, thinking we would use trucks and light aircraft to sneak supplies to the launch site.

The weakness of that plan was that it depended on Empress Ping's continued goodwill. She controlled the launch site, and all would be for naught if she turned on us. Apparently, she had.

Not that I would do anything silly based on that. Maybe JFK had been lying. I had to know for certain. Now how to do that without putting us within her power?

"May-ling, do you think your grandmother is in on this?"

"Rick, if she thought it best for China, she would do it."

"How do we know for sure where she stands?"

"By her actions after we get to safety."

We reached the garage, and the elevator doors opened to what looked like federal agents of some sort just exiting a black sedan.

There were two of them, and they were coming toward the elevator. I didn't hesitate and charged them. It was anything but elegant as far as hand-to-hand combat went, but it never is.

I crashed into one, bowling him over. When he landed, his head hit the concrete and bounced with a dull thud. He was out for the count. I hoped I hadn't killed him.

The other guy was standing there in surprise. That only lasted for a heartbeat, but that was all I needed as I hit him in the nose with the palm of my hand in a straight punch. A hit like that will stun a person.

From there it was easy to grab him and search him quickly. He had handcuffs in his back pocket, so I used them. His partner had the same.

May-ling, two aides, and her so-called bodyguards had just started to move when it was all over. I had them place the cuffed agents back in their sedan. We put them in the backseat, which had a cage between the back and the driver. The one I had knocked down had woken up, and his pupils weren't dilated, so it looked like he would only have a headache.

A quick discussion and a promise of a large bonus had the two aides act as decoys. One was to drive our limo to the airport. The other was to follow closely behind in the Fed's car. I hoped this would confuse the chase enough to make our escape.

After giving the two vehicles enough time to clear the area, we followed in a Lincoln Continental. It was the perfect car for DC. There were hundreds of them on the road hauling self-important functionaries around.

The bodyguards were up front. There was a street map in the glove box, so one gave the other directions to Rock Creek Park. This gave May-ling and me time to talk.

"Rick, what you have accomplished in the last half hour is incredible. You made all those phone calls to set up our escape and captured two men. How did you know how to do all that?"

"This is how I have been living for the last five years. From that first bank robbery in Colorado to my escape from Siberia, then my action in Korea, and many other incidents, I have learned to act quickly and decisively."

"Husband, I'm impressed."

"Thank you. Just think how embarrassing this will be if I'm being paranoid and no one is trying to capture us."

"Do you believe that?"

"No."

"Well, then, you have taken the only sensible actions possible. If you are wrong, little harm is done."

The drive to the park was tense as we expected to be stopped by police cars at any moment. Our fears proved groundless as we arrived at the park after a half-hour drive.

The road to the old mill was well-marked, so we easily found the parking lot. We had no sooner gotten out of the car than an ungainly-looking platform descended from the sky.

If the nickname of the Pregnant Guppy hadn't been used for the new 737, it would have received the title. What looked like the body of a Greyhound bus had been merged with the GC platform. On the back of the platform were two hyper-speed engines. On the front was a cluster of small steering engines. They reminded me of one of those balls they used in ballrooms to have moving lights.

The driver locked the car and left the keys on top of the right front tire at my direction. I didn't want to have to buy Mum or Dad a new car if I could avoid it.

We boarded the strange craft as fast as we could. It had settled to the ground. A ladder like those used in swimming pools fastened to the side enabled us to climb. Later I asked and was told it was a swimming pool ladder.

There were many tourists in the parking lot with cameras, so the GC cat was out of the bag. Anne was the pilot, as I had been told. She didn't mess around. As soon as the airlock doors were closed, she lifted straight up.

It was weird that we were going to orbit, and there were no g-forces on us. It was then that it hit me that I had never thought about May-ling being pregnant and that she shouldn't go to the moon because of the stress of taking off.

I expressed that to her.

"Rick, I thought of that at once but decided the risk had to be taken. Then I realized it would be no risk at all."

"Well, I'm glad one of us can think in an emergency."

She laughed at that.

We had buckled up with the airline-type seatbelts. I removed mine and moved up to talk to Anne. She didn't seem too busy as she was using a nail file.

"How do you like being the first GC pilot?"

"It's okay, a bit boring if you want the truth."

"I can see that with the up and down portion. What about using the engines?"

"Again, no problem. The controls are very simple. You have to input your destination, and the guidance computer does the rest."

"How does the computer know where to find your destination?"

"All your space stations and the moon colony have been programmed. There is a full radar suite on top of the bus, so we know where we are at all times."

"Neat. What do you do if there is an engine problem."

Anne got a weird look.

"Call AAA?"

"As soon as possible, we must have you undergo pilot training if you want to keep this job."

We arrived in orbit in ten minutes. This would revolutionize space travel. Not stopping at any of the now obsolete space stations, the computer fired up the hyperspace engines, and we headed directly to the moon.

Two hours later, we docked with the colony. The setup was inside a huge cavern. An extendable, air-tight boarding ramp like those now in use at larger airports allowed us to deplane. I doubt a new term would come into use. De-GC? No, that sounded stupid.

May-ling's stomach revolted as soon as we stepped off the platform into the moon's much lighter gravity. She spewed all over the place. So much for the wonders of modern travel.

This must have happened a lot as a gurney was available to move her to our palace. When we arrived at our suite, May-ling was given a sippy glass of Seven-Up to settle her stomach. When she could move without hurling, she went to the radio room.

Messages were waiting. The first was an announcement from the launch center that all operations had been halted due to technical problems. I now knew where the empress stood.

The next one was from Dad. The newspaper's reporter watched my 707 being seized by men in dark suits and my limo being stopped and searched upon arrival. My two aides were handcuffed and taken away.

Before we parted, I had instructed them to tell the truth about everything they knew. I hoped it was enough. I hoped the two agents I had disabled were okay.

There was a one-word message from Dad. It was Omega. This meant the family had all gone to ground. We had several safe houses around the world. They would be in a cabin on the Willamette River in Oregon.

Anne checked and found no listing for the safe house in the GC computer database. I gave her the coordinates, which I had memorized: 43.924274° N, -122.991135° E.

It would be nighttime when we arrived, so Dad would turn on two World War II surplus searchlights to guide her.

Those things could be seen for miles. There would be no trouble bringing my immediate family to safety. My aunts and uncles and many cousins had never been that close, so they would have to take their chances.

Aunt Sybil and Popeye were currently in Australia, and if all went to plan, they were on the way to Lasseter Station, where Anne would pick them up before returning to the moon.

The close staff at all my residences had their escape plans in place. If captured, they were to cooperate in every way, as they were victims of that evil King Richard Jackson.

Chapter 9

Wonder of wonders, the pickups all went smoothly. My immediate family was safe on the moon. The news made much of my disabling the two agents sent to arrest me and then my sending decoys to my jet. Obviously, the evil king had been planning this all along.

A one-word message from Jim Williamson told me that plan Delta was in progress. He managed to get this off before my offices were seized, and he was detained.

Our team of lawyers was on the case and assured us the government didn't have a leg to stand on.

The move of all GC equipment and personnel had occurred the day before my aborted visit to the White House, so all was well there.

They were in the process of setting up their equipment in the secure area and were planning to make enough of the pigment mixture to provide one gravity to the entire moon base. After that, they would do the same for our ships and stations.

I met with Mum, Dad, and May-ling about the recent events and how we should proceed.

My first question was, "Am I at war with Earth, all nations?"

Dad, who owned many of the major media outlets worldwide, gave his opinion.

"Rick, I think you are at war, but not a shooting war yet. Let's hope that can be avoided. This is more of a grab by the largest nations for your economic power. They feel threatened by what they can't control."

"So, what action should I take? My initial reaction was to decapitate, but I realized that would be extreme and lead to disaster."

Mum laughed as she replied, "That was my first thought also, but you are right. That would start us down the path of total war and the possible extinction of the human race. There are other ways.

"They have seized your launch site. Why not deny them the ability to go into space?"

"Destroy all the world's spaceports?"

"Nothing so extreme. Move your space stations. That way, they would have nowhere to go."

"I see. They don't have the capability yet to send manned missions directly to the moon. They would have to seize a station to set up a waypoint. If we see them launching towards one of the stations, we could move it."

We then had a long discussion about how to let the major nations know that I was denying them the use of the stations so they were earthbound.

The consensus was that I make a speech broadcast over all of Dad's networks, telling the world my side of the story and that we wouldn't allow any Earth nations to dock their vehicles at the Lunar Kingdom's stations.

It was a short declaration, but it took me hours to develop the right words. May-ling wrote the final draft, which met everyone's approval.

While this was going on, May-ling received a message from her grandmother, Empress Ping. It was a demand that she return to Earth at once.

That message resulted in May-ling giving her announcement after mine. She basically told the whole world that she was standing by her man.

Since the empress had taken my launch center, which I had built with my funds and used for the benefit of the Chinese people, she couldn't support these actions and would be staying on the moon with her husband.

She also added that anyone who tried to fight against the empress didn't have her support. There wasn't to be a civil war in her name. The Chinese people were waiting for the empress to come to her senses.

Man, my wife can be tough!

Once our broadcasts were made, there was an immediate reaction by the United States. Congress voted, and JFK agreed that all my U.S. assets be frozen.

The government reregistered the stock I had received in selling my companies as U.S. property. In a pen stroke, I had lost almost ten billion dollars. They didn't realize that that wouldn't hamper my operations at all.

The Australian goldfield was the only thing on Earth that could slow things down. The Australian government was holding back on confiscating that despite the pressure being exerted by the British government in the name of the Crown.

I didn't know the queen's position on this, and it really didn't matter. Even if the Australians nationalized Lasseter Station, it wouldn't starve the Lunar Kingdom.

I had too many hidden assets on Earth spread all over the world. With the GC vehicles, we could keep the colony well-supplied for a long time to come.

Since I didn't want to tell the Earth nations that, I had to do something in retaliation for the illegal appropriation of my property. I turned off all the media outlets that were using my satellites except Dad's. He realized it wouldn't take the government long to shut him down, but that was bound to happen anyway.

The dumbest thing the United States did was to take over the fusion generation companies in my name and block all contracts with independent power generation corporations.

This nullified the contracts I had in place that they would pay for the unskilled labor putting all the U.S. wiring infrastructure underground. That immediately increased the government-enabled power company's bottom line.

It also caused unemployment to skyrocket to five percent. This didn't sound like much, but it had to hurt when the country previously had full employment.

Left to their own means, the power companies started the process of raising their prices back to the old rates when using coal and oil.

Some state power commissions resisted this, but California, a bell-weather, allowed it. The eastern seaboard states immediately followed this, so most U.S. populations saw an increase in the bills.

JKF just thought he had taken a midterm hit in the ratings. It took a better month to play out, but it was ugly.

During the month, the moon colony had been painted with the GC pigment and had one earth gravity all over except in a few training and play areas. The biggest problem and joy simultaneously was changing the entire toilet system over.

Our earth supply system was working as planned. Those people manning the warehouses thought they were supplying remote mining bases. We kept the demand down at each warehouse to make it seem feasible.

We were becoming independent on most food items, but some we still imported at need. I had to cut the ribbon at the opening of our dairy. We had enough cows now to provide the milk needed for all dairy products. This included the most important of all, ice cream!

We still imported yak butter for May-ling's tea.

While these actions played out on Earth, we weren't ignoring the outer reaches. Particularly the asteroid belt. The colony had ships out exploring for minerals, especially evantonium. The independents were out in force.

That led to our first major problem. Claim jumping had occurred. An Earth corporation sponsored the claim jumpers. They had followed an independent family ship back to their claim.

The claim jumpers didn't realize that samples of ore all had their own fingerprints. We could tell if the ore came from a known source. A simple spectrograph showed it was from a filed claim when they brought the ore in.

When challenged, they claimed they had purchased the claim from the family but hadn't had a chance to register it yet. They had no proof of purchase, so a ship was sent out to check on the family, a man, and his wife, with two small children.

The family had been murdered. The stupid claim jumpers could have sent the family's ship off into space but left it in place on the asteroid.

It was an open-and-shut case. My people documented everything thoroughly. The claim jumpers demanded lawyers and received them.

Their first request was to be tried on Earth, which was denied. The four of them turned on each other and attempted to rat each other out for a reduced sentence.

This also was denied. We didn't need any of their testimony. They were brought before me as the final arbitrator on their fate in three weeks.

It was a simple decision. Besides claim jumping, they had committed murder. I sentenced them to death to be carried out at once. The entire proceedings were televised to all the Kingdom and the Outer Reaches and transmitted to Earth.

Everyone watching saw them put in an airlock, then me opening it to vacuum.

A few people on Earth declared me a monster. Most agreed that they deserved their fate. In my kingdom, it was seen as justice. I didn't face elections, but my poll ratings would have ensured my remaining in office. In many ways, we were like the frontier of the Old West.

Chapter 10

After executing the murderous claim jumpers, I banned all Earth-sponsored exploration. Only Lunar residents were allowed to explore and enter claims.

As expected, this was popular among my citizens and considered high-handed and arbitrary on Earth. At this point, that meant nothing to me.

The corporations that leased exploration ships were refunded their lease money and security deposits. The non-citizen workers were all returned to Earth by conventional rockets. I didn't want them in close contact with the GC machines.

Once the groundhogs, as they were called, were returned to Earth, all the different spaces they had access to were checked for bugs and other spy devices. Many of the devices were found. I think one hundred percent of the companies were spying on my colony one way or another.

While this was happening, the United States government kicked us out of the banking system. Our routing numbers were canceled, and the Lunar citizens' accounts were seized.

At least they tried to seize them. In turn, we announced that we would stand behind our citizens and deposit a sum equal to what they had lost in the Bank of Luna. At the same time, we broadcast that the notes that were on deposit would no longer be legal tender. We had records of everything issued, so the money was withdrawn from the U.S. banking system and put into the Bank of Luna.

This had a terrible effect on U.S. banks. Those that had heavy Lunar deposits were now over their loan limits. By U.S. law, they had to keep loans within a deposit ratio. Now they were out of balance and required to call in loans.

This caused enormous hardships for their borrowers. One large bank was brought to bankruptcy. Some people in Congress declared the bank was too large to fail and that the government would have to bail them out. The majority of the U.S. House was against this, so the bank went under.

Other nations watched this play out, and there were no other attempts to seize accounts.

The postal system was also attacked. The U.S. demanded the Kingdom be dropped from the International Postal Union. The Union rejected this move. The United States refused to accept mail with our stamps on it. They were informed that they would be the ones losing postal exchanges if they refused any member's mail.

The postal denial bills died a quick death in Congress.

Through cutouts, I bought the bankrupt U.S. bank. I now own the largest bank in the United States.

I approved all the steps taken but didn't come up with many of them myself. My many teams brought these forward. There were long-serving teams but no permanent teams. This would help keep a bureaucracy from forming.

When issues were addressed, the team would be dissolved. If the issue came back, another team was appointed with very few of the original members. This brought fresh thinking to the problem.

Our system of obtaining supplies for the colony was working well. Australia, Argentina, and Hong Kong proved to be our mainstays. Their governments were actively supporting us. They weren't notified that those supplies were being staged and shipped from their countries. At the same time, they weren't actively looking for shipping points.

No one was firing weapons, so the world generally wasn't taking things too seriously. Maybe it was like the phony war preceding the action that started between England and Germany in World War II.

Because of this, some things were considered funny.

I was directly involved in the most famous. During a news conference call, it started with Hodges, JFK's Secretary of Commerce.

"We have established an embargo of the moon for critical supplies. It is the simple things that will bring them down. They have fuel, air, and water. With us seizing the launch sites, we deny them life's essentials. Toilet paper, for example."

He droned on for another half hour about how we would soon yield. I had a brilliant idea. At least, I thought it brilliant. I made a call to Jim Williamson and explained what I needed. He made all the arrangements.

Descending near one of the supply warehouses on a GC ship, a load of Charmin toilet paper was waiting to be loaded. A television camera crew had accompanied me from the moon.

As the TP was being transferred to the GC ship, I picked up a four-pack of the TP and squeezed it. At this point, Mr. Whipple came from behind a tree and yelled, "Don't squeeze the Charmin!"

As he yelled, I jumped back on the GC ship, and we ascended quietly into the sky. We could push this close to the earth against the planet and move up. After the first hundred thousand feet, we used hyperspeed engines to return to the moon.

The GC repelled itself from large gravity fields when close. More like the planet pushed the ship away. Not creating enough speed to achieve orbit.

Our artificial gravity field did maintain the gravity setting at all times. Once in orbit, we could use the hyperspeed engines to give a thrust of ten or more gravities, while inside the ship, we were all at one gravity.

There were also inertial considerations. We could turn the ship on a dime using the directional thrusters and never feel it inside.

We had much more investigating to do, but the gravity field prevented small objects in space from hitting our ship. The shape of the ship's field would cause them to curve around the ship.

There had to be limits to this, or technically we could move the moon itself to avoid a crash. Somehow, I didn't think it would work like that. At the same time, it did provide a huge safety net.

A huge fee had been paid to the Charmin people to use Mr. Whipple in the stunt. After yelling at me, he did his trademark squeeze himself. The actor gained a trip to the moon at his leisure plus his usual advertising fee.

All of Dad's stations played it, making a laughingstock of the embargo on the late-night show circuit. I wish I had bought stock in the company.

Hodges retired soon after for health reasons.

There was a benefit from this that hadn't been planned. I received a radio-telephone call from Empress Ping.

"King Richard, I loved your toilet paper ploy. It allows me to immediately release our hold on the launch facility."

"I don't understand. Why does this allow you to do that?"

"You have proven that the moon can be resupplied without a launch facility, so now there is no need to stop launches if needed."

"I thought you were in favor of reining in my perceived power."

"No, silly boy, I had to go along with the Americans to prevent war between us. Now they can't complain that the launch site needs to be shut down for an embargo."

"Thank you. When will launches be allowed again?"

"Starting right this minute, I have sent the orders out and made a statement for the world."

"Again, thank you."

As soon as I was disconnected from the radio-telephone call, I returned to our suite where May-ling was dictating to one of her aides.

"Dear, could I have a private minute?"

She excused her aide to the hallway while we had our conversation. I explained the call from her grandmother.

"She didn't want to support the Americans but felt there might be a fighting war between China and the U.S. if she didn't go along with them."

"I love you, Rick, but you are so naïve in many ways."

"Huh?"

"Grandmother sees that the U.S. cannot achieve its goals, so she has to find a way to back down without losing face. Demonstrating the ability to resupply the moon gave her the perfect excuse."

"Oh."

At times I'm not the sharpest tool in the shed.

The Charmin run also showed the world a new space vehicle as it became known. Our escape from Rock Creek had some pictures taken, but they didn't make much of an impression. TV pictures of the GC machine drifting into the sky were more than impressive.

The event opened up speculation on what other powers we may have. Asked repeatedly for interviews, I remained silent on the issue. The more they had to guess, the better it was for us.

One side effect of the embargo was a halt to moon tourism. Well, almost a halt. With the launch center reopening, people would fly to China and lift off.

We got many requests for the GC ships to provide this service but saw this as an attempt by nations to get on board and potentially capture one. I even made a press release that anyone attempting to take over a GC ship would be considered a pirate and hanged by the neck until dead.

The execution would be held on the moon under the moon's natural gravity. In other words, slow, painful strangulation.

Once more, I was denounced by the UN. I thought about asking someone to keep track of the number of times I had been denounced. It might make the Guinness Book of Records.

May-ling talked me out of it.

Chapter 11

With the silent war between the United States and its allies and my kingdom, you would think the atmosphere on the moon would be solemn. Instead, it was like a snow day at school.

Most people still had to work, but many jobs were on hold as earth-linked operations slowed down. This gave people more time off from work.

The parks were overflowing with people on picnics.

The parks had all been dug up, and the solidified underlying moon rock was coated with the liquified evantonium. The grass was rolled up, the six inches of dirt scraped, the surface cleaned, and the paint applied.

This was a lot of work but went amazingly fast as extra hands were available due to the work slowdown.

After several hundred experiments, we found that we needed GC coating on all ceilings higher than ten feet. That was as far as the adjusted gravity went. We knew this but were shocked when the ladies' softball team started hitting underhanded pitches out of the park.

When the softball went above ten feet, it was now under the influence of the moon's gravity: up, up, and away!

Coating the high ceilings of the ballpark didn't resolve the problem, as the upper coating only extended down ten feet. This led to strange flights of the softballs.

A line drive would be like an Earth hit at one gravity all the way. A hit with the loft would really take off. A towering foul would leave the Earth's field, go moonshot, as it became called, then reenter Earth gravity near the ceiling.

It was mind-bending to try to work out the mechanics of flight. The ball would take off, then transition from Earth's normal to the moon's normal gravity, which would change the trajectory and height of its rise and slow the speed of its fall so that it would rise higher and sail farther than if it had stayed at Earth normally.

Starting relatively slowly, it rises abruptly after crossing the gravity threshold if it has not already reached the top of its arc. Then the ball drops faster until it slows its downward acceleration as it falls into Luna's normal gravity.

The seeming fluctuation in the gravity field made the ball appear to float on the moon and then accelerate as it once more neared the ground. Add to that the torque applied to the ball as it changed fields, and it was a brave infielder who dealt with these.

The ladies shattered the Earth record of over five hundred feet for a softball home run by a man, with a thousand feet considered normal.

Six positions were added to each team. They were called deep fielders and would fan out at about the nine-hundred-foot mark behind the outfielders. It made for some interesting games.

That all was on the moon. Our spaceships also had coatings on the ceilings and floors. The upper coating acted to compensate for high acceleration. We found no practical acceleration limits. In an excess of caution, we painted all interior surfaces of the ship so that sudden changes in direction wouldn't affect the passengers or mechanical units.

The exploration ships were converted first. They were looking for evantonium-containing asteroids as fast as they could.

I read one message where a miner spoke of an asteroid they had just left.

"It only had gold and platinum. We staked the claim and skedaddled looking for the good stuff."

So far, only one other asteroid had been found to contain evantonium in large quantities. The evantonium, as a trans-uranic, surprisingly wasn't radioactive. Mary thought it had something to do with the dimensions it was linked with, but she wasn't certain.

I expressed surprise to my little sister that she was uncertain. She knew everything.

"Rick, it is either the dimensional link or magic. I'm hoping for magic."

That's what the world needs—a ten-year-old who can throw fireballs!

I received a hand-delivered message from Frank Sinatra. He rightly didn't want this sent by radio to the moon. He and his buddy Dean Martin wanted to come to the moon for the experience.

I had no problem with this; it would be a propaganda victory if it leaked out. Since I wanted to keep the GC as low a profile as possible, I had them scheduled from the Chinese launch site.

I met them at our L2 station, where we boarded a capsule for the moon. We had fun during the four-hour trip. Frank and I did a duo of "Fly Me to the Moon". Then Dean and I went all out on, "That's Amore".

While on the moon, they gave a concert in the park for our people. This went over so well that I decided to bring groups up from Earth for future concerts. Heck, the t-shirt sales would pay for it all.

We ended up turning it into a charity event, where the performers got a free trip to the moon. Our people got a free show with big-name groups. The broadcast rights and merchandise sales profits were all donated to international charities. None was given to the United States, only charities. We were at war, you know.

I should have known better than to trust Sinatra and Martin. They were clowns from way back. Our singing in the space capsule was recorded. The record was released as a single. The B-side got as much airtime as the A-side. Of course, Frank and Dean argued about which side was A or B.

So once again, I had an international, or maybe interplanetary hit. There was even an inquiry about when I planned to go to Venus, as one artist wanted to do a song titled, "Venus". I turned it down even though I considered him a friend.

People's ingenuity fascinated me. I said yes to the Chinese ping-pong team that wanted to play in the moon's gravity. They normally would stand ten to fifteen feet from the table. Now they were ten yards from the table. It was crazy.

Mary came to me one day and asked if she could put on a fashion show on the moon. She would use as many kids as she could from the moon for the show. I couldn't see why not and told her to go ahead. If I only had known.

The clothes she wanted to show were on Earth, so she needed a GC landing to pick them up. That would be in England. I assumed she meant northern Scotland, where we had one of our pickup points.

I should have written the order to flight control more clearly. While Mary was still in my office, I filled out and wrote "England".

She thanked me and told me I was the best brother ever! That should have warned me of what was about to happen.

Later, I realized she had told me "As many moon kids as she could."

I took that at the time as working as many locals into the show as she could. No, she informed me I needed to sharpen my listening skills. She meant that she would import someone if she had an outfit that didn't work for a moon kid.

Again, the TV cameras were brought out. The warm-up for the show was a group of German gymnasts performing in moon gravity.

They worked with safety ropes for a week before trying some spectacular stunts, which would have been impossible on Earth. One girl named Ell Donasii was incredible in what she could do.

The fashion show went off without a hitch. I watched it with Mum and Dad. The first hint that I got was Mum saying, "She is grounded forever!"

I looked around and couldn't figure out what was wrong. Then I looked at the stage. Do you know how it takes a moment to register without expecting something? It took all of ten seconds to realize that the model for the new Princess Collection was Princess Anne of England.

The political fallout from this would be a disaster!

We had the TV on with the sound turned down. Dad turned the sound up, and the broadcasters were going nuts.

Even as this was happening, a message was being handed to Mum. It appeared that the Queen of England wanted her wayward daughter back so she could literally be grounded.

Breaking every rule, we used a GC ship to drop Princess Anne off at Windsor Castle within two hours.

Mary and her partner in crime, the pilot Anne, were summoned immediately after the show to explain themselves.

In her defense, Anne showed my handwritten order to do a pickup in England, not Scotland. I wished she had questioned that order, but it was my mistake.

Mary, on the other hand, was guilty as charged. She wanted to add some excitement to her fashion show, or as she put it, class it up a little. I swear I would drop a Rod from God on that sorority house.

She and Princess Anne had their own private code and had arranged everything without anyone being the wiser. It demonstrated that it was impossible to embargo the moon if nothing else. Two kids had bypassed it easily.

Chapter 12

I happened to be in the room when Mary explained what she had done. I was interested in how she got Anne, the pilot, not the princess, to land in England instead of Scotland at the normal site.

"Ricky, I have your written order to land in England, not Scotland. It didn't say where so I had to explain to Anne that we were landing in the back garden at Buckingham Palace to pick up a passenger.

"I told her you hadn't designated the pickup spot because you didn't know for certain which castle or palace Anne would be at that day. That made sense to her."

I'm going to have to clarify some things to any and all pilots who might be running errands for Mary. I needed to extend that to Denny for his many girlfriends and sports cars for Eddie.

Since I was nearest to the door, Mary had to pass me to reach Mum and Dad. I couldn't help noticing how padded her rear end was. She must have had dozens of handkerchiefs in her underwear. It looked like she was wearing a diaper. I wished I had a camera.

Before Mary arrived, Mum and Dad discussed what they should do about Mary. I didn't think Mary would like what they decided.

Dad started out with, "Mary, you are getting too old to spank. A swat on the butt is to get a young child's attention. You are past that."

Mary smiled at that, "Good to know. Do I have to do dishes for Mum on the moon?"

Her smile was more like a smirk. Bad move, Mary.

"No, you know how to wash dishes. Instead, you will be working with the groundskeeper at all of the parks here on the moon every day for the next two weeks."

"That's not so bad."

"You will be doing it all day long."

"What about my experiments in the lab?"

"You are banned from the lab for the next two weeks; security has been notified."

'You can't do that to me!"

Mum spoke up, "Do you want to try us?"

Mary suddenly got smart and quit digging the hole she was in.

"No, Mum. Can I go to the lab after hours?"

"You are banned, period. Keep trying to change things, and it will be three weeks."

"May I be excused?"

"No, what did you think when you arranged all this? Do you realize what trouble you have caused Richard?"

"I was the one who brought Anne up here. Why would Ricky be in trouble?"

"The British government will blame Richard because his spacecraft picked her up. They will not believe that you were behind it. They are already accusing him of attempting to kidnap the Royal Princess."

"I will tell them it was all my fault."

"Do you think they will believe a ten-year-old girl did this? They will likely say that he is hiding behind his little sister."

"Have Dad broadcast the truth."

"He can't; they have shut down all of his stations in England. The United States has also shut down all its TV and radio stations. They have also grabbed all his newspapers and magazines in the country."

"I'm in big trouble, aren't I?"

"Yes, but not for this. We knew they would do this, using any excuse they could."

"I'm sorry. I just want to go back to Jackson House and my life there."

"We can't. We will be arrested if we go back to Earth. Besides, they have taken over Jackson House in the U.S. We hope they don't find the subbasement."

"I'm so sorry. It's all my fault!"

"Mary, it is not your fault. It is the fault of greedy people on Earth wanting what we have."

"I still feel bad."

"And you should. It would help if you thought about the consequences when you do things. You are in the real world now, not playtime."

Dad spoke, "All the radio and TV stations are back on the air. It seems people get upset when you pull the plug in the ninth inning of the seventh game of the World Series when it is all tied up.

"The government is trying to blame it on technical difficulties, but the public isn't swallowing that as the government announced why they were taking my stations before they went down."

I had to snicker, "I bet the screams were something."

Mum added, "It may be the end of the Democrats as a party. They certainly are going to lose big in the upcoming midterms. JFK may get lynched by his own party."

Dad replied, "No, dear, JFK is smarter than that; he made LBJ the face of the effort to embargo the moon."

Aren't politics fun?

"Mum and Dad, it is bothering me to no end that I'm in an unofficial war with the United States. It has always been my country, and I don't like what is happening. If they resort to violence, I don't know if I could order a response in kind. I could be killing kids I went to school with in Bellefontaine or worked with in all the cities I visited."

From Dad, "What do you want to do, Rick?"

"I don't know, I don't want to hurt the U.S., but I know that the politicians and business people will misuse our knowledge if we give in."

"I agree," replied Dad. Mum nodded her head in support of his statement.

"Do you have any ideas on what we could do to bring this to a conclusion without fighting breaking out?"

Sitting quietly as a church mouse during this exchange, Mary said, "You told me I always had to share, or the other kids wouldn't like me. Why aren't you sharing?"

"You heard we can't trust any country to behave if they have this knowledge."

"I always had to bring enough cookies for everyone."

Mum, Dad, and I looked at each other. Could it be that simple? The United States and other major countries were trying to pressure us to give up our knowledge of producing fusion-powered electric generators, hyper-speed rocket engines, and GC coating. What would happen if we shared it with everyone? Open up the source material to the whole world.

It would play heck with the world's economy, and the rush to space would be like the Oklahoma land rush. Maybe more like the California gold rush with the prospectors coming in like crazy, and we would be the merchants selling picks and shovels.

It would result in the dislocation of many industries, which we had been trying to avoid, but no matter how we tried to help, they seemed to try to make it worse. Maybe we should let the chips fall where they may. It would get us out of the line of fire.

We could control the supply of evantonium until someone other than us made a major find.

Releasing how to build the fusion generators would hurt the people trying to take our knowledge. It wasn't as though we needed the money. We were holding back to enable the transition of the world's workforce.

What would come if we released that knowledge could hurt a lot of people, but not as much as a shooting war. Maybe the time had come to let market forces sort everything out. It would be poetic to give our enemies what they demanded. They would be the ones destroyed.

The hyper-speed ships were important, as they enabled access to the solar system. Though fast, without a source of evantonium, no one could compete with us.

We talked long into the night about handling this and the possible ramifications. Mary fell asleep in her chair. Mum decided that maybe she could be restricted for half a day from her labs instead of being banned. She may have prevented a world war.

We decided the faster we moved on this, the better it would be. We didn't want to dither and let a war start by accident.

In the morning, Mum and Dad talked to Mary about the fusion generator and making it public knowledge. She had no problem with that once she realized she was getting lab time back.

One nice thing about being an absolute monarch with total control over external relations was I didn't have to go to my parliament for permission. This would eventually change, but right now, I set the policy.

After cleaning up and changing clothes from our all-nighter, I went on TV. It went out to all of Dad's channels through the satellites we control. Basically, the whole world.

I explained that the current tensions were created by greedy people trying to take what was ours from our hard work. Rather than risk violence, I, as King of Luna and the Solar Reaches, was giving the knowledge to the whole world rather than a greedy few.

Chapter 13

During my speech, I gave the websites where the plans for the fusion generator and hyper-speed ship were to be found. We hadn't thought it completely through, and the sites crashed twice before we had enough servers online.

What the JE R&D people called browsers made it possible to post messages that anyone could see. A separate company had been set up, named "Find". It was all for free, but I was told it could be monetized by selling advertising.

I hated junk mail. I suspected these ads could be worse.

I also wondered how many people would build their own generators. The spaceships would be more difficult.

The first week was hectic as all get out. Mum, Dad, and I met with our top advisors to see if we understood all that was happening.

The first report was from the fusion people.

"There have been no disasters as the pundits on Earth have predicted. The process is such that you get fusion or you don't. There is no chance of a meltdown or release of radiation, so all is good on that front.

"We cannot know how many, if any, generators have been produced yet. We have received questions from legitimate governments and corporations. We have answered those as you announced we would. Those from private individuals have been declined. That said, some individuals may be successful without asking any questions."

I replied, "It sounds like things are proceeding as we all thought on that front. How long do you think it will be before we know how well they are being introduced?"

"We should see the first signs in three months or so."

"Please keep the group posted if anything changes."

"We will, Your Majesty."

"How often do I have to tell this group that I'm Rick in these meetings? I'm Rick."

"We will call you Rick, Your Majesty."

Since throwing my coffee cup at him would have been an overreaction, I let out a large harumph and let it go. For some reason, everyone else, including my traitorous parents, snickered or outright laughed.

Changing the subject, I asked, "Have we seen any sign of spaceship construction?"

"A few questions from the militaries of the major powers and international aircraft builders, but it will be six months or more before any launch."

"Now, for the sticky part, what about our relations with Earth's governments?"

"All have announced the blockade has been lifted."

"What about the United States specifically? They had taken the most action."

"There have been no offers to return your property they seized. At the same time, they want you to redeposit the funds to their banks."

Mum, Dad, and I exchanged a brief look. Without any words, we agreed on the next step.

"Redeposit the bank's funds in that bank that was too large to fail as a show of good faith. Tell them the rest of the banks will be taken care of when my physical structures and seized funds are returned. Also, all of my employees at Jackson Enterprises are allowed to return with no repercussions."

No one at the table except my immediate family knew I was now in control of that bank that was too large to fail. It was in my best interest to keep it afloat.

"Your...Err, Rick, what about the people that you had been paying to put the world's infrastructure underground? They are currently unemployed."

That kicked off a discussion. The U.S. government had seized the generating plants that were funding the operation. They had, in fact, given them to the power companies that had run them for us.

Would the government now take them back from those companies? If they did, should we use those funds to continue the program?

If the government didn't return the plants to us, did we owe anything to those workers we had displaced?

They returned the program to us but not the plants. Still, paying for the program seemed to be the right thing to do. However, it was announced that we were reinstituting the program at our cost; there would be no incentive for the United States to return our property.

None of the other countries in the world had gone so far as to seize and give away our generation plants. They took physical control, yes, but didn't give them to their business allies. These countries had relinquished control back to us and unfroze all of our banking accounts.

It was only the United States that was still trying to make trouble. Unfortunately, the only trouble was for them as midterm elections were approaching. The party currently in power would pay for the country's economic problems.

It was suggested that we announce that the return of paying the displaced workers would depend on the outcome of the U.S. midterms.

After a quick huddle with Mum and Dad, I told the group we weren't going to get involved with U.S. politics and that we would reinstitute the underground infrastructure project immediately.

This was to go out as a worldwide announcement with all the details that we were doing this despite the U.S. not returning our property.

The next item on the agenda was a request to build a Le Mans-type racecourse. A group of investors thought they could make it a profitable venture.

"I'm not against the idea. The problem is the supply of evantonium. To have one gravity of an area that large would take all of our ore supplies. If a large deposit is discovered, we can revisit the issue."

My brother Eddie had to be involved, but we couldn't spare the ore for a family member.

The meeting was interrupted by a messenger. This was highly unusual. The note handed to me reported that there had been a hijack attempt on one of our GC ships.

Since this was a high-level meeting, I shared the information with the staff and departed for the communications hub.

My head of security Hugh Paton, who had been in the meeting, accompanied my parents and me. It was a short hike made in silence.

We had anticipated something like this and had plans in place. I'm telling this like I had a part in the planning. Actually, the plan was presented to me by Hugh in a security review meeting.

The crew on the GC ship making the pickup were Royal Arms, an over-the-top description of our combination police force, army, space navy, and marines. There were different squads within the Royal Arms with training in various areas.

One didn't send Marines to perform police work. Marines were trained to assault. Civilians took a dim view of this practice.

Over time, the groups would separate into their own services, but keeping them as one from an administrative point of view was easier.

Anyway, the landing GC ship crew was our space navy type. Out of sight was a second GC ship with a squad of Marines. The second ship shadowed every landing.

My group and I arrived at the communication center at a critical juncture. Part of the landing procedure was to exchange messages between the pickup group and the warehouse.

Depending on the message, warnings were given. In this case, the statement, "Glad to see you," told the GC crew that armed enemy forces controlled the warehouse but that they were limited in number.

If it had been, "Glad to see you on this nice night," it would have meant, "Get the heck out of Dodge, overwhelming force."

"Glad to be here," in response, told the warehouse that the message was received and that steps were being taken.

The warehouse crew thought they were loading supplies for remote mining operations, which was correct. They didn't know how remote.

Because of this, they weren't aware of what would take place. Only the warehouse supervisor was in on everything.

"This is Marine GC One. We are going in."

"This is Warehouse GC Two, landing as per procedure to create a distraction."

There was a nervous wait for the next message.

The Marines surrounded the building and, in best assault tradition, started with flashbangs and broken doors and windows.

"This is Marine One Actual, situation under control."

Whew!

The five would-be hijackers were taken alive. They were both stirred and shaken, as Mr. Bond would describe, but they were alive and in handcuffs.

They had no identification and weren't talking, so we concluded this was a professional operation rather than a gangland attempt.

The supply ship took on its load, and the Marines with the prisoners all headed for the moon.

It took several days, but the story emerged. Our police squad landed and investigated the area. These were retired police department detectives, so they knew what they were doing.

They found the hijacker's transportation. They had left a van parked half a mile away and walked in. The van was from a rental agency.

Further investigation revealed the rental was by a front company registered in the State of Delaware. This went nowhere.

The breakthrough was a used matchbook on the floor of the van. It was from a restaurant in Langley, Virginia. I wonder who was headquartered there. Maybe those people had a Virginia Department of Highways sign in front of the building.

I had made a trip to our small jail to view the prisoners and burst out laughing when I saw who had been caught. The group leader was my old friend Rip Robertson, who was supposed to teach me how to recognize a tail.

This was going to be fun!

Chapter 14

"Rip! Fancy meeting you here. How are things going?"

It was mean of me to say this as I entered the cellblock where Rip and his crew were being held. No one has ever said that I was always a nice guy.

Rip didn't reply to my snarky statement. He glowered and turned away. He was always a sore loser.

"The only question I have is one you won't or can't answer. Was it a CIA-sanctioned operation, or have you gone rogue? I know they will deny you, so it is a moot point."

A tired look crossed Robertson's face, and I felt a pang of sympathy.

"Rip, you and these guys are being returned to Earth today."

One of his crew spoke up.

"In body bags?"

"No, alive and well, not even a little torture for form's sake. It might be embarrassing, but that is all."

I didn't tell them they would be dropped off on the front lawn of CIA headquarters. They would be handcuffed, nude, and have bowling ball bags as hoods. This would send a message.

A special trip to Earth had to be made to pick up the bowling ball bags as we hadn't installed a bowling alley in the colony. In the low gravity, it would have made no sense, but now we planned ten lanes and associated equipment.

The front lawn of the CIA headquarters was visible from the access road. Dad would have a TV broadcast van set up to record the return.

It was a timed operation as the CIA didn't appreciate the publicity. I had considered the White House lawn but realized that the GC ship would be vulnerable to fighter jets out of Andrews or Pax River.

It would be a race between the Air Force and Navy to shoot the intruder down.

Dad's talking head would read a copy of the statement the operators were carrying with them. It was simple and direct.

"CIA headquarters should be vacated at noon Eastern Standard Time tomorrow as it will be destroyed."

I wasn't going to act against the small group of men who tried to hijack the ship but the organization that supported them. If they were truly rogue operators, the CIA would have to learn to rein them in.

I suppose that delivering them nude, hooded, and in handcuffs was an action, but it was not proportional to the crime.

I also called the White House and left a message for the president. It briefly explained what was going to happen and why. I had no idea if this was a CIA brainchild or if they were acting on higher-up orders. With them, you never knew.

I thought I had planned this out, so it would be highly embarrassing for the U.S. government and the intelligence community in general.

I had forgotten how ruthless the CIA could be. At noon the next day, the building had been evacuated. Robertson and his crew were chained in place on the front lawn.

The CIA was willing to sacrifice them to show that I was a murderer. They thought that I would either back down or destroy the building and lose any public backing I had.

They didn't count on my real plan. I could have dropped a Rod from God on the building. That is what they were expecting. The explosion would have blown the building and the chained men to bits.

Instead, a GC ship descended and turned on the downward-facing gravity field that had been installed the day before.

The building was flattened bit by bit as the ship went its length. There was no damage outside of the gravity field.

It was funny watching the world's reaction on TV. In the U.S., it ran the gamut, from how King Richard could do this with no proof that it was an act of war, to good for him; that would teach the CIA to try their dirty tricks.

The rest of the world cried crocodile tears with the help of schadenfreude. There was never another attempt to hijack one of my GC ships.

The CIA director resigned in disgrace. I had it through back channels. He was the sacrificial pawn for the White House. Even knowing that I didn't know if the president was involved.

A side effect was that we received requests to demolish buildings. It seems four gravities leave a pancake that can be cleaned up easily without other damage.

I authorized a couple of the Space Ladies to start a business. I insisted they have an extremely loud warning system installed that would sound off before crushing the site. The site had to be roped off, inspected, and guarded by off-duty police to ensure that no one was accidentally or deliberately inside. I could see the mob using it to get rid of problems.

I heard Rip Robertson retired with a full pension, so I knew he hadn't gone rogue. Even though he had been an ass to me in California, he had served his country well.

There were some questions in the news about using bowling ball bags. The consensus was that we didn't have any hoods handy. Those in the know got the message.

Chapter 15

All this international recognition led to requests to establish embassies in my kingdom.

We would normally rate a small embassy to facilitate communications between our two governments of our size and population. There would be an ambassador and a small support staff. There would be little need for consular functions to aid U.S. citizens in my kingdom.

That was the norm. What was requested was a fully staffed embassy. Why the U.S. Navy wanted an attaché on the moon made no sense. Maybe they wanted to spy on us?

Since money wasn't a problem, I had embassies being set up in every country that recognized us. Then to add insult to injury, I had consulates established in every major city in those countries.

The consulate had all local hires to represent us. Most of them were "honorary consuls," lawyers with their own practices and offices who displayed a seal and provided consulate services in exchange for a) good networking, b) a diplomatic passport, always handy, and c) a modest pension, but no salary. This gave all host countries the headache of figuring out who our spies were, costing us little or nothing.

None of them were. Why bother to have spies on the ground when no hostile country could reach you? Let them plan, plot, and maneuver all they want. We were beyond their reach. We had given them all the information their spies would have been trying to obtain. Knowing how to do something and having the raw materials to do it were two different things.

A new cavern was excavated to host Embassy Row. This cavern also included housing for its employees. We allowed them to use our medical facilities, schools, library, and recreational facilities but could isolate them at need.

The employees usually hired locals. In this case, they had to be imported. We didn't have the excess population required. We liked the additional headcount. They liked the opportunity to include more spies.

Most cities hosting an embassy face the problem of civil fines like parking tickets. On Earth, those with diplomatic immunity didn't pay them. It wasn't a problem on the moon because there was no private transportation.

Out of necessity, I had to create a Department of State. I loved the title, the Department of State of the Lunar Kingdom and the Solar Reaches. Try to make an acronym out of DSLKSR. How did I know that DSL is a Nikon camera and KSR a particular model?

Never underestimate the bureaucratic mind. They had unlimited amounts of time to think of these things. Thus, my ambassadors were known as Nikons. A subsequent result was that I had to reach an agreement with the Nikon corporation so I wouldn't be sued for trademark infringement. The Nikon camera became the official camera of my kingdom.

Fortunately, they made some of the best cameras globally, so it wasn't a big deal.

The result of establishing the embassies was immediate population growth. We were now over a thousand people, the same size as the Vatican. This made us small fry, to say the least, in numbers. In area, we were larger than New York City.

I was in a meeting on how to delay the embassies and the subsequent spying attempts. All the governments wanted to design and erect their own buildings instead of using our one-size-fits-all Quonset huts.

This was fine with us as they would have to bring all the materials from Earth. Even the easy-to-set-up huts came from Earth, but they wanted wood, concrete, brick, and other materials.

We gave them the go-ahead. They were going to have to launch everything from China as we weren't making the GC ships available. This would make the timeline much longer and the cost out of this world. No pun intended.

The meeting was interrupted by a high-priority message for me. One of our exploration ship's fusion-pile had shut down. A family, the Robinsons, were stranded in a ship hurtling past Jupiter.

They weren't in immediate danger as there was enough battery power on board to last them for over a week.

I decided on the spot to go with the rescue tug.

"I have to leave on a rescue mission. A ship has lost its fusion pile, and we need to know what shut it down. This has never happened before. Carry on with the meeting."

Have I mentioned that I have learned to hate meetings?

The tug captain updated me as we boarded. It was one of the new models. It had hyper-speed engines with GC installed. It would easily be able to bring the ship and family back to the moon for close inspection.

As per standing instructions, no titles other than captain were used in this event.

"Richard, the family managed to stop their ship using most of their emergency power. They are at rest on a small moonlet."

"Any idea how large the moonlet is? To my knowledge, we don't have any recorded out that way."

"From their best estimate, it is about fifty miles in diameter. They have filed a claim but haven't told us what they think their find is."

"We will see in a few hours."

It was more than a few hours before we were able to dock with the family exploration/prospecting ship. Eight hours later, we were docked with the ship on the surface of the moonlet.

The family wasn't stressed at all. They had been in contact and knew that rescue was on the way. They had never been in danger of losing their life support, so all was good.

I was most interested in looking at the fusion pile that had shut down. When the technician who came along, well, I guess I came with him, opened the cabinet, it took him about five minutes to find the problem.

A small piece had fallen through a grate on top of the cabinet and had shorted across two wires. It looked like a small ray gun.

The technician showed it to a young child standing there. He was excited that we had found his toy robot's ray gun. Robbie had missed it.

Neither the technician nor I said anything. We would leave young Will to his parents. Something as simple as screen door screening fixed to the underside of the grate would have prevented the problem while still leaving airflow.

The parents were embarrassed to no end. I told them we would write the whole thing off as a learning experience all the way around.

The father then asked if he could speak to me in private. I excused us from the group. When in his office, he opened up.

"Are you aware we have staked a claim on this asteroid?"

"I was told that before we left. What is the find?"

"From the samples taken, this whole thing is seventy percent pure evantonium."

"What!"

"Seventy percent pure evantonium."

"You and your family's wealth may have just exceeded mine."

"You're not going to seize it for the kingdom?"

"No, but I'm going to insist I'm your only customer. We will have to work out the price, but you will not lose out."

"That's a relief. My wife and I thought you might take it all for the good of the kingdom."

"I hate the fact that you even had that thought. Is my reputation that bad?"

"No, it was just playing to our greatest fears."

"Some of the people I have dealt with would not only take it but also make your family disappear to keep it a secret."

He looked green at that.

"You would be declared lost in space. No fear, though. We are going to publicly announce this find and credit you with it. We won't give the location. It is far enough from the standard orbits that others will find it hard to stumble on it."

"Others will just follow us out here."

"I think setting up a full orbital living station here would be best. You realize that you can't return to Earth once this news gets out?"

"The girls will hate it when they hear this. They have been pestering me for a trip to Earth for some real shopping. My daughters the most, but my wife doesn't stop them."

"Then consider this, I buy the asteroid from you plus pay a royalty on tons mined. We keep your name out of it."

"How much are you offering?"

"I'm not certain what the true price per ton will come out to be, but would you accept ten billion dollars plus ten percent of the market price?"

"I think the ladies could have a nice shopping trip on that."

"I will offer my mother's service in introducing them to Rodeo Drive and Fifth Avenue. Now that things have calmed down on Earth, she and the rest of my family will be returning to Jackson House in Beverly Hills."

"We'll take you up on that offer. Going from middle class to filthy rich is mind-boggling."

"Welcome to my world."

"If you excuse me, I will give my wife the news."

From the scream I heard later, it appeared to be taken well.

Chapter 16

The Space Ladies on the trip made a more detailed surface investigation of the asteroid, moonlet, or whatever. It was larger than most of the asteroids in the belt, but it wasn't a moon since it was in a free obit. Someone else would have to sort out what it should be called.

One of the Space Ladies, Linda, called me on our private channel.

"Hey, Boss, I have found something you should see."

"It will take me a few to suit up, but on my way."

When I arrived at the spot where her beacon was blinking, it was at an opening to a tunnel or cave. We could see about fifty feet into the opening from our helmet lights. It was natural-looking, not constructed by men or even aliens. Of course, if it was aliens, maybe they made tunnels like this.

Telling Linda to stay outside, I went into the cave. I told her to let me know when I was about to leave her sight. Before that happened, the cavern opened up. Now I was inside. It was apparent this was a natural cavern in the asteroid.

My lights didn't begin to reach the sides of the cavern in any direction except the one I came from.

I returned to the entrance and asked Linda to leave a beacon so it would be easy to find the opening again. The beacon was a small battery-operated radio like those used at airports.

Returning to the rescue tug, the crew had attached cables to the family's ship. Checking that all were accounted for, we returned to the moon at a much more leisurely pace to not strain the cables.

There was business to be conducted once we were at the colony. First and foremost was the official transfer of the claim to me. This was a purchase by me from the family, not a purchase by the government for the government.

Once the claim was registered and funds transferred, I started arranging for an exploration team to be set up to map the cavern. Again, this was on my dime. I wanted it clear that it was mine, not the Lunar government's.

I even paid for the rescue call and tow.

My next step was to seal the claim record so no one could obtain the body's path. Once the files were sealed, I had them transferred into my private safe. All anyone could find out now was that a claim existed. Even the people I bought it from no longer have the orbital information.

The caverns on the object were large. What was its official type anyway? Later I was told it was an asteroid, plain and simple. The fact that it wasn't in what was considered a normal orbit wasn't considered abnormal. Since it wasn't big enough to be a planet and didn't orbit a planet like a moon, it is an asteroid.

All is well and good. Since it didn't have a name, I could name it whatever I wanted. After some thought, I decided not to name it. A name makes an object more real. It would develop a name in time, but the longer I could keep it a secret, the better it would be.

We had enough evantonium to complete our current projects, so there was no hurry to develop the new find.

I could justify not providing lift capability to other nations by continuing the illusion of a shortage.

My parents hadn't left for Earth yet, so I filled them in on the find. We had an interesting conversation. My mum surprised me by suggesting that I convert the caverns into my own fortress like Superman's. While I liked that idea, we would have mining operations there so that it wouldn't be hidden.

While that wasn't possible, we could make safe quarters for the family to retreat to if things got really bad.

Also, Dad wondered if it would be possible to smelt the ore on-site using a fusion-powered furnace. We then could ship the ore ingots to the Colony for conversion to the coatings.

I took it one step further and said we should convert the ingots on-site to the coating and only ship what was needed when needed.

We talked about this for over an hour and finally decided we were getting ahead of ourselves. First, we needed the exploration results, then we could come up with a plan of action.

It seemed like I had spent the last five years finding new places to live and creating safe retreats for the family. I wonder where the one after this would be.

The next morning, I had to sit in judgment on several court cases that had been elevated to my level. Fortunately, no one needed to be executed. I would have made an exception for one lawyer but was so glad when he shut up, I found his client guilty and to be returned to Earth and bolted from the room.

It seemed like I bolted. Actually, I think I looked distinguished in the robes I had adopted for my court appearances as I strolled from the room.

Mary, who had been watching the trial, asked why I had run from the room.

Later that afternoon, I said goodbye to my family as they returned to Earth. Except for Eddie. He was staying to work on the racecourse they had developed for low-gravity outside racing on the moon.

It was nothing like my first attempts. This one looked like it would work and be as safe as any on Earth. That's not saying much.

May-ling told me that she had received a message from her mother. Her mother and grandmother would like her to come down to Earth for a visit. It had been several weeks.

A trip from the moon to China was now the same as a driving trip from Bellefontaine to Columbus. Totally insane.

The next day I received a preliminary report from the cavern explorers. They had mapped out the entryway and the first large cavern. It was enormous, according to them. They had installed lighting around the rim. It was large enough that it could park every GC ship we had and then some.

This went well with the plan to make the place a manufacturing center and refuge. They further reported that three other openings were branching off the large cavern, heading deeper into the asteroid. They planned to string lights as they went deeper into its depths.

Trying to be proactive, I ordered a group to be formed to set up a plan of action to turn the asteroid into a manufacturing center and refuge. I also set up a requirement that it was to have a defense against incursions.

The defense would be heavy weapons for attacks on the ground and missile defense from incoming spaceships. This would include a full radar suite surrounding all approaches to the asteroid.

You would think with this going on, there wouldn't be time for any more excitement in my life. The excitement wasn't directed at me, but May-ling and I could be affected by it.

There was unrest in China. Somebody was stirring up the people against the empress. To further complicate matters, some of her province princes were starting to think they were warlords and adding to the unrest.

I asked May-ling if she still thought it wise to visit her family at this time. She was adamant, as only an expectant mother can be insisting; she was going on a visit.

I hadn't been married long, but I was learning to recognize those battles that couldn't be won. Or, if won, the price of victory would be beyond Pyrrhic.

Considering it would only take hours to land in Beijing, it was an all-day affair packing for the trip. Our pilot Anne had checked with the authorities at the Forbidden Palace, and we were cleared to land if we did it promptly. The political situation was deteriorating so quickly that they wanted us in the safety of the palace as soon as possible.

Once more, I asked May-ling if this was wise. I should have kept my mouth shut as I ended up with a crying wife telling me that I didn't love her anymore. This was proven by my not wanting to see her family.

I once more silently thanked my mum for her talk on the vagaries of a pregnant wife. I shut up and took it.

Acting, bull riding, being in fights for your life, and escaping from Siberia were all child's play compared to keeping an expecting wife satisfied. I was finding out that being a husband could be difficult.

The trip down was uneventful. I thanked the stars for gravity control. The trip gave May-ling time to recover from her hormone imbalance. Dad had taught me to blame all female crankiness on that.

She apologized for her inappropriate accusations. There were a few kisses and cuddles, and all seemed right in our world again.

Looking back, it would be some time before things were right again.

Chapter 17

We landed at the designated landing square in one of the courtyards. Something didn't seem right. Usually, there were ten or fifteen attendants to help us. Today there were none.

I went to the flight deck to give an order to the pilot.

"Something is not right here. No one is waiting for us. I will exit first. If there is a problem, take off and return May-ling to the moon."

My security didn't like my decision, but I held firm.

"What about you?"

"Do not delay for me. This is an order from your king. If there is trouble, return to the moon at once."

I thought I was overly concerned, but I was spooked.

"Yes, Your Majesty."

Returning to the main cabin, I told May-ling and her two ladies in waiting to stay on board. I would signal when safe to deplane.

"Be careful, Rick."

"I'm probably overreacting, but you are carrying our child."

From there, I opened the first hatch in the airlock. Since there was pressure on both sides of the doors, I could open the second door after securing the first.

There were controls that would allow us to keep both doors open, but I didn't use those.

The ramp was deserted, with no one in sight.

I took one step forward, and a man came running toward me.

He was yelling, "It's a trap."

With the sound of a gun firing, he collapsed in a fountain of blood. He was beyond help, so I turned to reenter the ship when a stunning blow hit me.

Falling to the ground, I saw the hatch closing. I was too stunned to move and think. The ship lifted as I watched. At least something was going right.

Rough hands brought me to my feet. A beanbag lay on the ground. When I regained my senses, I knew what it was. The police now used bean bag rounds in shotguns to incapacitate without killing.

Stumbling along between my captors, I regained clarity of thought.

"What is going on?"

I saw no use in blustering my way out with a muddled mind. This was a planned event.

There was no response. I tried to ask questions several more times but was ignored.

I was taken to an area of the Forbidden City that I wasn't familiar with. Stumbling into a building between my captors, I realized the palace had its own police station.

Without ceremony, I was locked into a cell.

It was with relief I lay down on the bare cot. At least May-ling had gotten off safely. I was alone in that cell for several hours. Just about when I thought I was forgotten, the doors opened, and a group of men came in.

The one in front was obviously their leader.

"How are you, Your Majesty?"

Have you ever noticed how a shift in tone can completely change the meaning of words? There was no concern in his question. It was more of a mocking statement.

"I've been better. What is this all about?"

"Straight to the point, I like that."

"Perhaps you could return the courtesy?"

"My name is Wang Gāng. I am the rightful Emperor of China."

"I think Empress Ping might dispute that."

"I have her head on display. She has said nothing."

At that, I shut up. I needed more information.

"You will have the false Empress May-ling brought to me."

"I won't. She is my wife and carrying my child."

"Then you will die."

"So be it. If I die, the Rods from God will destroy all of China."

"I have heard of your so-called Rods from God. I do not fear them."

"Kill me and learn."

"First, we will let your wife know we have you. She will be given a choice. Hers for yours. You can always marry again and sire more children."

"What about May-ling's mother? Is she okay?"

"She is fine. Her head is next to the former empress's."

"You will pay for this."

"Brave words from a prisoner. Think about this overnight. We will talk again in the morning. In the meantime, a message is being sent to May-ling."

This man must die. I didn't know how or when, but he must die.

He and his companions, who had said nothing, turned and left.

I spent my time exploring my cell, trying to find a way out or something to use as a weapon. It was well constructed, and I found nothing.

An hour later, a meal was served. It was a bowl of rice with small bits of chicken. Being hungry, I ate it all. When I finished, I examined the chopsticks I was given. Could I use them as a weapon?

They were round on end instead of pointed so that they couldn't be used for stabbing. While sturdier than those used in Japan, they had little value as a weapon.

The bowl was a poor ceramic that would break easily. The bowl could have been used as a fight scene prop in a Western.

The little sink in the cell had a thin stream of water, and I couldn't think of how to use it. The same with the hole in the floor toilet. There was no toilet tissue, so I would have to use my left hand and wash it thoroughly.

The bed, suspended from the wall like in American prisons, had a thin mattress and thinner blanket. There was no pillow.

There was not much in the way of the comforts of home. This was a holding cell in a police station, not a cell for permanent occupancy. Not that they would have been much different.

I spent the evening hours wondering how this would all work out. I hoped my parents could prevent May-ling from trying to trade herself for me.

Obviously, this madman would kill her and my unborn child, so there would be no contestants for the throne.

I finally realized that I had no control over these events and should try to get some sleep. Easy to say, hard to do. Somewhere along the line, I did drift off.

My name, spoken softly, woke me up sometime in the middle of the night. They had taken my watch and other belongings.

I struggled awake and sat up. A man was standing in front of my cell with a set of keys. I recognized him as one of the empress's guards.

"King Richard, I'm here to get you out."

I stood up, ready to leave. I might be going from the frying pan into the fire. Not being in a jail cell was the preferable route.

"Where are we going?"

"First, we have to get you out of the Forbidden City. Then we can talk."

"Lead on."

He had opened the cell door and led me out of the cell block. When we entered the entry office of the police station, three men were waiting. A dead man was also in a pool of blood on the floor.

I knew this was serious, but now it was real. I saw my watch and wallet on a desk, so I picked them up.

I blocked my savior's view with my body as I picked up a pistol from the desk. I stuffed it inside my shirt before I turned around.

"Follow us."

I followed without comment, as they were the only game in town at this point.

We crossed several streets outside the station and turned down an alley. We had to stop once at a cross street and hide in shadows as a ten-man patrol marched through.

At the end of the alley, our leader knocked softly on the backdoor of what appeared to be a warehouse.

Someone had been waiting inside as it was opened immediately. A few words were exchanged. We entered and were led across the room to a descending staircase.

As we crossed the warehouse, I realized it was a pumping station. Probably for the sewage system.

The staircase led down to a closed metal door. Once opened, the smell validated my sewage system thoughts.

There were powerful flashlights for each of us and rubber boots to slip on over our shoes.

We followed a walkway for what seemed several miles. Only in one place did the sewage channel overflow the walkway. It wasn't more than two inches deep, but it made me thankful for the boots.

We made one right turn into a connecting channel and followed it for several hundred yards. Our leader stopped and then opened a door built into the sidewall.

There was another staircase leading upwards. A landing at the top had a dim ceiling light. We removed our boots and turned off our flashlights.

Giving the shave and a haircut knock, the door opened to let us into a small storage closet. Opening the next door brought us into the back of a dry-cleaning establishment.

This brought back memories of my first meeting with the then Lady Ping. I set them aside. Time for mourning later.

I stopped in the center of the room and asked the leader.

"Now, fill me in on what is going on."

Chapter 18

"We are loyal to the new Empress May-ling. The rebels under the traitorous General Wang killed her mother and grandmother. He intends to declare himself emperor after he disposes of May-ling."

He continued, "We had to free you so that May-ling wouldn't trade herself for your safety."

Though I agreed with his reasoning, hearing why I was rescued was still deflating.

"Where is the nearest radio that can reach the moon?"

"There is a military base outside of Tianjin that is still under our control. We will head there."

"How far is it?"

"It is about eighty miles to the base."

"I suspect my escape has been noticed by now. They will have roadblocks set up."

"I'm certain of it. We will be riding bicycles on the backroads."

Internally, I groaned at the thought. The Chinese bicycles were heavy and didn't pedal easily. But needs must.

"I thank you and your troops for rescuing me. I agree with all your reasoning. That is why I need to get to a radio to let May-ling know I'm not in captivity."

"She knows by now. We do have radios that will reach Tianjin. They, in turn, sent a message to the moon."

"How does she know the message isn't a ploy?"

"What purpose would it serve?"

"You're correct. I'm not thinking clearly."

"If you follow me, we will get started."

There were bicycles in the corner of the warehouse. No three-speed racing bikes. They made the heaviest Schwinn bikes look like toys.

Once we started our journey, I realized they pedaled better than I thought. Not by much.

To exit Beijing, we went through every back alley imaginable. Even this late at night, there were people out and about. They ignored us as we ghosted through the night.

Saying we ghosted through the night might be an exaggeration. Our bikes rattled and clanged as we went.

After two hours, it was getting to be daylight, and we had only reached the outskirts of the city. This had been planned, for we finally pulled up to an old, broken-looking warehouse.

It looked like it was about to collapse from the outside. Inside it was well maintained. There was a hot meal waiting for us.

As we ate, I asked, "What is this place?"

"It is one of the safe houses maintained by the Palace Guard."

"Nicely done."

I was too tired to say anything else.

My exhaustion must have shown because my rescuer showed me cots lined up inside a stall.

I still didn't know his name.

"When will it be appropriate for me to learn your name?"

"After we reach safety. You, not knowing me, may let me go free if you are recaptured."

Good spy craft but poor in practice. I already knew he was in the Palace Guard. If recaptured, I would be shown pictures under torture to identify him.

"Makes sense."

Never insult your rescuer.

I almost staggered over to the cots. It didn't take long for me to fall asleep. Pass out was more like it. I woke hours later. I felt more alert, but I had muscle aches everywhere. Running and bicycling use different muscle sets.

We had a small meal and used the facilities. Back on the road at nightfall, we still had a ways to go. It was a cloudless night with a full moon. That worked for us and against us. We could see well, which was a plus. Others could see us, which was a minus.

One of the guards rode ahead to scout. He had a much newer, lighter bike that didn't make as much noise.

At one point, he came back and signaled us to dismount. There was a checkpoint ahead. They must only work during the day as they are all asleep. There wasn't even a sentry posted!

We wheeled our bikes through the checkpoint and when a mile or so down the road, took back to riding.

The walk did me good as it helped me stretch out my abused legs. It didn't hurt my back, either.

That night we made almost forty miles. We would be in Tianjin by the next nightfall. Stopping at another safe house, we ate our only meal of the day.

For lunch, we had a thick slice of bread. We ate this while riding.

There were even crude showers in the safe house. I noticed they didn't have one of my showerheads. You can't have everything. I soon found out they didn't have hot water either.

It worked wonders on my tired, sweaty, stinky body.

After cleaning up, I had a brief conference with my savior.

"Is there really a resistance, and how organized is it?"

"That is what we are sorting out now. All of the military bases are locked down. Loyal guardsmen scout each to find out who the leader supports."

"What about the lower ranks?"

"They will follow their leaders."

"Can the staff against us be replaced?"

"Yes, but it will take bullets or the garrote."

"Can we still radio the base at Tianjin?"

"Yes."

"I would like to send a message to the moon. I'm going to arrange a pickup by a GC ship. That will save us a day of riding."

"That is a good idea. We are far enough from Beijing that the ship can get in and out before troops arrive."

I gave him points for not smirking. My discomfort at the end of the day was obvious to all.

A message was sent. They were to pick us up in the evening. The pickup point was far enough from the safe house that it might not get blown.

Once more, I fell asleep quickly. I was aroused at twilight. We had a quick meal of rice and some sort of fish. It was suspect enough that I didn't inquire what sort of fish or how old.

After the stress of escaping captivity and leaving Beijing, the pickup was anticlimactic.

Within three hours, we were at Colony. May-ling was waiting for me with open arms. Once the loyal guards were settled into their new quarters, we retired to our home.

"May-ling, I have bad news. Your mother and the empress have been killed."

She already looked pale and worn.

"I was afraid of that, husband. What will we do?"

I started to say something and then stopped.

"What would you like to do? Do you want to recover China and be the empress?"

"Not that I want to, but I have to for the Chinese people. My grandmother had her faults, but she was improving the lives of the common people. It was making a stronger China."

"That's settled then. Now the question is how to accomplish that?"

"I don't know. I just don't know."

At that, my lovely wife lost her composure. She fell against me, crying her eyes out. I did the only thing I could. I held her tightly.

Soon she was able to quit crying and compose herself. She went to wash her face. I was thinking hard about what to do.

Until we had more information, there was nothing we could do. It dawned on me to get the information to formulate a plan.

That meant we needed information from inside China. The one best suited for that was the royal guard who had rescued me. I had yet to learn his name.

I arranged for a meeting with him and Jerri Cobb. She is the head Space Lady and would be a key player.

Before the meeting, I asked his name.

"Qin Shi Huang."

"It is nice to finally meet you, and I give you my thanks once more for my rescue."

May-ling was more direct in her giving thanks. She named him Lord Qin Shi Huang on the spot. She did add that she would have to ascend to the throne for it to take effect.

After bringing Jerri up to date on the situation, I started the meeting with the question, "How do we discover China's state of affairs in all provinces?"

Qin Shi told us that they were in contact with at least one army, navy, or air force base in each province, and he should be able to get a sitrep in hours. May-ling asked what a sitrep was.

He replied, "A situation report."

He continued, "I do have some preliminary information, and it is both good and bad."

I gestured for him to go on.

"Various of the princes in the provinces have declared themselves the rightful ruler of their area. Two of them, the one in Beijing and one in Shanghai, have declared themselves Emperor. Their forces are fighting as we speak."

I interjected, "As Napoleon said, never interrupt your enemy when he is making a mistake."

Qin Shi chuckled at that, "That would be a very rude thing to do."

No one else laughed; we were all feeling the pressure.

Qin Shi told May-ling, "There are 35 provinces and administrative divisions now, counting Siberia. Strangely enough, there is no unrest in Siberia."

She replied, "They are too busy developing the land and getting rich to bother with a civil war."

I had to ask, "So we have an idea of what we face. How do we take it all back?"

May-ling smiled for the first time since the troubles had started, "Like eating an elephant, one bite at a time."

Chapter 19

The first bite of that elephant was figuring out what we had on our plate. We needed to know what forces we had available. Then there was the pesky fact the enemy had an unknown number of troops. Plus, we didn't know their disposition.

That afternoon, it took some scrambling, but we set up a war room. Its centerpiece was a ten-foot square table with a huge map of China.

While that was happening, Qin Shi and several of his troops were on the radio to every concentration of our troops that we knew about.

Each location was told to put together the information we were requesting. They were not to send their response by radio. It would be picked up. They were given the morning to provide a summary of what they knew.

So that we weren't fed erroneous information, it was explained that we understood some of it was the best guess. All we asked was for them to differentiate between known facts and estimates.

We had to do this because of cultural reasons. In China, they never wanted to give bad news.

The next morning our GC ships were busy landing and picking up the requested data. Only one ship came under fire because someone had been smart enough to realize how the retrieval would go.

The ship was able to lift off without damage. We had to come up with a better method of communication.

The data retrieved was encouraging. From the best estimates, we had enough forces to overwhelm any location. The downside was the distribution of our forces.

While we had them outnumbered and outgunned, our assets were scattered over the map. We needed to figure out how to bring a significant force together without leaving any of our bases vulnerable.

As our group pored over the possible avenues, I looked around the room. All good people, and not one professional military man among us. Qin Shi was a captain in the Empress's Bodyguard, not a soldier.

I realized that I had the truest military experience of any present. I knew that I didn't have the knowledge to run a war.

"Captain Qin Shi, does your background include commanding troops on the battlefield?"

"No, I was recruited from the Beijing police force, where I was on the VIP bodyguard detail."

'We need to find an active general to lead our efforts."

"I agree. We are amateurs playing at war."

"Please send a message to all our bases asking them to list the top three military commanders with actual experience."

"Why the top three?"

"I assume that each base commander will think they should have command. They will put their name at the top of their list. We will select the one with the most overall recommendations. Also, put a two-hour turnaround on their recommendations so that little politicking can go on."

"That sounds like a plan. I will get right on it."

In three hours, we had a list from all bases. As expected, the first name on the list was the submitting base commander in most cases.

No problems with egos in the Chinese Army. This probably was true in all armies.

The most recommended general was Sun Wu. He was number two on almost every list. Undoubtedly, he would be the best choice for overall command of the Chinese Army after reconstituting.

We had to reconstitute the army as one hundred percent of the general staff were involved in the civil war, all on other sides. It spoke volumes about how the previous empress had neglected that portion of her reign.

The man who had the fourth most mentions was Cao Cao. He was noted as a brilliant logistician and staff officer. We selected him to fill the role of Chief of Staff for General Sun Wu.

May-ling chaired all of these discussions as the empress. It was her power that was being contested.

While all these discussions were going on, a larger room had been set up. This room had thirty-five sandbox tables set up. In the center of the room was an even larger one, twenty feet by twenty feet, with a large map of China.

Each political area had its own table.

We had raided several Risk game sets to collect figures to represent our troops. Larger and more appropriate figures were being developed.

Off-duty Space Ladies were placing the figures. This kept them in the loop of what was going on. It also helped familiarize them with areas they might be flying into.

They moved the figures with croupier sticks we had sent up from Las Vegas.

The two generals in question were brought up to the moon. May-ling interviewed them. I had sent backchannel messages to Whitehall and the Pentagon asking for their opinions on the two generals.

The response was almost embarrassingly positive. It seems we had what was considered the best leaders of all time on our side.

May-ling accepted and promoted the two generals to overall command. She permitted me to broadcast their names to all commands. We did it over an open channel. Maybe we could strike some fear and cause uncertainty.

The two generals spent the next two days poring over the boards, considering troop placement and various known enemy weaknesses.

They had told May-ling that a quick and easy victory would be the best way to kick off the campaign.

General Cao cornered me with a question.

"How many of these GC crafts do you have so we can move men around quickly?"

"We have fifty active crafts currently. I can have one hundred and forty more available in a week."

His look of disappointment told me that wasn't enough to help.

I asked, "Are you looking to move large masses of men and material?"

"Yes, we would need over a thousand of your ships to move an army."

"You don't need a GC ship capable of interplanetary flight. You need the equivalent of a flatboat."

"Yes."

"Last year, we kicked around an idea. Let me call Jackson R&D on Earth to see if they did anything with it."

Fortunately, my timing was good. It was still business hours at the R&D center. We kept EST on the moon. A leftover from our early days. Once away from the Earth's day-night cycle, it didn't matter what time you kept.

I imagined we would use EST no matter where we settled in the solar system. The twenty-four-hour days were what the human body was used to.

Previously we had noodled around making a large cargo platform for use on Earth. There really was no limit on size other than available evantonium.

I didn't know how far they had taken the concept. It didn't take long to find out they had a fully developed plan but hadn't built a prototype.

The next morning the generals and I went to the R&D center. I had cleared it with the U.S. Embassy. They wanted to know the purpose of the visit. I explained it was to review a concept vehicle. They didn't push the issue.

The U.S. and other countries in the world were watching China closely but not doing anything to interfere. It was pretty clear they were waiting to see how things would develop.

At the R&D center, they had the plans all set out. The concept was simple. Make a platform of the desired size, coat the underside with evantonium, and mount a fusion generator for power and large jet engines to push it around.

Many science fiction novels describe it as a giant gravity sled. The engines didn't have to be super powerful as neutralization of gravity and inertia resulted in atmospheric drag being the only resistance. We did what streamlining we could, but drag could not be reduced to zero. Still, engine power was not necessary to keep the sled in the air, which was the big power requirement in ordinary aircraft.

There were several designs. The first was a simple platform. It had possibilities. You could drive a division of soldiers on board and take off to your destination.

Other variations were fancier. There was one that was a moveable airfield. Another is a portable artillery park. The largest, which covered three square miles, was all of the above.

Since we needed transportation quickly, we chose the simple design. We could put five thousand troops on one platform. Two to four platforms would carry a full motorized division. There was another platform that would have artillery on board.

The artillery platform was a tremendous asset. We could set it at any height up to ten thousand feet. After that, supplemental oxygen would be needed. This gave new meaning to the term, having the high ground.

Only specialized anti-aircraft fire, which was unavailable to most of the warlords, could reach our people while we shelled them with impunity.

We did include an airfield platform for air defense. This gave us the most powerful army the world had ever seen.

Now, all we had to do was build them. Australia agreed to my using the Lassiter Station as the construction site. Concrete slabs were poured in forms suspended eight feet above the ground. When the concrete was set, the bottom was coated with evantonium. Power was applied, and the slab was towed to an assembly area.

The first platforms assembled were dedicated to hauling building materials. Jet engines were coming from every airplane graveyard that had workable engines.

As the world press called them, it took three weeks for the "fortress platforms" to be completed. Thousands of temporary workers had been flown in from worldwide.

Our army was getting ready to move.

Chapter 20

Nothing can change for months in the war, as in the phony war before the Battle of Britain. Or everything can change in minutes, as Pearl Harbor proved. There was some change during the three weeks we assembled our flying platforms.

Two provinces had a turnover in leadership. In one, a warlord prince was replaced by a commoner who proved to be a better warlord. The other was a prince overthrown by a May-ling loyalist.

We considered both wins. The two warlords fighting had weakened the victor significantly. The other was a plain win for us.

In most cases, the control of each political group was tightened. Their downfall was that the controlling warlords were greedy and immediately set out to conquer their neighbors.

Again, we all favored these actions as their armies were weakened in the aftermath. Only a few were consolidating their power and preparing for Empress May-ling to take her empire back.

Our generals were inventorying available assets. They made several trips Earthside to inspect the troops and materials that were reported as available.

Most reporting officers exaggerated what was available. One base commander had been stealing and selling everything he could get his hands on. His inspection resulted in his being stood against a wall and shot.

This execution was videotaped and shared with all base commanders. Revised estimates poured in. None were revised upwards. The downward revisions weren't disastrous but could have caused problems if not known in advance.

We had requests from every major military power to allow observers. They were all aware of our GC platforms and wanted to see their effect on warfare.

After a stormy session with our generals, May-ling agreed to allow this. The generals were reluctant to share any information outside of their staff.

May-ling's stance was that we might need their help in the immediate future, and it was advantageous to have them at our side. I kept out of this one.

This was May-ling's battle for her empire. Of course, I wanted her to win. At the same time, she had to demonstrate she was in control. What we talked about in the bedroom was no one's business.

At my suggestion, we had a duplicate war room for the observers. They were encouraged to separately come up with their own battle plans.

This led to interesting discussions between the officers from different armies in that room. We had bugged the heck out of the rooms, so we got some interesting insights into the different countries' thinking.

We also got some good ideas that several of our staff officers came up with, wink, wink. Nothing earth-shattering but useful. I imagine their reports to the various headquarters made us seem like military geniuses. After all, one who agrees with you must be very smart.

General Wu laughed himself silly when he realized the full extent of this program. He told us he would add it to his book, *The Art of War*.

Lists were made of every unit available. We weren't going to leave any base so weak that it couldn't defend itself. Once this list was compiled, the generals had an idea of what they had to work with.

Next, they had to plan the order in which to bring the provinces under control. One constraint that most armies had to consider was creating a beachhead. Normally beachheads were well-defined areas that could be defended.

With the GC flatboats, we could attack any province in any order. Like a game of Go, the ideal attack plan was to create a center and attack outwards. Always keep the lines of defense as short as possible.

Two provinces in the north of China had declared for the empress. They weren't adjoining. They did adjoin the Gobi desert, so the north didn't require a strong defensive line.

If we pacified the province between them, we had the beginnings of reconquering China. Then we would go for the province just south of the newly acquired one. Thus, the newly defeated one would be surrounded by provinces under our control.

By this method, the generals and their staff proposed to conduct the war. Troops would have to be left in each conquered province. Because of this, we had a shortfall of available manpower.

Once we had over half of China reoccupied, we would have to figure out how to continue.

The rest of the world didn't stop while these events were going on. For us, the biggest thing was a report from the evantonium finds survey team.

They had mapped the caverns that were accessible in the astertoid. I hadn't wanted to give the body a name to help conceal it from others. In the report, it was called Planet X. Some days you can't win.

The caverns were extensive. They were large enough to hold everything we had talked about. One note in the report made me go back out to Planet X. Once I was there, the lead surveyor took me inside the cavern.

"The inside looks like it has been finished."

"Come see for yourself."

She was right. The floors and walls were as smooth as cut marble.

"Any idea how this happened?"

"Aliens?"

I had hoped she wouldn't go there. That, on top of all else, would be too much.

"If so, did they leave anything behind?"

"Nothing. Like a rented apartment, they left it broom clean."

"Broom clean doesn't mean all signs of wear and tear have been repaired."

"There are scuff marks at various intersections as though large equipment touched the side as it was moved."

"Please show me."

We went to an opening from one large cavern to another. The opening itself, while large, showed signs of being hit on its edges. As though a large piece of equipment barely made it through.

I told the Space Lady, "Have someone try to scrape the residue off the wall as best as possible and analyze it."

"Rick, we have already started the process. Samples are at Jackson R&D as we speak."

"Good job. Do many people know of this?"

"Only the survey team. We didn't even tell the R&D people where it came from."

"Please keep it that way. There is no way this could be a natural phenomenon. If word got out, we would hear every government in the world screaming to have their people take a look."

"Is there anything else?"

"Not a thing."

"I wonder if there is any way to date this whole place. If there were aliens here, how long ago was it?"

"Rick, I would like to suggest that we comb the entire surface of this place, hunting for anything else."

"We also should use ground-penetrating radar to explore the entire asteroid."

"Again, we are ahead of you, boss. It should be here tomorrow."

"It's nice to have a great team in place. Is there anything I can do for you?"

"Not at this point. We have a GC field being set up, so we have decent living quarters. This is going to be a long-term project."

"Be certain to do it right. This will be a permanent base."

Back on Earth, various governments noted that all of a sudden, we were using evantonium as though we had an infinite supply. Inquiries were coming in to see if we would release any to them. Our standard reply was that we were digging into our reserves as a wartime measure.

On returning to the moon, I was given an update on the retaking of China.

"General Wu, I understand that congratulations are in order. The first province has been retaken."

"Yes, Your Majesty. This one was easier than predicted."

"Why did the show of force convince the leaders to surrender?"

"The building demolition company approached us with an idea."

"What was that?"

"For a fee, they would flatten the rebel's headquarters with them in it."

"I didn't see that coming. I gather it worked."

"Splendidly. It decapitated the rebels in one crushing blow."

General Wu is a very serious person. I was not going to accuse him of making a pun. The big smile that followed this statement told me he wasn't as serious as I thought.

"What happened next?"

"I sent a team in under a flag of truce. The remaining junior officers were only too glad to surrender to us."

"That is wonderful."

"More than wonderful. We have left soldiers from another province to keep order. The resident troops have been loaded on a platform. They will keep the order in the next province we take. Our manpower problem has been resolved."

"What's the next step?"

The demolition team is in the process of flattening every headquarters we know of before the word gets out. This could be the easiest victory in the history of warfare."

"I hope you haven't jinxed us."

His puzzled look at this statement spoke of another cultural difference.

Chapter 21

Soon after we had retaken the first states, other states declared for us. Two of them invited us in, and the princes reaffirmed their pledges. We still transferred their troops to the main army and placed ours with them.

Then three leaders saw the handwriting on the wall and departed for parts unknown.

My best guess was Brazil. They weren't my concern, but May-ling put her secret police on the trail. That wouldn't end well for the princes.

Once more, we switched troops around. After many interviews, we determined that only the highest officers were part of the revolutions. The average Joe couldn't care less who was in charge as long as they got paid.

Two of the renegade provinces were fighting each other. They were also raping and pillaging along the way.

After a serious discussion with her generals, May-ling decided to end them next. Waiting until the two armies were fighting each other in a relatively small area, I had the Space Ladies drop a Rod from God.

It was a full-size rod, and the impact was tremendous. It registered as an earthquake all over the world. When the dust settled, there was no trace of either army or their leadership.

It certainly got the attention of the world. Hearing about a theoretical weapon and seeing it used in real life were two different things. The damage was the same as a midsized hydrogen bomb, about nine megatons.

There was no radiation released, but there was a dust cloud. Dire predictions were made of nuclear winter, but they failed to materialize. The so-called pundits had failed to realize a large volcano eruption would do worse. This has occurred several times in recorded history.

One bit of fallout from dropping the rod was the immediate surrender of all the other provinces. It was almost humorous how they couldn't message May-ling fast enough.

She summoned them to the Forbidden City she had reoccupied and promptly imprisoned them. They would be tried and probably executed.

China is China.

I was by my wife's side during all of this. The decisions were hers, but we discussed them in depth. Nothing was done on impulse.

In the reinstated China, there were no princes other than any future royal ones. They were replaced by governors who served at the empress's pleasure. They would serve a limited term and be rotated or retired. They wouldn't be allowed to stay anywhere long enough to build a power base.

The same with the army units. Officers would be transferred routinely and whole units on occasion. Again, the idea was that a long-term power base wouldn't be allowed to consolidate.

This even reached large cities. The mayors and others who were political were term-limited. The only people who could count on remaining in their jobs were the technical people.

We even discussed that but realized you could only take things so far without causing disruptions. Whoever heard of a revolution led by electrical workers or trashmen?

From start to finish, the whole mess took three months. When it was finally over, May-ling allowed herself to mourn her mother and grandmother. A state funeral was held for both of them.

The disgraced princes received a bullet in the back of the head and a pine box. This was done publicly to demonstrate the consequences of revolt. Of course, the world decried the actions. It was felt that I was a bad influence on May-ling. Little did they know I had to talk her out of their deaths by a thousand cuts.

While the revolution was going on, the United States offered to help in exchange for a large amount of evantonium. We declined, saying that we could handle things by ourselves.

I received a message from the U.S. Joint Chiefs of Staff explaining that they had examined our logistics problems and there was no way we could move our troops as needed plus supply them.

Rather than argue with them, I detailed a GC platform over American Samoa to show what we were capable of. En route, the platform accidentally overflew the U.S. 7th Fleet.

The fleet scrambled jets to check us out. They were surprised when they realized that this particular platform was a base for the Chinese Air Force. There was a lot of wing waggling, and no harm was done.

It didn't take long for the Joint Chiefs to figure out that warfare had just changed. I was asked if I intended to support the Chinese in any undertakings.

I replied that I was supporting my wife in recovering her empire. The Lunar Kingdom and the Solar Reaches had no ambitions beyond that goal.

The more I used that name, the more I liked it.

As China came back under control, there was a new issue. May-ling had to be crowned Empress of China.

It would take time to set up a coronation. Her grandmother had just assumed the throne and crowned herself with no fanfare. This didn't seem appropriate at this time. The country was reeling from the civil wars, and people were starving in some areas of the country.

My brilliant wife came up with a good solution. She announced that it would take several millions of U.S. dollars to put on a formal coronation. She didn't feel right about doing this, so she would spend that money feeding her people.

All seven hundred million people in the country would be given one pound of rice. This was about a week's supply for one person.

The troops would distribute it in each area. There would be audits of what was sent out and delivered.

It cost more than sixty million dollars to buy the rice. GC platforms had to be sent worldwide to collect the huge amount.

Some dealers tried to capitalize on this and raised prices beyond reason. We published their names in the newspapers of their home country and made no purchases. We managed to get what was needed anyway.

To avoid starvation, it would cost close to a billion dollars. The Chinese treasury hadn't been looted, so the money was available. This was due to the fact that a large portion of their gold reserves was kept in Australia.

It was nip and tuck, but disaster was averted.

On the appointed day, May-ling crowned herself in front of international TV. She had the highest approval ratings ever recorded for any world leader that day.

The Russians foolishly chose to launch an invasion of their former Siberian territory that day. They sent troops into the Ural Mountains with a three-to-one advantage over the defending forces.

It only took a few simple radio messages for the GC platforms to bring in supporting troops accompanied by artillery, armor, and the Air Force.

After three days of stiff fighting, the Russians were sent packing and lost another one hundred miles off their eastern border. They never seemed to learn. As some wag put it, "At one time, the Russians had the second-best army in the world. Now they have the second-best army in China."

One important announcement had to be made to the world.

"The GC sleds that will be moving worldwide to collect food to prevent starvation in China will not be made available to any government or commercial entity. Exceptions will be made on a case-by-case basis for humanitarian reasons.

"This decision was reached to prevent the collapse of the worldwide transportation system. Airlines, railroads, and ocean freight company stock would become worthless overnight. This would throw the world into a depression like none other.

"Study groups will be created to see how these can be integrated with the world transportation system without massive disruptions. All major governments and industry groups will be invited to participate. Later, there will be an announcement about when these groups will be formed.

"It is not too early for each government to start identifying their representatives to their national working group.

"When a National working group comes to a consensus on the actions best taken for their nation, they will have one representative to present their case to the international working group.

"When an international plan is formulated, it will be voted on first by the international working group, then the governments of each country represented.

"When the final plan is approved with a majority vote, the GC sleds will become available for leases. That is right, 'leases.' The Lunar Kingdom and Solar Reaches will not sell any sled with GC capabilities outright. This is so we retain control and can prevent their misuse for warfare.

"I hope this announcement puts the fears in the marketplace to rest."

The announcement will keep the world's governments in a tizzy and off my back if nothing else.

May-ling told me this was wishful thinking. She turned out to be correct. The backchannels were buzzing as everyone possibly tried to gain an advantage over their competitors.

Chapter 22

One thing that puzzled me was the Russian attempt to take back Siberia. I thought the new government was more democratic and peaceful. It turned out the newly elected government was all the old hard-liner wolves in sheep's clothing.

These hardliners didn't bode well for the world. My private prediction that I didn't share with anyone, even May-ling, was that it would take a Rod from God on Red Square when their congress was in session to solve the issue.

I wasn't going to do anything about Russia but would keep an eye on them. I didn't understand the culture that would allow such leaders to come into power. The tsars were understandable because that was how the world was run at the time.

The Soviets made promises that weren't kept. It took over fifty years for the people to rise. The election cycle in the United States made changes much easier. That is why a Republic is a better option.

Hmm, I had better watch myself. Kings were changed by beheading.

While all this was going on down on Earth, things were happening in space. There had been a discovery on the evantonium asteroid that could shake the foundations of our thoughts on man's development. It started with a radio message to me.

"King Richard, we have found something on Planet X that you must see. I can't tell you over the air, but it is interesting."

I wish we could standardize a name for that place. Currently, Planet X is the forerunner. I should have named it upfront.

"I will be there in six hours."

Space travel had become like a trip to the corner store. Upon arrival at Planet X, my pilot followed a beacon to the exploration crew.

"Now that I'm here, what is so interesting?"

"Your Majesty, it is more than interesting. I didn't want to give a true description over the air. It may have set off a worldwide panic."

"Well, show me what is so important."

I hoped I wasn't brought out here on a wild goose chase.

The first sign that I wasn't was that there was a metal door in the face of a nearby cliff. It was man-sized. We hadn't built it. It opened with the simple push of a button next to the door. With this location, security wasn't an issue.

Going through the entrance revealed that it was an airlock. After closing the first door, some atmosphere was pumped in.

"What gas is this?"

"Air, sir, good old earth-type air."

"Call me Rick, for goodness sake."

"Yes, sir."

I could see that we would have to codify how to address me so I wouldn't go nuts with all the formality. Certainly, it was correct when holding Court or other formal occasions, but out in the field, no way.

After the second door was opened, we went into a hallway that led to an open room. It appeared to be a lounging area. It was sparsely furnished. The furniture looked like it was made for humans.

"This is interesting, but I don't see how it could cause worldwide panic. Also, where is the air coming from?"

"The air is easy. There is an equipment room at the back of this complex with several large, pressurized containers. The gauges show the air moving back and forth between them and the airlock."

"What is important is in this room?"

As she spoke, Billie, the Space Lady in charge of the exploration team, took me into a large room off the lounging area.

She was right. It was jaw-dropping. On a large table in the middle of the room were models of the Great Pyramids of Egypt, Stonehenge, and the Nasca line paintings in the Peruvian desert.

This discovery would set every conspiracy nut in the world off. Heck, it set me off. Who had done this?

Were they humans? Another question is, how does this station (for want of a better word) have power? This place was probably over a thousand years old. We had no batteries or power generation sources that would last that long.

A nuclear fission plant fuel lasts six years if not changed out. Nuclear fusion would go indefinitely as long as fuel was added. However, this Planet X would have been consumed totally in the time frames we were looking at.

"Have we identified the power source yet?"

"We think we have, but it makes no sense."

"Show me."

She was right. It made no sense in our frame of experience. After tracing out all the connections, what appeared to be the power source was the size of a large refrigerator.

The strangest thing is that no evidence of fuel was provided to the box. Where was the power coming from?

"Are there any signs of radiation?"

"Extremely low levels, safe for the human body. We have to test, but the only type of element that would meet the criteria is protactinium 231. It is safe for the human body as it only releases one proton at a time, and its half-life is thirty-seven thousand years."

"How do you know this?"

Billie continued, "A misspent youth and a Ph.D. in nuclear physics. After all that, I decided that flying was more fun. Then came this opportunity to be in space."

"I think we are lucky to have you, Billie. You have a new job, figuring out how this thing works. You will still keep your stick time, but when not scheduled, I want you here."

"Sounds like fun."

"You may want to consult with my sister. She may have some thoughts on this."

"I would be delighted to work with Mary. She is a hero in my world."

"Is there anything that hints about who may have made this station?"

"Not a thing we have found except that everything is scaled for humans."

"I'm not certain what to do about this. I would like it kept a secret until I have time to think about what to do. This will have to be shared with the world but must be done carefully."

Billie replied, "I understand. It is only my copilot and me in on this, and we will keep it quiet until you say differently."

We were having this conversation in front of the table where the models were. I was absently looking at the pyramids when I noticed that there appeared to be a wind blowing sand around.

"Billie, do you see the sand moving?"

"Yes."

As she answered me, the wind exposed something shiny in one of the many dunes surrounding the largest pyramid. I picked it up. It looked like the gold caps that were reported as topping the Pyramids. They had been gone for a long time, probably looted.

Since it seemed to fit, I placed it on top of the largest pyramid. It was a perfect fit, so I left it in place. It made an imposing edifice even more imposing.

"Let's go check out the equipment room one more time. That power-generation device is driving me nuts. There is no way that protactinium 231 could be powering that thing. One proton at a time wouldn't do it."

"Maybe it is an isomer of protactinium."

"It could be. What's an isomer of protactinium?"

"A rare form of the material. Most elements can form an isomer. However, they aren't considered useful and, in some cases, they are harmful."

Billie took many pictures of the entire structure while I explored looking for hidden doors. I found nothing, so we returned to the ship for our trip back to the moon.

It took us four hours to get home. I returned to the palace where May-ling was waiting. She had an incredible story to relate also. It was being told all over the solar system.

It seems there had been an event at the Great Pyramid of Giza. A gold cap had erupted from the desert and settled atop the pyramid.

Witnesses described the event. Since it was a tourist spot, there was even a 16mm film of the event.

The Egyptian Army had been moved in to protect the site. This was after experts had quickly identified the cap as solid gold.

I made a strangled sound. May-ling turned quickly to me.

"Rick, what have you done?"

"You had better sit down to hear this."

I then proceeded to relate the entire find to her.

"How would moving something on a model cause something on Earth to move?"

"Have you heard of Albert Einstein calling something a 'spooky action at a distance'?"

"I may have. It sounds familiar, but I don't know what it means."

"Neither do I. I do know that that was spooky action at a distance. I need to talk to Mary. This is too sensitive to talk about over the air, so I'm going down to Earth."

"It will have to wait until tomorrow."

"Why?"

"In California, it is past Mary's bedtime. This will wait."

I contacted Billie and her copilot, Jane, and told them what was happening and that they would take me Earthside first thing in the morning. The flight crew would notify the U.S. State Department of my trip and ensure they understood it was only a family visit.

I also called Mum and Dad and told them I would be there to talk to Mary about an important issue. Would they please let her miss school?

"No problem, Rick. Tomorrow is Saturday."

Chapter 23

At Jackson House on Saturday morning, we met for breakfast. An offhand comment by Mary brought forth an incident May-ling and I hadn't heard about. It seems Mary had been involved in an attempted robbery!

After our sounds of astonishment at not hearing about this earlier, we got her to relate the story. Mum and Dad looked ashamed that we hadn't been informed of this event.

Mary told us about her shopping trip in her own words.

"Mum's birthday was coming, so Jim and Sally took me shopping. Jim always drives and stays in the car."

"He preferred that rather than going into the stores. Sally and I agreed that men and boys didn't know how to shop.

She said this was because men were hunters. See food, kill food, and come home. They shopped the same way."

"Women are homemakers. We would look for the best, check the rest to ensure we were correct, then buy if on sale and go home."

That made sense to me.

"We had an appointment at Van Cleef & Arpels on Rodeo Drive. I wanted to buy Mum a tennis bracelet.

"We had to ring the doorbell to get in as they kept it locked. They only wanted serious buyers.

"A guard was sitting in a chair beside the door. He didn't get up when we came in. He was fat and looked lazy. I doubted he would be much help in a robbery.

"The saleslady who let us in was very nice. The room decorated. I had to ask what the style was because it was so ornate. Sally used the word ornate. I said over the top.

"The nice sales lady said it was called Baroque. She admitted it was over the top but worked there every day and didn't notice it anymore.

"She took us over to a strange little couch called a settee.

"The lady offered us refreshments. Coffee, tea, soft drinks, or juices. I asked for orange juice, and Sally got coffee.

"I wondered if I would be given a chance to buy anything. I realized there wasn't very much jewelry on display.

"The jewelry pieces on display were each in a separate display case. Looking around, I suspected they would charge more than most stores.

"The saleslady returned with a tray with our drinks and some pastries. One chocolate donut was yummy. While we were having our snack, the lady asked what Sally was in the market for.

"Sally corrected her, 'It's Mary who is shopping today. She is looking for a tennis bracelet for her mother's birthday.'

"'I'm sorry. I thought Mary was your daughter.'

"The lady turned to me and asked if I had a budget. She asked as though I would say five or ten dollars.

"I felt ornery. I replied, 'Somewhere between five and ten.'

"'I'm afraid we have nothing in that price range.'

"Sally was snickering. When she quieted down, she told the lady, 'I think Mary Jackson meant five or ten thousand dollars.'"

"The saleslady closed her mouth, then said, 'Oh, you are one of those Jacksons. I didn't understand. Certainly, we have items in your price range. Let me fetch a few.'

"She stood to leave when there was a crash at the front of the store. I looked in time to see a man with a small sledgehammer step through the remains of the front door.

"I don't think he or the two men behind him had an appointment. The fat guard started to stand up but sat back down when a gun was held to his head.

"I looked at Sally, and she told me to sit still. I did. I noticed her taking her pistol out of her purse and sliding it under a fold of her dress where she was sitting.

"I have to get a handgun!

"I did sneak out my Fairburn fighting knife and place it under my dress.

"While this was happening, the three men came to the back of the store. They weren't wearing masks. I had seen enough TV to know this wasn't good. They had hit the poor guard in the head, so he was out cold. They also took his revolver so that I couldn't retrieve it.

"One of the guys said, 'This is a robbery.'

"How redundant!

"He continued, 'You ladies sit still, and we will collect the jewels and leave. No one needs to get hurt.'

"I guess guards don't count.

"One guy used the handheld sledgehammer to break the display cases, grabbed the jewels, and put them in a pillowcase.

"The other two went into the backroom. There was a lot of crashing and banging.

"All of a sudden, there was a single gunshot. Then one of the robbers in the back was shouting, 'Why did you do that? Now we can be charged with murder in an armed robbery.'"

"Sally and I exchanged looks. Now they wouldn't want to leave any witnesses.

"The guy with the sledgehammer had his back to me, so I stabbed him deeply in his right kidney with my knife. He let out a strange noise and collapsed.

"The other two guys came out of the backroom. One had a sack in each hand which was poor planning. The other had one sack and his pistol.

"Sally shot the guy with the pistol first. The other guy dropped his two sacks and went for a handgun in his belt. She shot him before the sacks hit the floor.

"Sally checked and made sure all the bad guys were dead. She then went into the backroom but came back shortly. She was shaking her head.

"The manager didn't make it.

"All this time, our saleslady was sitting there frozen with a teacup halfway to her mouth. I reached over and took it from her.

"She promptly collapsed into tears.

"The guard was coming around but was in a daze.

"Sally went to a phone in the corner to call the police. Before she could dial the phone, they came in with guns drawn.

"It took a few minutes to sort out what had happened. One of the policemen told me they had been on the lookout for this gang. They had been doing 'smash and grabs' where they would be in and out in five minutes or less.

"Sally and I had to give separate statements. At first, they didn't think they needed to talk to me as I was just a kid. They changed their tune when they found out I put the knife in the guy's kidney, and then they interviewed me.

"They wanted to know where the knife was. I had cleaned it off and returned it to its sheath on my leg.

"They took the knife as evidence. I was told I would get it back. I replied it was okay because I had more at home.

"One of the officers joked, 'You will be defenseless until you get home.'

"I showed him the throwing knife covered by my dress sleeve.

"The policeman got a really strange look.

"By the time it was all done, I never got to buy Mum's present. Maybe we can go to Zales tomorrow.

"When we got home, Mummy and Daddy had to hear the whole story. They were glad we were both safe. Daddy told Sally she had earned her Christmas bonus. Jim was there and looked a little put out. He had missed all the fun.

"Daddy took me to our library the next day and asked how I had slept last night. I told him fine. He wanted to know if stabbing that guy bothered me at all. I told him no, as it was those guys or us.

"Daddy told me if I had any problems, please talk to him about them.

"Daddy, I do have a question."

"What is that?"

"Will people think I'm bragging if I put a notch on my knife handle?"

As Mary related this question she had asked Dad, I laughed. It wasn't that funny; it released the tension building in me as I realized how close I had come to losing my sister.

I also realized that my sister was a very good storyteller. We all were sitting on the edge of chairs, leaning forward as she told her story. Even Mum and Dad who already knew the story.

May-ling asked Mary, "What was his response?"

"He told me it wasn't bragging if you had done it."

At that, a knife appeared in her hand as though by magic. It had a notch in the handle.

Chapter 24

Both May-ling and I were shocked beyond words. We stared open-mouthed at Mary. My little sister had killed a man with a knife!

How could she have done this? Not that it didn't need to be done, but perform the deed? I started questioning her on that subject when I realized that I had killed men myself and that our parents had done the same.

Maybe Denny and Eddie were the strange ones in our family unless they had a story I had never heard.

"Good for you, girl. Just don't knife Patty when you are mad at her."

"I wouldn't dream of it. I have filled some balloons with India ink and saved them for her."

"Neat."

"How is she anyway?"

"She is mad at her grandfather. He wouldn't start a war so she could settle it and get a Nobel Peace Prize."

Maybe grandfather had mellowed in his old age.

"Mary, I came here for a reason. Are you real busy at the moment?"

"If you mean this moment, I'm busy talking to you. Professor Einstein and I correspond on that odd happening in Egypt, if you mean busy in general."

"Smart aleck."

"You need to learn the meaning of 'is.'"

"Keep it up, sis, and I won't tell you what moved the pyramid cap in place."

She got all serious immediately. Leaning forward, she asked me, "What?"

Even Mum and Dad, silent during this exchange, leaned in to hear what I had to say."

"I moved the cap."

"How?"

"An airlock was found on Planet X. It led to a series of rooms with breathable air and gravity. There is a table with a model of the Pyramid of Giza and Stonehenge.

"I noticed there was a breeze blowing sand around on the model. It uncovered the tip of the gold cap. I picked it up out of curiosity and placed it atop the pyramid. Later I found that the action was mirrored on Earth."

Mary got all excited.

"That is what the professor and I thought. The two objects are entangled. Whatever you do to one occurs with the other. Spooky action at a distance."

At that, she did a happy dance. She is ten no matter what else happens in her life.

"When can the professor and I go to Planet X and check it out?"

"Let me know when you are ready, and we can make it happen."

Mary left the room at a run to call Professor Einstein.

She returned to tell us that she and the professor would like a ride to Planet X first thing in the morning. I told her that would be no problem. I had a GC ship on standby at all times. The crew had taken to calling it the Royal Barge.

I told them, "Whatever floats your boat."

It was unseemly of them to boo their monarch. I need to build a Tower of London on the moon.

While at Jackson House, I reviewed mail that had been held for me. The clipping service I used was still located in LA. Every week they sent me a package containing a synopsis of mainstream articles and any specific letters that were serious. This didn't include offers of sex, ways to make a fortune, or free donuts. Why donuts, I don't know, but they were offered occasionally.

One of the specific letters was an invitation to be the guest speaker for the 1965 Bellefontaine High School graduation!

At first, I couldn't comprehend why they wanted me. I said this aloud to May-ling, and she laughed for several minutes. It finally dawned on me that I was probably one of the more famous graduates of BHS.

It was easy to say yes to the request. I did put the caveat that other events might preclude my speaking and that I would confirm ahead of time.

After lunch, I drove one of my old reliable T-Birds to the movie studio. I was feeling a little nostalgic for the simple days of movie-making.

The sticker on my car was outdated, so the guard made me wait while he called the office. He had a sour look when he raised the bar to let me pass. He must have gotten an earful.

Mr. Monroe appeared at the front door while I was parking my car in the visitor's section. At one time, I used to have a parking spot, but no more. How the mighty have fallen.

Mr. Monroe was effusive in his welcome.

"Rick, may I still call you Rick? What do we owe the honor of this visit?"

"I have some free time this afternoon and thought I would like to look around at my old stomping ground."

"Let me walk you through."

"That would be great. I suspect the turnover has been enough that your security people wouldn't recognize me and would haul me away."

The first place we went was the stunt area where the guys I used to work with hung out.

I wasn't there more than a minute when I had saber in hand fighting for my life. Well, fighting for my life Hollywood style. Lots of jumping around, wild swings, and a clash of metal. With the dull sabers, the worst hit would leave a black and blue mark.

I want to report that I had no marks, but that would be a fib. I gave better than I got but still received a few stinging blows. It was great fun.

The guys tried to talk me into jumping off a five-story building onto an airbag. I declined the opportunity, but it got me thinking. Could you make a personal GC system? I would have to look into that.

It would be so neat to jump off the building with no airbag and slowly come to a stop just as you were about to hit.

It would have to be battery-powered. On second thought, I had too many batteries die on me. This would take some careful doing.

I was even allowed to be an extra in a crowd scene. This would be a no-credit appearance. Word would get out that I was in the scene, but it would be an insider sort of thing. The director assured me this scene wouldn't hit the cutting room floor as he intended to leak my appearance to one of the trade journals.

I had no problem with this, as this is how the industry worked. Besides, no one would go to see a weird movie called Dr. Strangelove.

All in all, it was a fun, relaxing afternoon. I returned to Jackson House to a happy group of women. They had been shopping on Rodeo Drive and had to give Dad and me an impromptu fashion show.

Denny and Eddie both found they had urgent appointments elsewhere. Lucky them.

The next morning Mary, May-ling, my parents, and I flew to Princeton to pick up Professor Einstein. He was waiting and ready to go. For the record, his hair was in its famous disarray.

Once we were underway, I got up and asked why he wore it that way.

"The girls like it."

Okay.

He and Mary then discussed the physics of what had occurred. They were both excited as this opened up many possibilities. I couldn't follow most of it, but my ears did perk up when a casual mention was made of faster-than-light travel.

They didn't have a direct conversation as such. One would make a statement, and then they would both zone out, thinking it over.

Mum, Dad, May-ling, and I talked about how the retaking of China was progressing. The military operations had been completed. All territory was now under May-ling's control. Now she had to put civil authorities into place.

The question was the form of the civil government and the controls that needed to be in place to prevent further problems.

I learned that the leader, Wang Gāng, who had declared himself to me as the rightful Emperor of China, had been killed in the fighting. His entire organization had been purged.

Several hours later, May-ling decided she wanted a local free election system for everything below the governors of each state. There would be tight controls on voting.

Each person casting a ballot would have their thumb dyed with indelible ink, so each person could only vote once.

The army would be in charge of the ballot boxes to prevent stuffing. Even the army would have checks and balances by having officers of different units involved with each voting center.

Tampering with ballots would be an automatic death sentence. Voting rolls would be updated frequently. There would be huge fines for moving and not notifying your local election office.

There would also be fines for not voting without a medical excuse. Employers were required to give one half-paid day for voting.

It all sounded good, but Dad wondered how long it would take for someone to figure out how to get around the system.

May-ling was not amused.

Chapter 25

On our trip to Planet X, we were in what the crew called the Royal Barge, my GC ship. It was painted in my colors on the outside, British racing green with my coat of arms.

These were my British coat of arms. Should I have a Lunar coat of arms created? I didn't want to have a heraldry group for my small kingdom. Small in population, not size. Maybe I could hire it done by the British College of Arms for a fee.

The entire upper lever was decorated in soft tones that would be found in an old English club. Even several of the paintings would be at home in a hunt club.

I had vetoed using modern pop culture colors. To me, they were too garish. One of the paintings they wanted to buy was a picture of Campbell's tomato soup. Who would want that? I passed on the original.

The conference area had a table that doubled as the dining room table. It could seat twelve comfortably. On the side of the area was a buffet, as all meals were served buffet style. Along the wall was a large whiteboard.

This board was currently in use by Albert Einstein and my sister Mary. My parents and May-ling were half-listening from the seating area while pretending to read. In Mum's case, a crossword puzzle. I was unashamedly eavesdropping.

Mary and the professor were discussing their theories on quantum actions. I had always pictured these discussions to be learned dissertations between colleagues.

They were learned all right. Colleagues, I'm not certain. Dissertations, no way, more like shouting contests.

Professor Einstein yelled at Mary, *"Du farkirtst mir di yorn! Dummes Madchen."*

I had no idea what they meant but did understand her, "Stubborn poopy head," in reply.

Mum and Dad did their best to ignore all this, but from their smirks, it was a good give and take.

Later I asked Mary.

"Why did you call him a stubborn poopy head?"

She whispered, "Because I would get into big trouble if I called him a stupid son of a bitch."

So much for a learned dissertation.

These yelling matches didn't seem to bother or slow down their discussions, so I did my best to ignore them.

Later, Dad tried to apologize for Mary's behavior, but the professor would have none of it. He told Dad he hadn't had this much fun in years. He added that Mary was a true genius and should never be stifled.

I wasn't certain about that, thinking about Mary's plans for her sorority.

I asked him if they yelled like that at Princeton.

"We only yelled when we were young and filled with passion about our ideas. At the university, we are all old and stuffy. I think that is why older scientists don't have breakthroughs."

"Because of not yelling?"

"We are polite to each other and stay within the accepted boundaries of current theory. No one is so rude as to advance a new idea. That is why being with Mary is a pleasure. She makes me think outside of accepted theory. Even so, she is the one who will have new ideas that work. I can just encourage her by telling her she will be the death of me and that she is a dumb girl."

"You weren't offended by the poopy head?"

"Surprised, yes. Offended no. She usually calls me a dumb son of a bitch."

"That doesn't bother you?"

"Compared to her intellect, I am a dumb son of a bitch."

What can you say to that? I left Mary and the good doctor to their learned discussion.

So far, they had decided that sterile neutrinos or natural leptons had to be involved. These neutrinos would have right-handed chirality. There was possibly a fourth state of neutrality that could only be detected in a gravity field by its lack of interaction. This lack of interaction would appear as a blank period in the detection tank.

Furthermore, it would have two spin states with one-half spin. There would be no weak isospin projection. Its B-L would depend on the L charge assignment with an X of -5.

Mum and May-ling wanted to know what I understood from the discussion. Rather than try to explain something I didn't have a hope of understanding, I sold Mary down the river on her language.

Mum frowned at Mary's language but was very pleased about Einstein's remark on her intellect. I suspected Mum and Mary would be having a conversation shortly.

I wondered what punishment could be given to a ten-year-old super genius. Take away her slide rule? Come to think of it. I had never seen Mary with one.

She and the professor seemed to be on a break, so I asked her about slide rules. She told me they were too slow; it was easier to work everything in her head.

I was feeling guilty about ratting her out about her cursing.

"That's okay, Rick. I have a Get-out-of-Jail-Free card."

"What?"

She reached into her ever-present Coach bag and pulled out a Get-out-of-Jail-Free card from a Monopoly game. On the back, Mum had signed it with a note saying it was a reward for donating items for one of Mum's charity auctions.

"When she asked for the donation, I presented the card to her to sign as payment."

"Brilliant, Mary."

At that, she pulled out another Get-out-of-Jail-Free card and asked me to sign it to her for ratting her out.

Nope, never going to play Monopoly with her again. I signed it and wondered what it would cost me in the future.

She went back to the professor with a new thought to present. It had something to do with left-handed chirality. That left-handed was a possibility made sense as they had been discussing right-handed before.

Out of sheer perversity, as they were getting back together, I asked loudly, "Why does it have to be right-handed or left-handed? Why not use a sphere of orientation to rotate between all the dimensions?"

I had no idea where I pulled that thought from other than trying to be a smart aleck. They stopped completely, and you could have heard the proverbial pin drop.

Doctor Einstein asked me, "Will you repeat that, Rick?"

"Why does it have to be right-handed or left-handed? Why not use a sphere of orientation to rotate between all the dimensions?"

Again, dead silence.

Mary finally broke the silence.

"Rick, your name will be on the paper. You have just earned your share of the Nobel Prize in Physics. You have given us the key to explaining dark matter and dark radiation. It also could be the key to true quantum entanglement like that used in the pyramids. As a grand prize, it would also tell us how faster-than-light travel could occur."

I had gone from smart aleck to genius in one simple step.

Mary and Professor Einstein started writing on the whiteboard. They would no sooner fill it up than erase it and come up with a new set of formulas. Fortunately, we had learned from the hard lessons at Stanford.

We had a steward with a Polaroid camera and a film one with black and white film taking frequent pictures of the board as it progressed.

Of course, my parents and May-ling wanted me to explain how I made such a groundbreaking discovery. I stuttered and finally admitted that I had no idea what it meant when I said it. I was just trying to be a smart ass.

They all agreed that I was a smart ass.

Chapter 26

Mary and the good doctor assured me that any comment that moved things forward should be rewarded, whether or not it was well thought out. They then proceeded to dive into the ramifications of my off-the-wall comment.

I tried to follow them but was quickly lost, so I turned to my parents and May-ling to change the topic.

"How do you think the way things are being resolved in China affects our position in the world? All the Earth's governments seem so skittish with me right now."

Dad replied, "From early news stories, the world is now even more concerned about your power."

"Why so?"

Dad replied, "Let me see; who holds the high ground and can waste any country from orbit?"

I thought it was a rhetorical question until I realized he was waiting for an answer.

"The Lunar Kingdom, but we have held that advantage for a while now. Something else has changed."

Mum asked, "Who has the economic power to bring down the economy of any nation?"

"The Kingdom, but again we have had that power."

Dad broke in, "Who can move an army to any place on Earth in hours?"

"I can have the army moved, but the Kingdom doesn't have the troops."

Mum asked again, "Whose wife controls the largest army on Earth?"

"What armies? The Chinese Army belongs to May-ling, not me."

"A fine distinction that is no distinction in most eyes."

I looked at May-ling, and she nodded, "Rick, we are one and the same."

Dad chimed in, "Who is an absolute monarch when it comes to the foreign affairs of his kingdom?"

"Oh."

"Now, do you see why they are nervous around you?"

This came from Dad, but Mum was nodding her head in agreement.

"Before, you were viewed as the power in space but unable to conduct a land war to seize territory. You are the most powerful force on earth with the huge GC sleds. No nation could stand against your armies."

This left me wordless for a moment.

"What will happen from here?"

"The world powers will wait and see how you use your newfound power."

"What if we release a statement of our intentions or lack thereof?"

"Only actions will be taken seriously. Many a dictator has promised peace and then turned."

"May-ling, what do you think we should do?"

"Nothing, be the sleeping giant."

"Shouldn't we send some sort of a signal?"

"There is one signal we can send that will drive them crazy without threatening them."

"What is that?"

"I was going to do this anyway but will make it very public that China is doing away with its nuclear energy program, including the production of bombs. We will also start dismantling those in our stockpile."

"I get it. With the Rods from God, you don't need the expense."

"It will be an enormous cost saving. That and the fact that you will volunteer to dump all the nuclear waste into the sun."

I had to think about that for a moment.

"Not only will I do it for free for China. It will be free for all nuclear waste for the world."

"Since the fusion plants are replacing the need for fission plants, there is little need for nuclear power, other than for medical uses."

"There will be a demand that we share the GC sled technology with the world."

"If things work out as I think they will, we can do that on a limited basis."

"How so?"

"We will operate small GC sleds in any country requesting them for emergency vehicles. We can even bring out large ones for natural disasters."

"How can you prevent one from being hijacked?"

"Quantum entanglement."

"Brilliant. If Mary and the professor can figure out how it works on Planet X, there will be a method of disabling any individual sled at will."

From there, our conversation grew more general. No solutions were generated, but we wondered what could be done to reduce the military-industrial complex. Shifting industries from designing and producing arms to commercial goods seemed a worthwhile goal.

We circled this idea for the rest of the trip but made no firm conclusions. In the meantime, Mary and the professor returned to yelling at each other, so I assumed they were making progress.

Once at Planet X, we immediately went to the control room. This was what we called the room with the pyramid and Stonehenge models. There were also the desert paintings, but we didn't want to mess with them.

I thought Mary would be the one to watch as she would want to pick stuff up and move it. It was Doctor Einstein who was the problem child. Before I could stop him, he picked up a lintel stone at Stonehenge and placed it across two uprights. It looked like a perfect fit.

The world news later confirmed this.

The Space Ladies who had remained behind to investigate the site took us to the equipment room. They had identified the function of almost all of the equipment. There was only one bank of instruments for which there was no apparent use.

Mary asked if this could be the equipment that entangled objects. With that thought in mind, we collectively tried to trace out the functions and order they might have occurred.

Dad, standing at the far end, made a significant breakthrough.

"It looks like this valve is the exit point of the process. The question is, what comes out?"

Mum remarked, "It would have to be a fluid."

I came up with, "If that is the output end, where is the input?"

With that in mind, we all stared at the rack of machines. The professor pointed out that there was an open hopper on top of the first machine in a row.

I know this all sounds obvious when talking about it, but we had never seen anything like this before and had no idea how it worked or what it really did.

Once we saw the hopper, the question was how it was filled. The opening faced the tall ceiling. We couldn't reach the ceiling from the floor. It didn't take much to figure out that the railing above the hopper opening must have been the track for a moving hopper to load the main machine.

It didn't take much backtracking to a large, almost empty room. There the rails stopped at the far edge of the room. At the end of the rails was a bucket from the attached cables that appeared to be able to come down and scoop stuff off the floor.

While we were looking up, Mary was looking down.

"There is evantonium dust all over the floor."

I confirmed this by the simple expedient of licking some of the dust off my finger. Yucky, I know, but the stuff had a unique taste, just as copper has. Once you tasted it, you knew.

"Where did they get the evantonium from?" Dad asked.

He answered his own question when he pointed out a large machine in the far corner. We traipsed over to it and realized it was a mining machine very similar to those we had used on the moon. It would grind away the face of the room we were in, leaving a pile of dust behind.

This would then be scooped up and dumped in the open hopper of the strange group of machines.

It took a few minutes for the import of this discovery to hit us. I'm not certain who voiced it first.

"This bank of machines can do what we were about to spend a fortune on. It can convert evantonium from raw ore to paint."

I noticed that all the machines were bolted together as though we had produced them. This said, whatever measurement system they were using wasn't the same. It seemed closer to metric than the U.S. standard, but we would have to measure a lot to create a set of tools to disassemble the machines and make drawings of the parts so we could produce more.

That opened up a whole new can of worms. Did we really want to disassemble the only working model that we had? I was assuming that it worked.

We returned to the seating area and discussed the subject. One of the Space Ladies asked how the equipment was powered.

We all raced back to the equipment room and checked out the machine. It was almost a whew moment when we realized it was electrical power from a fusion generator.

Mum observed, "It is a shame we don't have an operations manual for this place."

That sort of brought home how little we knew about this facility. If we weren't careful, we could destroy ourselves.

I made an executive decision, "We have to stop messing with anything here. I'm going to have a team of engineers from Jackson R&D map this place out before we touch anything else.

Mary spoke up, "But I wanted to move a pyramid a few feet. That would be so confusing to them on earth. I would write my sorority's name on the side so they would know who did it."

She is only ten.

Mum placidly replied, "Not today. Maybe later, dear."

Mary smiled at this and nodded her head. With my far superior knowledge of the world, I knew Mum meant, "No way in hell."

The reason we had come still had no answer. How was entanglement achieved? Once more, we explored the area but could find no additional machinery or hidden rooms.

One of the Space Ladies, Linda, I think, rushed into the seating area.

"Come quickly. Something has changed in the model room."

As a group, we rushed into the room. What had changed was an area of the model table, where it had been a plain surface before. There was now a series of hieroglyphs scrolling across it.

Since we couldn't read them, we all felt helpless until they started repeating themselves. Then it became a matter of taking pictures so we could have an expert translate the message.

It could have been everything from "Take me to your leader" to "Deposit another dime for ten more minutes."

Chapter 27

Mary and Doctor Einstein continued their discussions. Now they were talking about brains and bulks. This made no sense to me, so I asked why they were talking about brains. Mary let me know I was silly. They were branes. She went on to explain what they were.

All I got out of it was that gravity could extend into different dimensions, and maybe it wasn't as weak as it seemed.

I joked that gravity didn't seem weak when I was in freefall.

"Yeah, but you can pick up a telephone and overcome the gravity of the entire planet Earth."

Knowing when I was in over my head, I shut up.

Mary let us know that she and the Professor had seen all they needed and were ready to head back to Earth.

The trip back to Earth went fast. All of us had tried to ignore the message that came across the table. We decided to keep its existence a secret for as long as we could.

Too many people in our party had seen it so it would get out somehow. It was my job to explain to the family and crew why this should be kept quiet.

"If word gets out before we translate the message, it will cause worldwide panic. Please don't talk about this until we know what it says. I promise you that you will be updated as soon as we know."

Everyone agreed to keep it confidential, but I knew it would get out. It wouldn't take malice. An unthinking comment could let the cat out of the bag.

As soon as we landed, I called Mr. Norman in England. He has the contacts to get the translation made and the ability to keep it silent.

Fortunately, it was still business hours over there, so he was immediately available.

"Rick, it has been a while. How can I help you?"

"Could we talk about it in person? I can be there in half an hour."

Having a GC vehicle at your beck and call was very useful. As I was flying to England, I wondered if I could have my bus, as I referred to my GC, made to look like a Thunderbird. Probably not, but at least it was in my colors and arms.

That reminded me that I also owned a 707 that was now obsolete, at least for my purposes. It had been nice to have a traveling office with sleeping quarters. This prompted another note to GC maintenance to look into providing those facilities on this craft.

There was an entire upper deck to this unit that was virtually unused. Some nice quarters could be put there.

Rather than landing at Heathrow, we settled into a large open field behind the palace. As soon as I exited, a footman driving a golf cart took me to the palace proper.

I was escorted to Mr. Norman's room, where he greeted me profusely. He had a copy of those damned songs that Sinatra and Martin had tricked me into singing. Apparently, I was involved in another hit record. I gracefully autographed it for him. Well, not gracefully, maybe a little bit snarkily, well, a lot snarkily. I thought better of myself and apologized for my response.

He told me not to worry, that he had been young once.

I retorted, "Was that immediately after the Battle of Hastings, Mr. Norman?"

He got a very funny look on his face and replied, "Something like that."

No, it couldn't be, could it? I ignored his comment and explained that I needed a translator of some Egyptian hieroglyphics. I didn't give him the complete story.

"I'll call some people and see who would be best for this project."

"I will appreciate it."

"While I'm doing that, the queen would like to speak to you."

'My pleasure."

I was led to a very small room that was reserved for private conversations with Her Majesty. I assumed the room was checked for bugs all the time. Later I found that it was enclosed in a Faraday Cage. It was as secure as any room in the spy world.

"King Richard, thank you for stopping by."

I felt awkward for a moment.

"My pleasure, Your Majesty."

"Now we have got that out of the way. How is your family?"

"Fine, ma'am."

"An idea occurred to me that I wish to discuss with you."

"If I may ask?"

"I want to explore a military alliance between Great Britain, the Commonwealth, and all associated territories and the Lunar Kingdom and Solar Reaches."

Didn't see that one coming.

"Why?"

"Simple economics, You control the most powerful force on earth. All the nations together couldn't overcome your kingdom. Why should we finance a military when we can hide behind your skirts?"

"What's in it for the Lunar Kingdom?"

"More power. If we join an alliance, the rest of the world will be clamoring to get in."

"True."

"It would give us an excuse to get rid of our obsolete expensive nuclear program."

"Do you mean bombs or power generation?"

"Bombs, we are already shifting to your sister Mary's fusion devices."

"I like that thought. However, something afoot might require us to keep the bombs."

She achieved an alarmed look as she asked, "What?"

I went to explain our entire trip to Planet X. Well. I left out the way Professor Einstein and Mary talked to each other. I didn't think Her Majesty could handle Poopie Head.

"So, a lot will depend on the message translation."

"Yes."

'Do you mind if I tell the Prime Minister that you would entertain an alliance? As a socialist, he will love the idea of taking money from the military for his programs."

"Yes, but I ask that you let the Chief of the General Staff know that I would want to hire any officers or soldiers made redundant. They could be headquartered here as part of the agreement, but they would be part of my army."

"I will do that."

We ended our conversation on a high note, and I was escorted back to Mr. Norman's office.

"Rick, the man we need is Cyril Aldred of the Royal Scottish Museum. I have talked to him, and he is willing to look at your message whenever you can get there."

"Call him back and tell him we will be landing in Edinburgh at the museum's main courtyard in half an hour."

"We have a Messenger leaving for Edinburgh about now. May he hitch a ride?"

"Certainly, but don't try to make a habit of it, old friend."

"Who me?"

We both laughed at that, knowing him for the sly old bugger he is.

The Messenger joined me in the golf cart. I think he was in a little shock. I don't know why.

Everyone hitches a ride with a king when they can.

Twenty-seven minutes later, we landed in the main courtyard of the National Museums, which the Royal was a part of.

A docent was waiting and led me to Dr. Aldred while the Messenger fought his way through the gathering crowd, who wanted to see one of the fabled GC ships, the press's term, not mine.

Doctor Aldred (call me Cyril) led me to a workshop area set up as a translation area.

He grew very excited when I showed him the Polaroid pictures of the hieroglyphics.

"These first are perfect examples of the Old Kingdom. This group is from the Middle Kingdom. These photos are as important as the Rosetta Stone. We understand the Middle Kingdom glyphs quite well, but the Old Kingdom glyphs have some gaps. These will close many of them."

"How long will it take to translate them?"

"I will have a team start on them immediately. We should have our first translation in two days."

"Then I will go home and return in two days."

Chapter 28

"Where is home?"

That is when I realized he had no idea who I was.

"Home is on the moon, but my wife and I are visiting my parents in California."

You could see the wheels turn and connections made. Before he could say anything, I held out my hand and introduced myself as Richard Jackson.

As we shook hands, you could see the wheels still turning.

"May I ask what your connection is with these hieroglyphics?"

"They were found on one of my properties, and I'm curious."

Not a lie, but I was playing this close.

"As I said, it will take at least two days to sort these out. That assumes they are a true match of Old and Middle Kingdom glyphs."

I gave him one of my cards and told him to call me when he had the results. At that, we ended our meeting, and I returned to California on my GC craft.

Once home, I brought Mum, Dad, and May-ling up to date on my conversation with the queen. Their immediate reactions were positive.

May-ling saw this as an opportunity to do away with nuclear weapons completely. That alone would make the project worthwhile. Her theory was that once Great Britain allied with us, the rest of the nations would want to join.

She thought even Russia would apply, but I thought she was overly optimistic.

Mum had the idea of offering to dispose of all nuclear waste. We could toss it into the sun, which wouldn't even notice such small amounts. This would allow the continued use of radioactive elements in medicine and other applications.

It was brought up that the world's arms industry would take a huge hit if everyone allied with us. There would be no need for large standing armies and all their equipment.

Some units would have to be maintained to put down the occasional civil war or local invasion. Countries would still go to war over important matters such as soccer matches.

The economic dislocation would be enormous.

I reminded them that we might want to hold up on disarmament until we knew what that message in hieroglyphs said. That was no big deal because we would have an idea of its contents soon.

May-ling excused herself to take a nap. Her pregnancy was wearing on her. How she kept her schedule at all was beyond me.

My small kingdom, population-wise, kept me busy. How she ran an empire like China was impressive, to say the least. Granted, she had a huge staff to support her.

She was followed by two GC craft full of her support staff everywhere she went. She spent most of her time in meetings when not with me. I sat in on a few of her meetings and saw a common thread.

Every problem presented to her had to be accompanied by one or more solutions. Each solution had to have its pros and cons spelled out. The solutions weren't presented in a vacuum. How they would interact with the big picture had to be presented.

They couldn't say we would pay for this with money from another program. How would taking that money affect the contribution presented? This often led to other programs. Until all ramifications could be identified, she wouldn't order a change. Even then, unintended consequences occurred, leading to another meeting, and around it would go.

She paid strict attention to the financial details of her empire but even more attention to feeding her people. With its tremendous population, China had historically been on the verge of total starvation many times. She would move Heaven and Earth to prevent this.

Annexing Siberia had provided a new food source, but ensuring that the food was distributed to where it was needed was a logistical nightmare.

Officials who thought they could withhold food from the people and make their fortune found a public execution instead. It didn't take too many beheadings to keep any theft down to a dull roar. It was impossible to stop it all. The system worked well enough that there weren't any reports of starvation this year.

During my time in LA, I spent some time at the studio. While there, my friends and teachers illustrated how out of practice I was getting. This lack of practice was accomplished by beating me black and blue.

Unarmed combat was the hardest. I really had to work at it. My swordplay needed work but was fundamentally sound. I decided that I wouldn't spend any more time on boxing. The boxing I had learned was for the camera, not real life. Since it didn't look like I would be making any movies in the future, I dropped it.

Archery was my true love on the physical side of things. I hadn't figured out how to create an archery range on the moon. Like softball, we couldn't create a true gravity situation.

I ended up arranging for unarmed combat instruction on a scheduled basis. The instructor or substitute would come to me wherever I was for a session. Having money and GC spacecraft was nice.

There was no phone call from Doctor Aldred on the second day, but I received a call early on the third. He informed me they had what they felt was a good translation but wanted to know if I had any photographs besides the Polaroids. Having more detail would be helpful.

Pictures with regular black and white film had been taken, and I had them developed here at Jackson House. I managed to catch Denny without a date, so he took the time to develop them.

The detail on these was sharper than on the Polaroids. On several of the columns, which looked like hieroglyphics, there were depictions of the equipment in what we called the utility room.

The first in the series of photographs showed all of the equipment in its order of placement. The following pictures had exploded details of each individual piece. The hieroglyphs started with a picture of the piece, then individual components.

From these instructions, we could disassemble each machine, measure the components, and reassemble them.

We could duplicate the setup.

Additional hieroglyphs were maintenance and troubleshooting instructions. I couldn't read them, but their purpose was clear.

I was so excited by the fact that I had the GC crew take me to England at once. An hour later, I was knocking on the door of the professor's lab. No one answered. Why should they be there at 3 a.m.?

The crew and I found an all-night diner and ate an early breakfast or, for us, a late dinner and drank coffee until nine o'clock, normal university business hours. I went to the lab while the crew returned to our ship to nap.

This time the knock on the door was answered. The professor was surprised to see me as I was supposed to be waiting for his call. When I brought out the enlarged photos with sharper detail, he grabbed them from me. He had a grad student nearby start pinning them to a bulletin board.

I also brought a series of photographs of the equipment room to show the machines to which the hieroglyphs were referring.

It didn't take long for him and his three assistants to agree with my initial impression. He then told me to go away and wait for his call unless I had something else I wasn't sharing.

You could tell he wanted to know where the equipment came from and how it related to hieroglyphics. The machines were far ahead of anything developed in ancient Egypt, so why use hieroglyphics?

He wasn't going to get an answer to his unasked question, at least not now.

Returning to the GC ship parked in an open space near the lab, I had to wade through a large throng that had gathered to view the ship. The local constables had even arrived and were holding them back.

I wondered if I would have trouble getting through the police line, but apparently, they recognized me and let me pass. There were shouted questions from the crowd, but I ignored them.

I roused my now grumpy crew from their short naps and returned to California.

At Jackson House, I arrived just in time for dinner. I felt like I had been cheated out of lunch. Without too much whining about my missed meal, I brought the family up to date on the photograph findings.

My dear wife had no sympathy for my so-called missed meal. Something about many wasted breakfasts. I wasn't stupid enough to argue the point. Besides, Mum and Mary were both ready to defend May-lings' point of view. That was a no-win if there ever was.

My dad was keeping his head down while eating his meal. Denny and Eddie were watching as though at a tennis match. Thanks, guys!

I mumbled, "You are so right, dear."

I then followed Dad's example and concentrated on my meal. Later I couldn't have told you what we had that night.

Chapter 29

Each of us shared our plans for the next few days. May-ling had to return to China to hold court for some civil matters. Dad had the usual business rounds of his media empire. Mum was involved in a big charity event sponsored by Anna Romanov.

Denny was off to interview models for his photography studios. Not sure why he needed them, but he seemed happy with the idea. Enough said.

Eddie was off to the races, this time a NASCAR event. Then there was Mary. She had lunch with her grade school class and then a sorority meeting. She was giving a lecture on string theory to a class of graduate students at Caltech. Then a fashion show followed by an awards dinner.

She wasn't clear about the dinner. It was for a mathematical prize. She didn't know if she was receiving the award or giving it. Mary didn't appear too concerned either way.

Jim and Sally must be run ragged. I mentioned that and was told there was now a support team to arrange for transportation, meals, rooms, and the like. There were also another ten guards who rotated as her outer guard team. Jim and Sally remained her close team.

I then asked about Mary being limited in her time in the adult world. Mum told me that ship had sailed.

Since I had a few days to kill before hearing anything on the hieroglyphs, I decided I needed to address Kingdom business.

Like May-ling, I would hold court for public matters. She and I decided that we would work all week and get back together on Friday night. We would meet in Paris for dinner and then fly to Australia for the rest of the weekend. We now had a beach house near Bondi Beach that would be a perfect getaway.

May-ling and I retired to our suite for a pleasant evening which was nobody's business.

The next day we all met at the breakfast buffet and went our separate ways.

I held court on Wednesday morning. My staff made a few reserved comments about the short notice, but I regally ignored them. Sometimes it is good to be king.

Most of the petitions presented were boring requests for special treatment for a business proposition that would benefit only that business.

It was easy to reject them.

A lawyer from Nutt, Case, and Friend made an interesting appeal. He wanted to change the law firm's name.

With a name like that, I would want to change it, also. I asked what they would like to change it to.

"We have made two associates partners, so we would like to change it to Nutt, Case, and Friends."

Without comment, I approved the change. Did I say it was good to be king?

On a more serious note, there was a representative from Monaco. We hadn't established diplomatic relations with them, so I was curious about their presence.

They wanted to exchange ambassadors and enter into a military alliance with the Lunar Kingdom, and Solar Reaches.

I tried not to be rude in asking what they could bring to the alliance.

"How large is your standing army, and what are its units?"

"We have 255 members between the Corps des Sapeurs-Pompiers and the Compagnie des Carabiniers du Prince."

"What are their functions?"

"The Corps des Sapeurs-Pompiers are trained to handle civil emergencies on land and sea. The Compagnie des Carabiniers du Prince is the prince's protection."

"Why have you come to us? I thought you had an agreement with the French armed forces."

"Exactly."

Oh boy, do I make the French mad or Mum? Putting it that way made it easy.

"We would be delighted to enter an agreement with Monaco's Principality."

The French would get over being mad. I was not going to challenge Mum.

I asked the ambassador from Monaco to stay until the end of the court session. We needed to iron out some details. At the same time, my agreement in my Public Court made it a legal agreement, but it still needed to be formalized in writing.

It needed to be spelled out when one party would come to the aid of another and what the aid would consist of. It had to have an end or renewal date and method of notification of withdrawal. I had seen examples of agreements. They were long detailed documents.

There was also the pesky little detail that the ambassador probably thought that this agreement brought the Chinese armed forces in on his side.

The fact is, I didn't have an agreement with the Chinese. At least not a formal one. My help in putting down the recent revolutions was a husband siding with his wife. Not a formal action of one country allying with another.

After declaring the court closed, I sat with the ambassador and explained everything to him. He was way ahead of me. He presented me with a draft agreement.

It was one page in length and answered all of my questions. He knew I didn't have an agreement with the Chinese but thought it wouldn't take long to get one in place.

He had a draft of an agreement for an alliance between Monaco and China, plus a draft of an agreement between China and the Lunar Kingdom and the Solar Reaches.

I had finally gotten used to our long and unwieldy name.

He asked how long it would take me to get an agreement with China. He also needed to get an audience with Empress May-ling's staff. He thought it would take months.

I told him nonsense; come with me.

The Royal Barge always had a crew on standby. In two hours, we were discussing the issue with my wife in the Forbidden City.

She was all for a formal alliance with me and didn't see any risk in allying with Monaco. After all, we were agreeing to come to their aid if attacked, not helping them attack others.

With very few markups, the agreements were finalized. All signed fresh copies. Even a notification to the world of the existence of the agreements. No rationale for the agreements, just that they were in place.

I had the GC ship return the ambassador to Monaco while I spent quality time with my wife.

Our diplomatic venture had to set some records and would leave many diplomats worried about their jobs.

May-ling and I agreed that the floodgates had been opened. Most countries would be knocking at our door. Maybe there would be peace in our time.

I wondered how that would work out as I had studied the last time that had been proclaimed.

As delightful as the interruption had been to our week, she had to get back to work. Before I left, she had her regular examination, and her pregnancy was continuing well. I would be a father in a month.

Like all expecting couples, we considered names for a boy or girl. In May-ling's case, family and national traditions came into play.

We had a quiet weekend, but on Monday, it started. First in line was Great Britain wanting to sign a military alliance. When Queen Elizabeth presented the proposal to the Prime Minister, he almost flipped out.

First of all, it was not the done thing for the queen to present policy. Her role was to rubber stamp the government policies. Secondly, this was wonderful! They could defund the military and shift money to their socialist programs.

A draft of the government counter-proposal to my verbal agreement with the queen was sent to me on the moon. It did everything but make me responsible for their national debt.

I countered with a one-page document similar to the one with Monaco. Using GC craft to return my answer made it happen in one day.

In their eagerness to take advantage of the situation, they publicly announced the alliance as though it was a done deal. According to them, a new golden age was starting, a socialist paradise in the making, with the Lunar Kingdom and Solar Reaches bearing all the cost.

This news release may have garnered some votes for their upcoming elections but left them in a terrible bargaining position.

My one-page draft was returned with notes when translated from bureaucrat-ese told me to go to hell.

I released a public statement that there was no military alliance between us and Great Britain. They had rejected our proposal.

This statement set off a round of public whining or whinging, as the Brits say, about how unfair I was.

My counter reply was that I was willing to come to Great Britain's aid if attacked, but not willing to pay for what standing armed forces they chose to maintain.

The queen did an end run on history. She signed the one-page document on behalf of Great Britain and all nations of the Commonwealth.

This document left all the governments in a cleft position. Since I also signed the document, I would come to their aid if they were attacked. The queen couldn't force her government or those of the Commonwealth to come to my aid if the Kingdom were attacked.

This promised aid was a moot point, as no one was in a position to attack the moon.

Chapter 30

Sixty-seven different countries inquired about a military alliance in the next two days. Those embassies I had opened were all busy. Here I thought them a nuisance.

May-ling and I decided we would accept all offers using the simple form. Any attempts to negotiate would be rejected. No one else would if Great Britain couldn't get away with a lengthy document. I thought this would be a deal breaker for the United States. It wasn't.

Even though the U.S. Military-Industrial Complex squealed like stuck pigs, polling showed eighty-seven percent of Americans thought it a good idea. This rating was probably higher than those favoring sliced bread.

It took until Thursday for the U.S. to come around, and they wanted special terms. They didn't get them.

I called President Kennedy and asked him what their rationale was for joining. In short, it was to keep them out of small wars against Communism.

Plus, it would help to keep the American budget in balance. Again, there would be less spent on the military and more on social programs.

Kennedy tried to persuade Congress to put most of the money saved into infrastructure projects rather than handouts. He didn't appear to be having much luck. They loved handing out free things to their voters. Not that they were trying to buy votes. Of course not.

Our conversation turned to the Military-Industrial Complex, as President Eisenhower had dubbed it. This reduction in the possibility of war was a rare opportunity to shift away from the production of arms, which in turn led to a desire to play with the toys of war.

The fly in the ointment was that so many people depended on the jobs in those industries that it could bring a worldwide recession, if not depression if those jobs disappeared.

The president asked me if I had any ideas on what products could be made by those companies that would be losing their military contracts. I had to confess that I hadn't given it any thought.

"Rick, one of our think tanks has suggested shifting to electricity to power cars, trucks, and trams.

"The fusion plants could produce the electricity, but they are so big they wouldn't fit in a truck, much less a car.

"Our current battery technology is not up to the job. That may be our savior."

"How is that, Mr. President?"

"First of all, it is John in private, and second, we can issue requests for proposals to develop the technology. Any reasonable RFP could be funded, keeping many companies in business."

"That would take care of the design and engineering companies. What about people who build things?"

"That is where we will need your help. Could you see your way to allowing us and other countries to build your GC ships and establish research stations around the solar system? You could keep control of the evantonium."

"That might be possible. Let me pass it by my think tank."

"Tell your parents, May-ling, and Mary that I said hello."

"I will, John."

"Let me know your answer soon as the markets are getting jittery."

We exchanged a few other thoughts but didn't get anywhere, so we bid our goodbyes. I immediately got together and brought my think tank up to date. The president had accurately identified my think tank.

Everyone thought the basic proposal was sound. Some details had to be considered. The most important was making GC vehicles available on a wide basis. Several of them pushing on a chunk of rock would make them the equivalent of a nuclear bomb.

Mary had the solution.

"I can now entangle evantonium. We can control any craft that we coat. Since it is entangled, there are no distance limits."

Mum asked, "We will be able to control them, but how will we know there is a need?"

We all thought about that problem for a moment, then I had an idea.

"We will have to have an International Space Traffic Control system. All the nations of the earth will fund it, creating many jobs that didn't exist before. Even the planning for such an agency will create new jobs."

We thought we had the beginnings of a workable plan to shift arms production to civilian production without a huge dislocation of the economy.

I won't say May-ling was smug, but she did look pleased. The Chinese were starting to develop a military complex but weren't dependent on it so that events wouldn't harm them. They did have an enormous standing army, but its main purpose was to give its young men something to do.

She already had plans to shift them into developing mining and farming operations in Siberia.

I didn't pass up the opportunity to tease her about her spies stealing from the West, so they didn't need to design anything. That was one of the rare times I got my wife to blush.

Upon that delightful note, we adjourned our think tank. I did contact JE Research and scheduled a meeting for early Monday. I was going to create several research teams to explore the proposed actions' ramifications and possible unintended consequences.

Monday's trip by helicopter to the JE campus made me think of another job creation opportunity. Looking down at the smog-creating traffic snarl, I realized that with practically free unlimited power, bus lines or other transportation systems could be implemented to move people.

A larger GC barge could transport people and their vehicles along the current freeway system. They would stop at every freeway exit to allow cars to roll off and on. While in transit, people could stay in their car or go to an onboard restaurant for longer trips.

There would be express and locals. The GC barge would need drivers for safe lane changes. I went wild and thought about having grocery stores and other shops on board. It would allow people to use their time rather than fight traffic jams.

I even imagined having a moving community college where people who commuted the same route every day could take classes. That might be going too far in my thinking.

I met with the senior staff of JE Research. I explained to the group what had led to the current line of thinking and possible solutions.

I asked that each person now take the time to outline their first thoughts when presented with the situation. They could be concerns or additional ideas. Nothing was out of bounds.

At first, there were a lot of blank looks. Then a person started to write. Pretty soon, pencils and pens were flying across the paper.

I had time for some donuts and two cups of coffee before they were all finished.

We then went to the whiteboards. The ideas presented ranged from creating a space patrol to charging stations for electric cars.

A space patrol made me think of the old TV series I loved as a kid. What they were talking about was more like a highway patrol. That sounded like it would work.

The electric charging stations seemed like a no-go as people wouldn't want to sit for hours on a trip while their auto batteries charged.

I didn't share my thoughts as we kept writing the ideas down. This session was brainstorming.

We began to get duplicates as each idea was presented and written down. Since the idea generator may have had some thoughts written down in addition to the original proposal, we had them cut out that section of their notes and start to compile common thoughts. They would be consolidated after this session.

Some of the thoughts would create a bureaucracy. I was inclined to throw these away until I realized that jobs had to be created.

Not only would they be jobs, but they would be jobs at a solar level, above any separate nation.

There was the problem of the ruling body of this bureaucracy, as I didn't want to end up as King of the Universe. The moon was hard enough.

At the end of our session, it was agreed that a team would go through all the ideas presented, plus the thoughts from my overview. They would develop a list of pros and cons for each, and then if an idea were a go, a team would be created to identify how to implement the idea on a worldwide scale.

While my teams were doing this work, all the nations in the world had to be performing similar actions. Because I didn't want to be King of the Universe, we needed to be united and all ideas brought to the table.

I realized that I couldn't do all this work myself. I called President Kennedy and explained my thoughts and actions. He agreed that my course of action made sense and that he would be glad to lead a worldwide group. I hoped he didn't want to be King of the Universe.

At least I controlled the GC craft and evantonium. If Mary was correct about entanglement, it gave even more protection against a madman. We just had to hope I wouldn't go crazy.

Chapter 31

Over the next several days, all independent nations except the United States and Russia applied to join the military alliance. One pundit compared it to the situation before World War I. Entangling alliances had set off that conflagration.

Other pundits pointed out his error. The U.S. and Russia were the only two nations that could attack each other without having the rest of the world turn on them. The first to attack would bring the might of the world down upon them.

I think we may have taken our first steps toward true world peace.

I have offered to dispose of the world's radioactive waste twice by this point. It must have penetrated this time as nations got in line to have their waste hauled away.

There were enough requests that the GC sled took a month to pick up the materials, take them to orbit, then push them toward the sun. One side effect of this program was that my people got an insight into how far nations were in their programs to develop nuclear weapons.

It was frightening.

I thought the large nations were the only ones with nuclear programs, but when I discovered that countries like South Africa had them, it was scary.

The bureaucrats at the UN didn't care for this turn of events. The United Nations had been formed to discourage war between nations. I had just taken that off the board. The only reason now for their existence was for humanitarian missions.

Russia thought they could get away with some saber rattling. They threatened the United States. This threat of nuclear warfare was a bad move as Congress had been torn about joining the alliance. Now they passed a joint request motion to join.

The United States joining the alliance left Russia in a bad position. If they attacked any country, I would respond in kind. However, any nation in the world could attack them at will as they weren't members of the alliance.

I wouldn't help the attacking nation, but Russia would be doomed if it were a combination like NATO.

Another Russian government turnover, which was becoming all too frequent, occurred. The new government, a form of social democracy, requested to join.

Several nations objected to them joining, but I reminded them that the individual countries were allied with me and that I would do what I thought was right.

Some bright soul suggested that things would change with my sudden demise. May-ling, who would inherit my power, let the world know she would take a dim view of her husband's assassination.

That was nice to know.

There was no gridlock or any chance of an intervention war starting. Civil wars could occur.

Again, the pundits were up in arms. The colonies couldn't have broken away from England. It was again pointed out that the American Revolution was a civil war. Then it came up that in the American Civil War, if the Confederacy had immediately been able to join such an alliance, the United States would have to have let them go.

I made it very clear that I wouldn't take sides if there were such a division in any nation. I would prevent outsiders from attacking them but wouldn't interfere until their differences were settled.

I was a nasty dictator for not allowing countries to go to war.

Some days you can't win.

Though I was portrayed as a bad guy, the result was good. Oddly, no one tried to show that May-ling was part of the problem. I don't think anyone was stupid enough to pick on a pregnant woman. Especially one who controlled the largest army in the world.

No matter what was said, it would be impossible to attack another country without bringing the combined might of the Lunar Kingdom and the Solar Reaches, plus the Chinese Empire, down upon them.

Since all the alliances were made with May-ling and me, they weren't allied with each other. The world's peace required May-ling and me to remain alive and in power. Since we had no heir, the alliance would collapse upon our deaths.

Hurry up, baby.

It had been announced that my parents would serve as regents for our child if we died prematurely. This announcement lent some stability to the situation. There were some unhappy Chinese about having *gweilo* in charge of their country, but they were an extremely small part of the population.

I didn't ask any questions about their complaints suddenly stopping. May-ling did comment that they had found a new source of workers in the Siberian mines.

She didn't tell me how to run my kingdom, and I didn't try to tell her how to run her empire. Our child's education would be interesting.

While all the drama was playing out on Earth, my exploration crews found new knowledge of the solar system.

Up close, Mars was still the red planet. Venus wasn't a place to take a holiday. The surface of Mercury would be molten or frozen, depending on the time of day.

The day on Mercury was fifty-eight days and fifteen hours long. A Mercury year or one orbit of the sun was eighty-eight days. A Mercury calendar would be interesting.

The most important find was the confirmation at long last of the planet Vulcan. This planet was long thought to explain variations in Mercury's orbit, but direct evidence of its existence was never found.

French mathematician Urbain Le Verrier in 1859 confirmed unexplained peculiarities in Mercury's orbit and predicted they had to be the result of gravitational influences of another unknown nearby planet or series of asteroids.

Le Verrier had great credibility since, using mathematics, he predicted the existence of the planet Neptune.

A French amateur astronomer reported that he had observed an object passing in front of the Sun that same year. This announcement led Le Verrier to announce the long sought-after planet even though he questioned the capabilities of the astronomer's equipment. He named the planet Vulcan after the Roman god of fire.

There were many searches conducted for Vulcan. Even with claimed observations, its existence could not be confirmed.

The need for the planet as an explanation for Mercury's orbit was made unnecessary by Einstein's 1915 theory of General Relativity3.

Einstein's theory showed that Mercury's variation from the orbit predicted by Newtonian spacetime caused by the Sun's mass.

Now the question arose, how did the discovery of Vulcan affect the general theory of relativity? When I shared the discovery with Mary, her only comment was, "Uh, oh."

She immediately made a phone call to Professor Einstein. Without listening closely, I heard an uncharacteristically serious conversation without one "poopy head."

After she hung up, she approached me in a subdued manner.

"Rick, please have readings taken using every possible sensor. This discovery could destroy Uncle Albert's reputation."

Without making smart comments, I told her it would be a priority. I would have a GC ship land on the planet to retrieve samples. This situation was important to my sister, so it was important to me.

After the family discussed things, we decided to keep it confidential until we had some answers. We didn't want the scientific world to be in an uproar without reason.

Space Ladies, as usual, would provide transportation. Einstein and Mary would handle the science portion. The JE Research Center would support them.

We needed to establish some basic facts before attempting anything major around Vulcan. We knew it was fourteen million miles from the surface of the sun. This distance would place it outside the Corona, which could reach a million degrees.

The surface of the sun was only fifty-five hundred degrees. Only! We needed to know the temperature of the surface of Vulcan. It would be hotter than on Mercury on the sun's side. Its equator would be four to eight hundred degrees. Mercury rotates very slowly, so the side facing away from the sun would be approaching absolute zero or -387 degrees F.

Basic math told us the sun side of Vulcan could reach 6000 degrees F. The earth metal with the highest melting point is tungsten. Tungsten's melting temperature is 5432 degrees F.

This temperature differential gave rise to the question of why Vulcan even exists. It should have been sublimated by the sun eons ago.

That is unless a new element was involved. One could hope.

A heat shield was made for a smaller-than-usual GC craft at an enormous cost of time and effort. The heat shield was made up of multiple "sacrificial" layers, mirror finished so that most of the Sun's radiation was simply reflected away but sandwiched with ablative material which evaporated at a controlled rate when exposed to the Sun, carrying heat away in doing so, before exposing another mirror-finished layer. The structure supporting all this was tungsten, so it would remain solid even as it heated up.

The initial approach would be in the shadow of the planet. Once close enough for the onboard instruments to register, a pass would be made of the hot side. Once this information was collected, a safe approach could be planned.

A landing on the Earth side of the planet was considered, but for safety reasons, put off until later visits.

The mission planning team involved my family, Professor Einstein, the Space Ladies, and JE Research.

Mary and the professor were for full speed ahead. The Space Ladies who would be on the first manned flights, not so much.

Chapter 32

I ruled in favor of the Space Ladies. I hope they would have refused to go if I had told them to take the unsafe path. You never know. I wasn't going to take the chance when time was on our side.

They accomplished the mission with no problems. The pass in front of the Sun went smoothly. The craft lost a couple of layers of the heat shield, but the ablative layers created a dense cloud of, for lack of a better word, smoke as they burned away, keeping the Sun's heat from even reaching the surface of the shield until the gases had dissipated. The shield quickly resolidified as the craft returned to the shelter of the dark side.

After the tungsten cooled down rapidly and the loss was measured, it was determined that three layers of the shield were gone. It had taken fifteen minutes to make that pass.

The records did show an anomaly. The temperatures dropped below tungsten's melting point at the closest approach to Vulcan. They remained that way until the ship was the same distance from Vulcan as when the phenomenon had started.

This temperature zone was extremely strange as the temperature profile of the sun was thought to be understood. There was an incredible hot center. The cool surface (5500 degrees F) and the millions of degrees found in the corona. Outside of the corona zone, temperatures dropped back to near-surface temperatures. These temperatures decreased further from the sun.

The zone where mankind could live was known as the Goldilocks zone. Not too hot, not too cold, just right.

It was decided that it was safe to land on Vulcan. The planet was half the size of Earth's moon, which was strange. Its gravity should have more effect on Mercury than it demonstrated.

When the GC craft landed, and the Space Ladies prepared to exit, they reported that the surface had one Earth gravity. This was insane. This planet wasn't natural.

Samples were taken and returned to Earth for testing at JE Research. Within one day, it was reported back that the samples were one hundred percent new, previously undiscovered material.

Weirder and weirder.

A new mission for the exploration crew was to determine if the gravity and what appeared to be a heat shield around the planet were uniform.

Gravity and temperature were found to be uniform around the planet. Not only was this established, but equipment was found in orbit, which might explain why. The look of the strange equipment reminded us of that found on Planet X, with further confirmation by the finding of hieroglyphic identification on various parts of the large structures.

Each one of them was as large as the Pyramid of Giza. They were equidistant from each other and enclosed the planet in a sphere. An examination of their surfaces revealed they had evantonium coating on all sides. That would explain the gravity at the surface.

It also meant the planet couldn't affect Mercury's orbit. Professor Einstein actually punched his hand in the air for victory when he heard this.

We still didn't understand the temperature barrier, but we now knew it was manmade, or rather alien-made.

If those protections weren't in place, Vulcan would have disappeared hundreds of millions of years ago. That is assuming it was in its current one-year orbit around the sun. Talk about coincidences. I thought not. For all we knew, it had been towed into place last week, or more likely, five thousand years ago.

There was another mystery. Why could Vulcan only be detected once inside the orbit of Mercury? The logical thought was that there was something about Mercury preventing any detection.

That made me wonder. Was anything natural in the solar system, or had the aliens constructed the whole system?

It took another week before we got the first results from JE Research on the properties of the newly found element. Its discovery was going to require significant changes to the periodic table. Anything of its nature should be radioactive. It wasn't.

More mysteries.

Professor Einstein and Mary were excited about the possibilities. We were all back at Jackson House in California. The good doctor now had a bedroom of his own. Princeton was asking why he was spending so much time away from the campus.

He explained that he and Mary had new thoughts on the Unified Field Theory, and he had to stay at her house. Her mother wouldn't let her stay up late, so he had to work with her at her house so they wouldn't lose working time.

What a weak excuse, but Princeton bought it. I understood in a way. The two smartest people in the world would always be peculiar.

I could see that our secrets were hanging by a thread. Even so, I wanted to put things off as long as possible. The more we knew, the less chance of the world descending into chaos when the news came out.

While the investigation of Vulcan and Planet X continued, the world continued its business. To keep the world's economy from collapsing, my staff was buying up the stock of the major arms producers.

Word was passed down through those companies I now controlled that we were to continue all contracts with vendors and that this was to continue through the entire supply chain.

Gold production was increased from the Lassiter mine to support all these companies and their commitments to back the new currency being issued.

One of my fears was that there would be a huge amount of gold found by the many explorers. If they were my people, we could put a lid on it. If the gold find was by others, the price of gold would plummet, and my currency would devalue. This devaluation, in turn, would make the arms industry problematic.

So far, it hadn't occurred. Was gold naturally rare in our solar system, or was all this part of an alien grand plan?

The large aircraft manufacturers were now building GC craft. The only thing my people were now doing was installing the evantonium devices that allowed gravity to be controlled.

Some businesses could be shifted to other products. An example was the tank factory in Lima, Ohio. It was to be closed down with minimal security staff left behind. We might need a heavy vehicle similar to a tank in the future, so tools and materials were left in place.

One storekeeper was assigned to keep a perpetual inventory to detect any signs of theft. I suspected Berlin Bowsher would have an easy lifetime job. I met him on one of the many tours I was taking to ensure that things were going okay.

Being able to move around quickly was a boon. I asked Mr. Bowsher if he would be bored doing this job. He told me no. It left him plenty of time to try to solve a family mystery. The family name had been Bowser but had been changed to Bowsher.

This name change occurred in the 1930s. Not all family members had changed names, but no one was talking. We all have our mysteries to solve, some bigger than others.

My visits to arms design and development groups and manufacturing sites worldwide were like a dizzy merry-go-round. There were minor snags, but they were being worked out. By this time, I had a staff of over one hundred keeping track of the conversions.

I avoided meetings like the plague, but they couldn't be helped. When possible, they were held on the Royal Barge while in transit. Arrival at its destination brought the meeting to a close no matter where we were on the agenda.

Those staff members stuck on a fifteen-minute flight had to pick the most salient points and go for it. I didn't help them when I had all the chairs removed from the conference room.

This merry-go-round was but one of several I was on. There were meetings with world leaders, singly and in groups. I had broken down and provided the twenty most important countries, at least in this effort, with a GC sled.

The media called them the GC 20. I think Dad coined the phrase.

While in a meeting with President Kennedy, he asked all aides to leave the room. When we were alone, he spoke up.

"Rick, this is embarrassing for me. I am going to be awarded the Nobel Peace Prize. It should be yours, but the Oslo people have been listening to the United Nations staff. The UN staff hates you passionately and has convinced the prize selection committee to award it to me."

"I understand they hate me, for I have eliminated most of the need for their large funding."

"I know the United States provides a huge portion of the funds. If no peacekeeping missions are going on, it will cut the costs enormously.

"Of course, the UN staff is trying to keep the cash cow going for stupid reasons, I have heard. They want to send troops into Detroit on Devil's Night to keep the place from burning. Appropriately, I replied it would be a cold day in hell when UN troops were permitted in the U.S.

"They replied that they would only use U.S. troops. The troops would wear the UN blue beanies and be controlled by Swedish officers. I didn't know what to say to that, so I hung up."

"Don't worry about any of it. The two Nobel prizes that my sister is receiving are enough for any family."

"I'm glad you understand."

Chapter 33

"Rick, if they aren't going to present you with the Peace Prize, I'm going to turn mine down," Mary almost screamed.

I replied, "You have to accept them so I can attend the ceremony."

"Why would you want to go?"

"To watch their faces when they see me. Their type finds it hard to face the people they are mistreating."

"Ooh, I didn't think of that."

"Our whole family will be there, so we must have an honor guard."

"Men with guns? How many?"

"I was thinking two each for Mum, Dad, Denny, Eddie, and me."

"What about May-ling?"

"I think she would only need one."

"One!"

"Yeah, one mechanized division of the Chinese Army on the GC platforms."

Mary gave a small laugh, "That should keep things peaceful."

"Exactly my point."

"What if you are asked why you only have two bodyguards?"

"I will tell them I'm being guarded by my Rods in orbit."

"You are mean. No one will ever want you to visit."

"That is another point to be made. You don't want to do anything bad that may make me visit you."

"That's probably too subtle for most people."

"One of Dad's reporters will ask me the right questions."

"Now I want to go. This presentation will be fun. I was trying to figure out how to shock the prize committee, like streaking their stage, but this will be better."

"It will also save you from having a red bottom afterward."

"Why would my bum be red?"

"Spanking."

"Daddy told me I was too old to spank."

"Did Mum say that?"

"Thank you, Rick. You just saved me."

"That's what big brothers are for."

May-ling, who had been sitting quietly through this conversation, spoke up. "I will have to act the same when Rick's daughter tries to get away with things. She will have him wrapped around her finger."

I nodded my head. Who am I to argue against a universal truth?

After Mary left, May-ling and I both laughed. I could picture Mary stripping down before she was supposed to come onto the stage.

We both stopped laughing at the same time.

May-ling spoke first, "I will tell your Mum so she can keep an eye on Mary at the ceremony. She might change her mind."

"I'll warn Jim and Sally."

I ended with, "It's a good thing this isn't until December 10th. Our entourage will take a lot of planning."

One thing, life at the Jacksons is never dull.

The world's leaders kept contacting me. Or at least trying to contact me. Over fifty phone calls a day were too many for me to handle, no matter who was on the line.

My staff finally put together a conference call with most of them on the line. We opened with a roll call of those present. It was done in alphabetical order by country rather than the leader's name.

I'm certain there would still be complaints over precedence, but I didn't care at this point. All the leaders were jockeying for positions to gain an advantage for their country.

The tables were turned on them when I told them they were the working group to decide how this huge combination of the Military

Alliance and all the new bureaucracies, such as the Space Patrol and Space Traffic Control, would be funded and managed.

I offered the use of a conference room on the moon and would provide transportation. Setting a date one month in advance gave my people enough time to set everything up.

At that, I left the line. During the conference call, people had no way to mute an individual phone so it would be chaotic for the rest of the call.

My family think tank had devised this plan. I loved it. I couldn't wait to hear the screams from the UN staff.

It took two months to write the United States Constitution and two years to get it ratified. I figured this document would take two years to write and ten years to have all agree.

In the meantime, we would proceed to form all the various groups and put them into action. Various staff members were appointed to lead each group.

The groups would be semi-military in their organization. Ranks and uniforms would be used under civilian rules rather than military discipline.

The groups were all independent of each other. After they were formed, they would have to form working agreements with the other groups.

As titular head of all the groups, my new uniform had five stars. One of the uniform rules was that each person could wear all awards given by their respective countries.

By this time, my uniform looked like an advertisement for a circus. If nothing else, it gave me a certain amount of respect. All the medals I wore had been won in true warrior fashion. I didn't wear any good conduct medals.

The truth is I hadn't earned any good conduct medals. What does that say about me?

Forming and putting these organizations to work would take at least a year. What was accomplished immediately was to employ those being displaced by the dismantling of the Military-Industrial Complex.

A new problem arose. We did need to maintain a certain amount of armed forces readiness. Also, the capability to design and manufacture new armaments.

I had my staff put together a working group to address this problem. They were to identify a bare-bones structure of the companies to keep in place. I would then buy these companies. Salaries would be made attractive to keep from losing good people.

The trick was to have industries from many different countries involved.

My stand-up meetings became famous. Woe unto them who tried to drag a meeting out. I had to fire two staff members during meetings before the rest got the word.

Still, my feet hurt. If this kept up, I would have flat feet. I finally limited all meetings to six hours a day. One hour for the moon's business and five for forming the new organizations.

This meeting time included the issues of our trimmed-down Military-Industrial Complex. Doing it this way could maintain my sanity and physical fitness. Not that I felt sane anymore.

The minutes of each working group were made available to the public through news releases. This feedback resulted in an enormous amount of feedback from individuals and groups. Some of it was even useful.

In general, the groups were trying to grind their axes while the individuals were trying to improve the overall picture. There was now a staff group in place to receive and review all feedback and forward that to the pertinent groups, which seemed to have merit.

I, who hated bureaucracies, was creating a new one of considerable size. You would think I was running a government.

My old friends at the UN were having conniptions. All this power and money was floating around. They weren't at the hog trough.

The media, wonder of wonders, played it straight down the middle. They were reporting the facts and nothing but the facts. The opinion editors ignored the whole issue. This ignoring may have been because so many special interest groups were upset, the editors didn't know which way to turn.

Dad had a lot of man-on-the-street interviews. The general public had mixed emotions. They were all glad to see the tools of war being set down. The public of each country was afraid of losing their national identity.

That is everyone but the Canadians. The average Canadian response was, "Eh?" When quizzed about the response, they were Canadians, and no one could take that away from them. They wouldn't have to fight for it. They would just be.

How can you argue with that? I wanted to give Canadians hiring preference but was talked out of it, which was just as well.

Gold production at Lassiter's Reef had to be ramped up once more. I was spending more money than that proverbial drunken sailor.

That thought kept running through my head to such a degree that I found myself singing, "What do you do with a drunken sailor," in the shower.

I hoped my shower wasn't bugged. I couldn't take another hit song. It would be a hit because it was so bad that it would be used in schools as corporal punishment.

Updates on the investigation of Vulcan came in. No evidence had been found of what made Vulcan invisible to all sensors unless inside the orbit of Mercury.

Everyone agreed that it must be something about Mercury that was causing the phenomenon. Nothing had been found. Even radar probes of the subsurface hadn't found anything.

A contest was held at JE Research to name the new element found on Vulcan. The more they dug, the more it looked like the whole planet was a ball of vulcanite. The name made more sense than evantonium, but I couldn't point my finger at anyone since I named it.

Considerable discussion was held on the way Vulcan existed in the first place. The consensus was that it was a rare and valuable material. Otherwise, why go to such extremes to hide it?

Hiding it like that wasn't even within Earth's capabilities. Maybe for the aliens, it was child's play.

Chapter 34

Mary had mentioned earlier that she knew how to entangle things. I accepted that while I should have asked if she could do it. Knowing how and achieving something were two different things.

I checked the time and found it was late afternoon in California, so I hopped on a GC and went to visit her. She was in a good mood, as usual. She was always on top, bubbling over, or mad as all get out over something.

"How are things, sis?"

"Just great, Ricky. We just finished the next round of commercials for our puppy fund, and they look good. My winter dress collection is selling well. We had a food fight at my old school. Everyone got detention except me. Since I don't go there for classes, I was told not to come back next week. Patty was really mad that I got off so light. Then, my sorority was told we had behaved long enough to be off probation. This timing works well as we will be back on it next week when they find out that we have an all-male review show scheduled, someone called Magic Mike. I can't wait. Oh yeah, Professor Einstein and I submitted our paper on how gravity works, and you are named an author. The Nobel committee will have a cow."

This information came out in one long rush. I made a mental note to talk to Mum about this Magic Mike thing. I had never heard of him, but it sounded like bad news for a ten-year-old. I suspect Mum might have a problem with it after she checked it out.

"Mary, you told me you know how to entangle things. Is that theoretically, or can you actually do it?"

"Oh, it can be done, easy peasy. When we tried to send alternating current through the evantonium, it blew up. We were using way too much. You can entangle a batch of paint with extremely low voltage, and the paint will be entangled. You then paint the items you want entangled and Bob's your uncle."

"Do you mean if I paint three or more items with the entangled paint, they are all entangled?"

"We have messed with it in the lab. All items appear entangled with the first painted item but not others."

"So, whatever happens to the source happens to any other with the same batch of paint."

"You got it."

"This opens up all sorts of possibilities."

"The engineers at JE Research are way ahead of you. They are trying to entangle a power supply receiver in vehicles to the fusion power grid. Even without broadcasting power, as Tesla thought about, with entanglement, the electric power goes into the "entanglement box" at the power station and comes out in cars, buses, GC barges, etc."

"Yikes, Mary, this solves the battery problem and could create many new jobs. JE Labs can even come up with a combination "entanglement receiver" and electric motor that could be dropped into existing cars and trucks to replace their gasoline or diesel engines, connecting the power takeoff to the car/truck's driveshaft."

"That's what they plan to do."

"We must consider what this will do to the fossil fuel industry. We need to find ways to use more coal and petroleum as chemical feedstocks to produce a wide range of new materials for building, clothing, and even car and truck bodies. Or GC barges. That means many more new jobs. I like this."

I continued. "Natural gas, believe it or not, can be used to make fertilizer, so there would continue to be a market for that."

"Could we bottle farts?"

She is only ten.

"Maybe. We can make you a set of underwear to collect yours as a test."

"Eww!"

I'm her big brother; occasionally, my duty is to gross her out. I didn't want her to have a swelled head. Entanglement looked like another Nobel Prize to me.

Before contacting JE Research and prioritizing the entanglement project, I told Mum she should check into a guy called Magic Mike and his appearance at Mary's sorority next week.

Her reaction was different than I thought it would be. Her first action was to call Mary's sorority house and confirm that he would be appearing next Saturday night. Then she excitedly called her friend Anna Romanov and told her they would be going to a Magic Mike show next Saturday.

I could hear Anna squeal on the other end. Who is this guy?

Her next step was to let Mary know she was grounded a week from Saturday. Mary didn't take this well. I escaped while the two females went at it.

Dad had just walked in the back door as I escaped.

"Hey, Dad, have you heard of a guy called Magic Mike?"

"What about him?"

"Mum and Mary are fighting because Mum won't let her go to a show he is putting on at Mary's sorority."

"I would hope not."

"Instead, Mum and Anna Romanov are going in her place."

Rarely have I seen my dad at a loss. You could tell he didn't know how to react. All of a sudden, he got a big grin.

"Her seeing Magic Mike could be a good thing for me."

At that, he walked away before I could ask any more questions. I noticed he wasn't in the reception room where Mum and Mary were still going at it.

Hunting for a snack, I ran into Mrs. Hernandez in the kitchen. I asked her if she knew who this Magic Mike was. After filling her in on why I asked, she took off to find Mum. I heard her talking to herself about what she was going to do!

I was almost desperate as I called the information desk at our local library. When I asked if they knew of someone called Magic Mike, I learned he was a highly sought-after male stripper! The lady librarian asked me why I wanted to know. I got off the line. I didn't think the common room at Mary's sorority house could hold many more ladies.

Now I understood why Mum wouldn't let Mary go. It also explained why Mum, Anna, and Mrs. Hernandez wanted to go.

I had to think about Dad's sudden grin. When I put it together, I was embarrassed. Surely my parents didn't still do that!

I was glad that May-ling was in China. I lived with that thought until Mum told me that May-ling would be coming to town a week from Saturday.

Maybe this isn't a bad deal.

Setting aside the sordid lives of the Jackson family and friends, I called JE Research.

They had already performed the first multiple entanglements. Think tank teams were already exploring the ramifications of all this. Everyone in the world would love this, except maybe the Arabs. Their oil income was about to go down the tubes.

The Shah of Iran wouldn't be a happy camper, either. I wondered what effect this would have on the future of the world. I made a mental note to determine what could be done to ameliorate the effects. The world didn't need an uneducated discontented population.

What little I knew of Islam spelled trouble. Of course, that was from my Christian point of view. They probably thought we were the problem children.

Things had calmed down. At dinner, I found out Mum was arranging a Princess Party at Disney for Mary and her friends a week from Saturday. Mary would be the only real princess there. I bet she would wear her tiara. Eat your hearts out, Sleeping Beauty and Cinderella.

There was a slight change in bodyguard assignments. Sally was replacing one of Mum's male guards for that night. Poor Jim had to spend the evening with a bunch of ten-year-olds. Life can be hard.

Dad and I decided to take a GC sled to Augusta to play a round of golf on that Saturday. Dad was cool and got Jim out of his assignment, and he came with us. He was a pretty good golfer. I was rusty, and Dad had improved, so we had a good time.

After our round, where I had broken par but nothing else, we were at loose ends. With the time difference, it was still early in California. Dad mentioned they had a good Can Can show at the Moulin Rouge in Paris.

Using the bar phone in the clubhouse, I called the presidential palace in France. It wouldn't do to show up unannounced. I was put through to the president.

When I explained our mission, he told me we couldn't go without the proper accompaniment. It just so happened that his wife was out of town, and he could escort us.

With our sled, it was a hop, skip, and jump to Paris. Landing at the Élysée Palace, we joined the French president in a motorcade to the Moulin Rouge.

After an eye-opening show, we dropped the president off and returned to California in time to greet some amorous ladies.

I hoped Mary had as much fun as we did.

Chapter 35

I started the next day off with a grin on my face. I briefly thought about making Magic Mike a Knight of the Realm for services rendered. After thinking about how that might be interpreted, I set that idea aside.

At breakfast, I asked Mary how her Princess Party went.

"It was a lot of fun after we got past the awkward entrance."

"What was awkward about it?"

"The Disney Princesses presented all the girls with tiaras just like the ones they wore. They were very fancy-looking. I was already wearing my tiara with real diamonds. It didn't look as grand as theirs. Snow White told me to take my dinky old one off and wear a nice one."

Ouch, I could see what was coming.

"I told her I would rather wear the real thing than one of their fakes."

"I bet that went over well. "

"Not really. The actress suddenly dropped out of character and started to call me a brat.

"Lucky for her, a Disney attendant who was the Master of Ceremonies grabbed her and told her that I was a real princess and that my tiara was the real thing."

"How did she take that?"

"The actress playing Snow White is a real pro. Once she realized what was going on, she turned, gave me a deep curtsy, and apologized for her confusion.

"I told her not to give it a second thought. It had to be difficult to play her role as a storybook character and deal with the real world.

"She agreed with me and told me how one day in a line at the supermarket, she was ready to ask them if they knew they were keeping a princess waiting."

"That would have been embarrassing for her."

"I told her that even as a real princess, it wouldn't have helped her. I know because I have tried it in the cafeteria line at my grade school.

"We had a wonderful evening after that. The other princesses gave me a lot of good ideas about being a princess."

The princess's advice can't have a good ending, I thought.

"What was their main advice?"

"To always be gracious to people, even those who annoy you. People remember you kindly; those annoying are annoyed in turn, and you have the high ground."

That sounded like good advice for a king. Maybe Disney could run a school for royals.

All the silly stuff aside, I got a phone call from JE Research with an update on vulcanite. It seems the element makes a super heatsink for computers. Not only that, but it is also superconductive at room temperature. This totally violates so many laws of physics, it is insane. Where is the heat going? This is a Mary problem.

That means it can be used as the pathway for the electrons. The heat created won't escape, and the flow will be superfast. If we entangle everything, we will have computers that exceed our wildest imaginations.

I still thought there was something about the element we didn't understand. I voiced my thoughts, and they agreed with me. Various tests would continue.

If vulcanite wasn't useful for something extremely important, why was almost a planet's worth in orbit near the Sun? With the relatively small temperature difference between Vulcan and the Sun, it would take almost a billion years to sublimate off.

Several interesting tidbits crossed my desk. One of international importance and one personal.

The important one was the leadership of the House of Commons had resigned, and a new government had to be elected.

When the queen took the unilateral action of signing a military alliance with me, British law required one of two actions. The queen had to surrender, or the prime minister had to resign, and elections were held.

Reading between the lines of the report, the Prime Minister went to Buckingham Palace expecting to hear she was abdicating. It would have been royally polite, as only the queen could do, but she basically told him to pound sand.

The queen hadn't made any public announcements, as she never did on political issues, but there was a long report in the *Times*. Before approaching me, she had a poll taken of the House of Commons.

Because of Military-Industrial support, a vote to join the alliance would fail even though it was heavily weighted in the British people's interests.

It was reported in the *Times* that taxes would go down and public assistance increase.

The politicians were well aware of this but still would have voted it down. The *Times* went so far as to name names of those who would have voted against the alliance.

The anti-alliance voters wouldn't fare well in the by-elections.

Well played, Queen Elizabeth!

The second note to me was that Boris and Natasha had a baby. He was named Richard Boris Fatale Badenov. They wanted me to be his godfather. I sent a return note that I would be delighted.

Now what to get a baby Badenov?

Looking through a Sears catalog, I settled on a squirrel-shaped baby rattle and a toy stuffed moose. I don't know why I chose those. They were just cute. There also would be a fully paid college education fund established.

I was working in my office on the moon. I had to be here for an event the next day. I would have liked to have skipped it, but it would look bad for the king to skip his official birthday party.

Unlike the queen, I had elected to have my birthday celebrated on my actual birthday. I suspected her June date was selected because of the horrid April weather in England. I later discovered that it had been selected in 1748 for King George II.

Countries in the Commonwealth celebrate at different times to smooth out their holiday calendars and weather considerations. I wonder if the queen got presents or just official good wishes on all those birthdays.

I don't think we will let Mary know about all these parties.

There would be no Trooping of the Color at my party. There would be a picnic-style party on the Commons open to all. That was easy to do in my small country.

My family had agreed that we would only spend a maximum of twenty dollars on each other's presents. We were so rich that money had no meaning. This was one time it was the gift that counted, not its worth.

Of course, Dad and I agreed that when it came to our spouses, all bets were off.

I planned to cheat a little on my present to Mary on her birthday. I had what the people at JE Research called a supercomputer built for her. I would tell her I got it at the U.S. price of $19.95. The true price would be several million dollars.

I hoped she would use it for serious research rather than playing Pong.

Going back to my birthday celebration. An old British tradition that had been discontinued because of the population size was a gift from the monarch to the people.

The gift handed out in Toronto, Canada in 1859 was a ticket good for one free loaf of bread. The local government bore the cost, but I thought it was a nice gesture.

I could afford to do something similar for my people. At the party, tickets would be handed out for a ten percent tax rebate on their first income tax.

There was no income tax at this time because our local politicians couldn't get their act together. I hoped for two outcomes. First, the government would create an income tax. I was getting tired of paying for everything out of pocket. Yes, I could afford it, but I didn't want to have a kingdom living on handouts.

Secondly, I wanted people to work and pay a tax so the kingdom would be self-supporting!

There was an underground economy but not an official one besides my personal income.

These thoughts led me to how to create an influx of foreign currency. Maybe if we could get Magic Mike to have a permanent show here, it would attract tourists.

Nah. The same for casinos. Maybe tours of the moon with stops at each landing site. I had already declared all previous landing sites to be international monuments that were not to be disturbed.

Maybe it was time to fence them off. That thought turned into creating a Solar System Park Service. Again, more jobs.

These thoughts made my decision to allow the Hilton people to build a hotel at the base of Olympus Mons on Mars. The new Solar System Park Service could conduct tours to the top. That would help fund the park service.

Once I started down this line of thought, I called an aide in to take notes to start the ball rolling.

I would have to take that tour myself. Anything sixteen miles high, three times Mount Everest, was worth visiting. There wouldn't be the dangers of climbing Everest, but there would be bragging rights.

I wondered how the Century Club would handle this. Suddenly visiting one hundred different countries wasn't as impressive anymore. I can hear it now.

"I've been to Bora Bora."

"Well, I've been to Jupiter and Mars."

My aide noted that the new park service had to establish an Interstellar Visitor Passbook. Then they would have a station at each location to stamp the passbooks. More jobs.

More headaches. How soon would they become Interstellar Passports?

Chapter 36

My birthday started as a wonderfully clear day on the moon. It was always a wonderfully clear day inside our tunnel system. My wife gave me an early birthday present. A very private gift.

So, I got ready to face the day with a smile.

My immediate family had come up for the celebration. My family now included Popeye, Sybil, and Mrs. Hernandez.

We had a festive breakfast together. My presents from the family were given to me. They mostly come under the heading of gag gifts. Eddie's proved to be the most unique and popular.

Who would have thought to give someone on the moon a pogo stick? We guys couldn't wait to try it out in moon gravity. It should be a blast.

My parents gave me a new sports coat, along with custom shirts. They all had the Lunar Kingdom logo embroidered on them.

Mary got me cuff links for my shirts.

Denny had brought his equipment for a group of family portraits.

May-ling presented me with a *yìnzhāng*, a seal to stamp legal documents. It had the logo of the Lunar Kingdom and my coat of arms carved to form the stamp. Unlike the ornate carvings on the handle of most stamps, mine was plain.

She informed me that they would be carved on the handle when significant events occurred in my life.

Thinking of my life so far, I wondered what she considered significant. I must have looked bewildered because the whole family started to laugh.

My treacherous wife then unscrewed the handle from the stamp and threaded a new one on. It had small carvings that were hard to see because there were so many. Looking closer, I realized they were the history of my life to date.

She also presented me with a box to keep it in. It was velvet-lined with a recess for the *yìnzhāng*. There was also a chop for embossing documents. The *yìnzhāng* left a one-dimensional stamp, while the chop left a raised impression. One for simple documents and the impression for formal documents such as treaties adorned with wax and ribbons.

Popeye and Sybil presented me with an album containing many certificates. They certified the many crossings I had done. That reminded me that there was one important one that Popeye had done but I hadn't yet—The Royal Order of Purple Porpoises for maritime personnel who crossed the junction of the equator and the International Date Line at the Sacred Hour of the Vernal Equinox.

I had never related all of this to my family, so we had to go through the album page by page. I had many of them. Popeye had brought his album along with the following:

The Order of the Blue Nose is for maritime personnel who have crossed the Arctic Circle.

The Order of the Red Nose was presented to maritime personnel crossing the Antarctic Circle.

The Imperial Order of the Golden Dragon for maritime personnel who have crossed the International Date Line.

The Sacred Order of The Golden Dragon for maritime personnel who have crossed at the same time Lat. 00-000°, Long. 180.00°

The Order of the Ditch for maritime personnel who have passed through the Panama Canal.

The Magellan's Strait Jacket Club for all maritime personnel who transited the Straits of Magellan.

The Order of the Rock is for maritime personnel who have transited the Straits of Gibraltar.

The Safari to Suez for maritime personnel who have passed through the Suez Canal.

The Golden Shellback is for maritime personnel who have crossed the point where the Equator crosses the International Date Line.

The Order of the Sand Squid is for maritime personnel attached to army units or in the Middle East.

The Emerald Shellback or Royal Diamond Shellback is for maritime personnel who cross at 0 degrees off West Africa (where the equator crosses the prime meridian).

The Realm of the Czars for maritime personnel who crossed into the Black Sea.

The Order of Magellan for maritime personnel who circumnavigated the Earth.

The Order of the Lakes is for maritime personnel who have sailed on all five Great Lakes.

The Order of the Spanish Main for maritime personnel who have sailed in the Caribbean.

The Order of the Sparrow is for maritime personnel who sailed on all seven seas (North Atlantic, South Atlantic, North Pacific, South Pacific, Indian, Arctic, and Antarctic Oceans).

The Order of the Ebony Shellback for maritime personnel who have crossed the Equator on Lake Victoria.

Popeye had one thing that I didn't. He had all the tattoos for the awards. I mentioned that I should have them to May-ling. That got shot down quickly.

Even if we obtained the Royal Order together, Popeye and I could never equal the *SS Warimoo*.

In December 1899, the *SS Warimoo* was ferrying passengers between Canada and Australia.

While at sea Captain John Phillips realized he had the opportunity to do something extraordinary. He commanded that the ship steered for the point where the equator crossed the International Date Line.

The ship arrived in time to straddle that point as the clock struck midnight on December 31, 1899.

The forward part of the ship was in the Southern Hemisphere and the middle of summer. The rear part of the ship was in the Northern Hemisphere and the middle of winter.

Half of the ship was on 31 December 1899, while the forward half skipped a day ahead and into 1 January 1900.

The ship was not only in two different days, two different months, two different years, two different seasons, and two different hemispheres but also in two different centuries, all simultaneously.

If we lived until 1999, we might try that. Not only would we repeat all of the previous records, but we would also be in two millenniums simultaneously!

It would be ten thousand years of the Decem millennium before that record could be broken. We would have to invite the Guinness Book of Records people along in 1999.

Mary, the bright one in the family, told us she could earn all the above in one day. She would have ships posted at each point and time, then hop from ship to ship in a GC craft.

Spoilsport! I told her I would stamp all her certificates, but they would have asterisks.

"What will the asterisks say?"

"Cheater!"

Mary pouted so much that Mum told her a rooster would sit on her lip. That brought us a giggle, and all was well.

We had some time before the official event, so we sat around and talked about possible awards for visiting locations in the solar system.

Mum and Dad had one more present for me. It was a large golden key cut like an old-style skeleton key. Tradition in England was to present a golden key on one's twenty-first birthday. The key signified that you were now an adult and had the freedoms and privileges thereof. The normal birthday key was a cutout on a birthday card. I had come of age.

It was fun and silly until someone said we should have an Olympus Mons for climbing the mountain. That wasn't what shut us up; it was Mary's comment.

"So, if someone climbed a mountain on Venus. It would be the Mons Venus award."

I hope she didn't understand what she just said. After much coughing and quick sips of juice and coffee, the crowd broke up.

We moved as a group to the main commons area. We were right on time. I thought there would be other people on their way, but there wasn't anyone on our main road.

When we arrived at the Commons, I understood. It looked like the entire colony, which now stood at a little over two thousand people, had shown up early.

Our five-man band struck up "Happy Birthday" when I was spotted, and the crowd sang to me.

I shook hands along the way. There were cameras all over the place. There was even a TV camera set up. I didn't realize that my birthday would be such a big deal. Later I figured out Rick Jackson's birthday wasn't a big deal. The King of Luna and the Solar Research's birthday was a big deal.

There were tables laden with food and drink for all. I ascended the stage, normally used for outdoor plays and events. Immediately below the stage, the center table had a huge birthday cake set up.

It was so large it seemed to defy gravity. Mum told me the cake was sitting on its GC pad so it wouldn't collapse. I wondered if we could have it declared the largest birthday cake ever.

May-ling and I sat in the center positions of the main table. Then the speeches began. I was shocked when all five of them proved to be short and to the point.

The last one made by our temporary leader was the best. He was the temporary mayor because we had no real government. His job was to lead the people I had appointed to create a constitution and the basic form of government for our colony. The only provision I insisted upon was that we would be a constitutional monarchy with me as king. I had the last word as long as I financially supported the colony.

After the colony had an elected government and a tax code, would I surrender the power of the purse? The government funds were not to be confused with my fortune.

Chapter 37

The last speech was a shocker! The interim government speaker ended with a message to me. He announced that an income tax had been voted on and passed. It was to be a five percent flat tax.

We had taken our first steps as a country.

Looking at previous royal birthday celebrations, I liked the idea of the king, me, giving a present to his citizens. It was an open secret that I had certificates printed that would give the recipient a ten percent reduction of their taxes for the year they were turned in.

They had a time limit of twenty-five years. Since all citizens would receive one certificate, there would be children just born that would receive one.

The interim government could take a hint. I had been pushing for the tax to be enacted. Once the tax was laid out, people could decide if they would be taxpayers or not. Those who paid taxes got a vote in our affairs. Those who didn't choose to support the colony in our endeavors would have no vote.

This plan would prevent a welfare class from voting us into poverty. Thomas Jefferson would approve.

Once a person decided to be a taxpayer, they were locked into it for life. A person who elected not to pay taxes could change their mind once.

This rule would prevent tax avoidance by gaming the system.

Each certificate was issued to a specific person in their name. While there were over two thousand people in the colony, many were personnel with embassies or companies hired to perform special tasks.

One thousand five hundred fifty-four certificates had been issued.

Now that the tax was in place, people could declare whether or not they would be taxpayers. Those who chose to be taxpayers would vote for their representatives in the new government.

The election season would be a short two weeks. There would only be ten representatives in our new parliament. The representatives would elect one of their members as the first prime minister.

I didn't think any parties would be formed for this first election, but it wouldn't take long before they were formed.

Unlike the Queen of England, I had retained foreign affairs and the military.

Since we were a small group, the interim government had arranged for people to be able to declare their preference of being a taxpayer or not.

I cut the huge birthday cake that looked like a GC craft. Small figures on the board represented my family and me.

As ice cream and slices of cake were handed out, it was announced that we now had one thousand three hundred and forty-two taxpayers.

The floor was open to questions. I could see these taking hours.

The first question was a doozy.

"Can we sell our tax rebate certificates?"

This question was immediately dumped into my lap. Without time to think, I responded, "Yes, they can. If a child's certificate is sold, the money will be held for the child and not go into their parent's pocket."

Oncc I gave my answer, the person who had asked the question held his certificate and asked, "What are your bids?"

Before I could head it off, a bidding war had started.

I could have shut it off, but I decided to let it go. The first certificate sold for one thousand and fifty lunar dollars. That amount was a small fortune.

As soon as the certificate was sold, I took over.

"All right, folks. Let's do this right. I know that Pete is also an auctioneer in the interim government. Form a line, and he will take over.

Thirty-two people lined up, fifteen of them children.

The price bid held up. The going rate turned out to be around one thousand lunar dollars. People had to owe taxes on over ten thousand dollars for this to be worth their while.

People must be optimistic about our future.

It didn't take long for a professional auctioneer to run the show. Once settlement had been made to both parties, the certificate was registered in the new owner's name.

While all this was going on, I realized why my family was so interested in everywhere that Popeye had been. They were wasting time so the interim government could arrive at and vote on the new tax rate.

Two people stood there looking a little lost when it looked like the auction was complete, and all was settled. Tears were pouring down the ten-year-old girl's cheeks.

May-ling and I went over to them to see what the problem was.

Her mother said, "We need at least fifteen hundred dollars to pay our rent and feed us for the next month. The rent is due today. We hoped we could use Cindy's money to help out, but your rules say they must be held for her."

I was at a loss. May-ling stepped up.

"What do you do?"

"That's the problem. I'm a seamstress, and there is no need for one in the colony."

"How did you end up here?"

"My soon-to-be ex-husband brought us up here, then abandoned us for one of the Space Ladies. They both returned to Earth, and now I can't even afford a ticket home."

May-ling turned and beckoned Mary over.

"Mary, I remember you saying you wanted to have special clothes made here on the moon for your collection."

"That's right; it would be very high-end. Only originals handmade here on the moon."

May-ling turned to the mother, "I'm sorry I didn't get your name."

"Heather Johnson."

"Mary, Heather is a seamstress?"

Mary looked a little uncomfortable at this.

Mary asked Mrs. Johnson, "This is embarrassing to ask like this, but are you any good?"

"I made the dresses that Cindy and I are wearing."

"Do you mind?"

At that, Mary felt the fabric, examined the seams, peeked at the liners, and checked out the fit of the dresses.

"You're hired," Mary announced.

Heather got a faint look but managed to say thank you.

"Would ten thousand dollars a month be enough?"

"Oh my...gosh, yes."

I told Mary, "I think an immediate hiring bonus would be in order."

"How much?"

"I think a month's pay would be about right."

Mary didn't quibble. She pulled a folded check out of her little purse and wrote it at once.

"Your first job, Heather, is finding a place to set up shop. I think the designs shall be one of my company's names, but you will be the maker. The accounting people will figure out the best way to do it. We want to legally avoid old money bag's tax as much as possible."

I'm pretty sure sororicide is against the law on the moon. Maybe I could change the laws. Please wait a minute. We didn't have any laws yet. It was a royal fiat! Off with her head! Or better yet, tickle her until she pees.

I thanked Mary and May-ling for taking care of what could have become a sticky wicket. I did write a note to check into Mr. Johnson and his Space Lady. At best, the Space Lady would get a dishonorable discharge.

The guy was looking at child support in his future, even if I had to extradite him to the moon to serve a prison sentence. Since we didn't have a prison system, maybe I could hire one on earth.

The rest of my day was spent watching sack races, egg-on-spoon races, and other outdoor festival games.

While these were going on, many people came over to me and wished me many happy returns. There was a lot of casual conversation, but people seemed to respect my day and didn't make any serious requests.

Well, there was one that I took under serious consideration. One of the younger guys wanted me to invite the Swedish all-girl volleyball team for an exhibition match. He had pictures of them playing in bikinis.

I was thinking about it until my wife slapped me on the back of my head. It reminded me of what Dad used to do to the Harmon kid.

"I must pass on this. My advisors don't think it will help international relations."

The kid went away disappointed. May-ling told me that I had made a wise decision. I wondered if we could get Dad to sponsor it through one of his newspapers.

I know you can't read other people's minds, so I wondered when Mum told me not to think about it.

Meanwhile, two young ladies were having a good time. Mary and Cindy were rating all the guys their age. I kept track of the high scorers. They might have to be exiled from the moon.

Pretty soon, the two came over to Mum and asked if they could have a dance party. Considering my little sister is a genius, she didn't play it well.

Mum told her, of course, they could have an all-girls party. Mum and Heather gave each other a look and shook their heads. Their problems were just starting.

At least Mary didn't ask if Magic Mike could dance with them.

Chapter 38

I was given a list of all the world leaders who had sent birthday wishes. I thought about all the letter signing I would have to do. Not only that, each letter, though short, would have to be an individual composition. It wouldn't do to send a form letter.

The party continued all day long. A lot of people were having a good time. Later I was besieged by people wanting favors who thinly disguised themselves as well-wishers.

People who had good ideas and were willing to work for them got a fair hearing. Those who wanted a handout got sent away. They didn't know yet that we didn't need any freeloaders on the moon and that they would be sent back to Earth.

There were contests and prizes for all ages. My favorite was watching the little kids, six and under, dig in a mulch pile for money. It was only for lower denomination coins.

There were no gold loonies worth about four hundred dollars U.S. or silver ones worth five dollars U.S. We had to issue the lower coins in decimal values for everyday commerce.

We had copper pennies, and everything else was minted with silver and nickel. There was enough silver in each coin to match the face value. A dime would have one-tenth of an ounce of silver, so ten of them equal a one-ounce silver dollar. This ratio was true for the nickel, dime, quarter, half dollar, and silver dollar.

I had almost no input on the designs, which had me on the dollar, May-ling on the half, Denny on the quarter, Mary on the dime, and Eddie on the nickel. The penny had May-ling and me together.

When I asked why Mary was on the dime while Eddie was on the nickel, it was explained they went by the physical size of the coin rather than its value. Not sure I agree with that, but you can only manage so much.

While Denny and Eddie were acknowledged as princes, Princess Mary had worldwide recognition. That made sense. Who wouldn't love a cute ten-year-old financial genius who also was a true genius and was changing the world for the better?

Her coin wasn't even called a dime. It was simply a Mary. It was the most minted coin of our kingdom. Every young lady in the world hoarded her Marys. It didn't help when Mary replaced the penny in loafers. They still called them penny loafers but were only stylish with Marys in them.

Her dress company then had the same concept for purses, wallets, and anything else. These Marys didn't come back into circulation, so we had to have more minted to meet demand.

Then some independents made necklaces and bracelets out of Marys. These soon became mass-produced items. A small rise in silver price was attributed to the demand for Marys. We had a for-profit mint outside of Philadelphia producing our coins.

The mint was busy with our coins. They quit producing specialty items that they flogged to the public as collectibles. Our main coins, the Lunar silver and gold coins plus ingots, were still cast by the Australian government.

Silver is frequently found as an "impurity" in gold ores, and this was the case with Lassiter's Reef, so we had no shortage of silver, which appeared as a black sand waste product during the initial refinement stage of the gold. The silver-bearing sand then had to be smelted to recover the silver, but there was a lot of "pay dirt" in that sand.

I discovered that Denny could get dates just by handing one of his quarters to a young lady. I made a point of not making any two-bit jokes.

Eddie was still so wrapped up in his racing world that he appeared oblivious to it all.

May-ling ended up issuing her coin in China as part of their official currency. In China, the coin was as popular as Marys were elsewhere.

My silver dollar had almost no demand as a collectible. It was used the same as a U.S. dollar bill but had no other function. I didn't know if this should bum me out. I decided to remain above it all. It didn't bother me. Right.

My public birthday party continued all day and into the evening. The little children were taken home to bed while the parents returned for an evening of music and dancing.

I wondered who was taking care of the children. May-ling told me that teenage girls were charging a small fortune to babysit. Some boys were even doing it!

During the afternoon, I copied an English tradition. Birthday honors were presented. At this time, the new creation of a countess was the highest honor awarded. The new countess was my first Space Lady, Jerri Cobb.

There were several barons and a bunch of knights. I had decided that any employee who spent five or more years on active space duty would become a knight.

Another group of people were awarded knighthood but couldn't be present. First responders used GC barges and sleds to rescue people from disabled ships, forest fires, volcano eruptions, hurricanes, typhoons, raging flood waters, and burning skyscrapers. I provided the crafts and operators while the responders performed the dangerous rescues.

I could relate to several of these rescues, especially those from raging waters, and respected these people to no end.

None of the people on Earth were citizens of the Lunar Kingdom and the Solar Reaches, so their titles were honorary only. We would recognize them while on the moon, but none of their Earth nations would do the same.

To sweeten the pot, I included ten thousand Lunar dollars annually for their lifetime. They would also have the right to immigrate to the moon if they met our conditions.

Our conditions were simple. They must be able to support themselves. While we had short-term unemployment, no programs would allow an able-bodied worker to live off welfare.

I was almost paranoid about the subject. I didn't want any slums or underclass in my kingdom. Many on Earth declared me to be an elitist or cold-hearted at best. I noticed that those with that attitude met one or both conditions.

I wondered what would happen if I sent a busload of poor people to Martha's Vineyard.

We did have programs for those who became physically disabled or were born with deficiencies. Those people would have worked if they could.

I was a fan of Lee Kwan Yew and his approach in many cases. No matter how old you were, we had something that the elderly could do. Heaven help the child who threw a liter bottle on the playground in front of the grandmas who patrolled the area.

They were armed with brooms and were known to give a swat to the butt of an unruly child. Generally, that child would get the same when they arrived home.

There was another class of people that we gave shelter to on the moon. These people were whistleblowers who needed to be in hiding until they were called to testify.

We had been approached by the United States Marshal's Witness Protection program. We reached an agreement and soon agreements in place with most industrialized nations.

We wouldn't accept any gangsters who had turned against their gangs.

There was a special cavern set up for the whistleblowers. They were allowed to shop, play, or attend classes in the main area but had to spend the night in their area. This precaution was for their security and ours.

We watched these people carefully. If they blended into our population and showed a work ethic, they would be considered if they applied for citizenship.

The morning after the party, I was up early and out helping the cleanup crews. While most people picked up their trash, there still was a mess from the various games. The pile of mulch with money for the little kids was the worst.

Mary and her new friend Cindy were working on it. At least, I thought, they were helping. It didn't take long to realize they were searching for any coins the littles may have missed.

When they found one, they held it up in the air and did a happy dance. It reminded me that the princess, the millionaire, and the genius combined was only ten years old.

I walked through the area they hadn't searched and scattered golden loonies when they weren't looking. That would give a happy dance or two.

May-ling, who had now come out to help, saw me and told me I would spoil our daughter beyond belief. I told her to believe that I would spoil our daughter.

We said these words in jest. We spent many an hour discussing how to raise our children regardless of their sex. They would be heirs to the largest fortune in the world and rulers over most of the human race. We had to be careful to teach them about duty. There would be no spoiled brats on our watch.

Not that the kids wouldn't be allowed to have fun. We would be careful to be sure they didn't become entitled, arrogant snobs. We knew there would be plenty of people encouraging exactly that.

I liked to think our parents had done a good job with us, so we would use their actions to guide ours. My family never had servants when I was young, but May-ling's did. She would help our children realize the servants were there to assist and were people in their own right.

Chapter 39

The solar system didn't stop because of my birthday. An ongoing exploration of the planets made for some interesting discoveries.

The most fascinating was made in the high atmosphere of Jupiter. All observations were made by unmanned or unwomaned GC craft due to intense radiation caused by Jupiter's magnetic field.

After two trips each, we would scrap the GC craft because of damage build-up. It took a total of fourteen crafts to build the pictures that we obtained.

Jupiter is massive. It is eleven times wider than Earth. To put it in perspective, if Earth was the size of a quarter, Jupiter would be the size of a basketball.

It has rings like Saturn, but they are dim and hard to see because they are made of dust, unlike Saturn's, which are mostly ice. Its mass is more than twice all other planets combined.

It has seventy-five moons and more to be discovered.

The famous red spot storm has been raging for hundreds of years. Its diameter is greater than the diameter of Earth.

An interesting discovery was made at the bottom of the high atmosphere. That is a strange way to say it, but Jupiter is made up of many layers. Most of which we will never reach.

The upper atmosphere has clouds made up of water and ammonia. A late-night comedian suggested it was the largest bottle of Windex in existence.

The clouds floated in an atmosphere of hydrogen and helium. The atmosphere was a liquid because of the high gravity compressing the hydrogen/helium mix.

It was at the transition of the upper atmosphere to the next layer that the discovery was made.

The next layer was solid compared to the upper atmosphere. It was not a perfect ball but comprised of uneven heights and sizes of ridges. This transition zone appeared to function similarly to a reef in Earth's oceans.

There was a form of life there. Nothing like anything on Earth. The simplest description would be they looked like jellyfish. There were billions upon billions of them.

They came in all sizes and colors. The largest was as big as a blimp. The smallest was the size of a tennis ball.

What they used for locomotion was unknown. The current theory was that the Jupiter jellyfish moved like an octopus. However, they weren't observed swelling and contracting.

What was observed was that they swam in schools like fish. Like with like. These schools could be miles long.

The Jupiter jellyfish name was shortened to JJs by common usage. The JJs preyed on other types of JJs. How this was done was amazing.

When two schools of JJ of different sorts approached each other, the schools would break down into smaller groups.

These groups of individuals would cluster together to form a shape. There were many shapes, even from the same type of JJ in the same school.

The research people named the JJ shapes after familiar Earth animals. There were sharks, barracudas, snakes, lions, and tigers. These were just a few of those observed.

These shapes would attack each other. The winner was usually the larger or faster shape.

The most dominant shape was called a Maw. It was a huge mouth. They swallowed anything smaller than themselves. It was all mouth with almost no body attached.

How the shapes digested their food was still under debate. We had released all these findings to all of Earth, so many theories were being offered.

When a battle between schools was over, partial shapes would be absorbed by others of the same type.

There was a huge argument about whether the JJs swam in formation or combined physically into a new life form.

When schools reach a certain size, they split to form new schools. The few pictures we had suggested that it was the same as cell division.

Rather than lose GC craft, we sent in drones. These drones were to return photos to the craft, then to be brought out to the researchers.

None of the drones were ever able to make it back. We thought we would lose them to radiation damage. Instead, they were all eaten by the first school that came across them.

The schools, in turn, were immediately attacked by what was called a Moray Eel. They lurked in the reefs. A theory held that the various life forms considered the drone elements desirable.

The cost of this information was in the billions, so I called the project off; while extremely interesting, it was of no practical use.

The screams from Earth's scientists were heard everywhere. They seemed to think that I owed them the information for free.

No one took my offer to continue observing the JJs if they funded it.

One group of researchers thought I was unreasonable when I wouldn't send a manned GC craft down to capture JJs for study.

I offered them a craft if they would man it. There were no takers.

That offer was a bit of a gamble. The film from the last GC craft sent in was being withheld from everyone on my direct orders.

I didn't want to start a world panic over what they revealed. There was intelligent and maybe unfriendly life on Jupiter.

The Eels had collected the elements from drones sent. They had attacked the other JJs who had destroyed our drones.

The JJs were transparent. Previous pictures sent back let us see the parts of drones inside the original JJ attackers. When the Moray Eels attacked the first group, they now contained the drone parts.

Things changed on the last trip down. The Moray Eels attacked the drones directly. They didn't leave the vicinity of their reefs. Our sensors showed that they used weapons made from the first drone elements.

Our investigation was providing them with the means to manufacture weapons! That was the real reason I stopped all flights into the Jovian atmosphere.

At Jackson Research, they were working on developing a new type of drone from different materials. We needed to know more about these aliens without providing them with the means to harm us.

My adventures in the last few years have taught me to be ready for danger at any time. Another charge given to research was to develop weapons that would work against the JJ.

Some groups on Earth would have a cow about me being a warmonger. To them, I was a monster for wanting to kill innocent JJ. They would ignore that it was the JJs destroying our drones.

I wasn't going to commit genocide, but I wouldn't offer up Earth on a platter.

One of the first weapon submissions was a way to detonate the hydrogen/helium mixture in the first layer of Jupiter's atmosphere.

It took me a while to wrap my head around that. First, it might destroy the entire planet Jupiter. That might set off a chain reaction that would destroy us. I knew of no way to work the math to model the results.

I put a hold on that line of research. Maybe we would have to revisit it if the Eels broke out and were a true threat. Those were some mighty big ifs.

Another group wanted to drop small quantities of chemicals to see if they could poison the JJs. This plan held some promise as it wouldn't destroy Jupiter.

I had to keep reminding everyone involved that we had to determine if the Eels would be damaging to us.

There were now enough people working on the JJ project that it would get out. Because of that, I briefed the top ten world leaders one-on-one, as a meeting would have signaled a problem.

All of my travels were now documented by the world's press. Surrendering to the inevitable, my staff released my daily schedule. Each visit had a public version, such as a new trade agreement or cooperation in space development.

It wasn't until I was alone with the leader that I revealed the true reason. In our post-meeting press conference, the leadership's stress was construed to mean that their country hadn't done well on the new agreement.

When the terms were released to the public, the pundits were confused. At least I got a chuckle out of that.

The leaders agreed with my thoughts and plans in the follow-ups from those meetings.

I was glad about that but didn't care that much. My wife and unborn child were at risk, and I wouldn't take any chances with their lives.

May-ling knew the entire story from day one. She was of the "nuke'em first" school of thought.

Mum and Dad wanted to take it slow and see if we could establish communication with the Eels. That made a lot of sense, so that was another working group formed.

The attempt to see if we could communicate was a public attempt with working groups at every university and think tank that showed an interest.

The only information they weren't provided was what we knew about the Eels.

There were some interesting proposals. One I liked best was to dump different colors of dyes to see if they would attract the JJs.

These dyes would allow us to see if any JJs could differentiate colors. In the second part of that experiment, we could try out different substances to see if they were poison to the JJs.

Not very friendly, I know, but this was he human race at risk.

Chapter 40

After several drone launches, potassium permanganate was found deadly to the JJs of all types.

The drones had as few elements as possible, using wood as the main frame. We knew they wouldn't be retrievable and didn't want to provide the Moray Eels with more building materials.

The Moray Eels seized the first drones with potassium permanganate. Those involved died immediately. The PP, as we call it, is an oxidizer. Whatever the Eels were made of reacted violently with it.

The Eels didn't grab the next one sent down; they let other JJs seize it. After the predictable violent reaction, the Moray Eels collected the elements they needed from the JJ remains.

Their actions indicated some level of intelligence. The new question was how intelligent and whether they were belligerent to other life forms.

Now that we knew we could contain the Moray Eels if needed, there was no need to keep them a secret.

I introduced the lead researcher to the world. She presented the findings of the different committees. It boiled down to the following. We found life on Jupiter. It may be inimical, and we have weapons that will defeat them if needed.

We now were trying to figure out how intelligent they were and to open communication if possible.

She shared pictures of the different JJs we had identified and how they worked together. You would think with such a clear explanation, there would be a few questions.

After two hours with her growing hoarse, I called for the last question.

It was a doozy, "Do you think they will invade Earth?"

This question was after it had been explained how different their environment is from ours.

I jumped in and answered the question.

"There is less chance than the sharks in the ocean have of invading Denver."

He wanted a follow-up, but I shut the mike off and left.

Talking to stupid never gets anywhere.

The working groups came up with many methods to communicate with the Eels. They wanted to try blinking lights, lights of different colors, blinking lights of different colors, many different sounds at various frequencies.

They also wanted to try sonar. What the scientists were trying to find at this stage was something that would get the Eel's attention.

Once they had their attention, they would try different messages. Most of the messages would be based on fundamental math.

This project would be long-term; all we could do was keep trying.

While that was happening, my brother Denny dropped a blockbuster on the family. He was getting married.

His lifestyle had finally caught up with him. His girlfriend of the last six months or so was pregnant. As he put it, "We have to get married."

I wasn't there when he told Mum and Dad, but it must have been quite a scene. He told me they took it calmly when I asked him about it.

I know there was a question about my birthdate and Mum and Dad's marriage, so they couldn't get too worked up.

Their only question was, "Is this what you want?"

He told them he wanted this very much.

Our parents met with her parents. That didn't go quite so well. Her father was all upset about my parents' worthless son despoiling their innocent daughter.

First, Denny wasn't worthless. The last time I heard, his business was pulling in over a million dollars a year, and he was about to go to international.

From what I understood, the innocent little girl had been a willing participant. I wondered if she was a gold digger trying to get into the Jackson family.

After meeting Janet, that fear was set to rest. She is head over heels in love with Denny. Luckily, he seemed to be gaga over her. They were sickeningly sweet with each other. So much I wanted to puke.

I asked Mum if May-ling and I were like that.

"Worse."

When the women, no men allowed, talked over the wedding plans, Janet expressed a desire to be married on the moon. The other women jumped all over this idea as it made for a much more exciting wedding.

What happened to the low-key wedding when the bride was pregnant? Wisely I kept my mouth shut and went along with all their plans. Woe unto the man who got between a bride and her wedding.

Even worse was my mum, May-ling, and Mary were in complete agreement. It would be the first wedding on the moon.

The small details, like how to get all the guests to the moon and to build a church to hold the wedding, were left to me.

It didn't work out that way. I had lined up a bunch of GC crafts to pick people up. I was informed that my scheduling was wrong, and the craft needed to be spruced up to carry wedding guests.

Discretion being the better part of valor, I asked Mum and the bride's mother to handle the scheduling as I, being a mere male, couldn't understand the social nuances involved.

I delivered those lines with a straight face, though Mum gave me a sharp look.

May-ling and Mary were given the job of redecorating the GC craft. I attempted to give them a budget but was laughed off. I was beginning to understand the game's rules and told accounting to allow all expenses. After all, how much could a wedding cost?

Then there was the small matter of not having a church in our country. I had called us a colony, but we were well beyond that now.

You would think putting up a building and calling it a church would be simple. Did I have a lot to learn about religion?

The Christians, Jews, Muslims, Hindus, Confucianists, Taos, and others all had differences in the temples, churches, or whatever they called them.

I tried the nondenominational airport model. That went nowhere quickly. Everyone knew they were only used to announce a plane had gone down, losing all souls on board.

I chickened out and formed a committee of the major religious leaders and had them lay out a plan for a religious district. Each leader would be given the same funding for their church. The small denominations would have to share one of three facilities.

It seemed like we had as many religious variations as people.

What seemed like a pain to me at first proved to be a blessing in disguise. And yes, the pun was intended.

I didn't know, but one of our growing population's discontents was the lack of facilities for marriages, christenings, funerals, Sunday school, and bingo.

In fairness to the others, the Catholics missed their bingo the most.

I was glad to take that off the table. I also took off-the-table support for a religion other than the original structures. They would have to pay for and build their monasteries, houses for priests, salaries, and whatnot. Any latecomer religions were on their own.

The Mormons cried foul as they would have to pay their missionaries' way. I suggested they split the cost with the Seventh Day Adventists. What language!

The Wiccans approached me through an intermediary asking for my position on witchcraft. I replied that I had dealt with several witches in my life and didn't view them in favor but had nothing against witches in general.

An application was made for an opening in the woods for a coven to meet. They also wanted high walls around it so they could dance sky clad.

I shouldn't have given May-ling that last piece of information as I was forbidden from ever attending a ceremony. When Mary learned about it, she didn't think it was a big deal. Her sorority went streaking all the time, and wasn't that the same thing?

Mum wasn't happy. I suspect Mary's sorority would soon be on triple-secret probation.

Expanding our tunnel system and allowing a religious district opened the floodgates for other requests.

While we had some shops, we didn't have what could be called a business district.

We needed dentists' offices, doctors' offices, pharmacies, hair salons, barbers, bakeries, tailors, dry cleaners, seamstresses, hat stores (men's and women's), coffee shops, and numerous others.

Yielding to the inevitable, I had a business district built with stores and offices for rent. I didn't see how the hat business could make it in an indoor environment of the moon, but I learned they could.

Human nature being what it was, people independently decided if they weren't in a building or the home, they were outside and must wear a hat.

President Kennedy wearing his famous fedora in his inauguration parade made men's hats more popular than ever.

I refused to wear a hat. I did have to wear a small gold circlet when attending to my royal duties, but that was it.

While all these jobs were heaped on me, my brother Denny had the typical groom's duties. Make certain he had a tux. He owed me big time.

As it turned out, the new church district wouldn't be ready in time. I approached the wedding committee with some apprehension. It was for naught. They laughed and told me that none of the buildings would be big enough.

The wedding would be held outdoors in the Commons. All I had to do was have bleachers set up. When I asked how many, I was told to plan for a few thousand guests!

This headcount went well beyond a small wedding.

When I questioned it, I was told that Denny was a very important figure and that many world leaders would attend, along with the brightest and most famous in many walks of life.

This was my brother Denny we were talking about. What are they thinking? When I expressed that thought, I was reminded that he was my heir until my child was born. He was effectively Crown Prince Denny until my child replaced him. Then he would still be a Prince of the Realm.

I knew this but had never given it any serious thought. Should I come up with a title system such as the English used? I didn't know if Denny had ever been made a moon citizen.

Chapter 41

I must be getting old. I had previously declared the members of my immediate family citizens of the Lunar Kingdom and the Solar Reaches. Denny's passport even identified him as a Prince of the Realm.

I had declared Mary a princess and, in fairness to my brothers, made them princes. Mary took it very seriously. They didn't.

I elected to also give them titles based on the English system. The titles were based on the English translation of major features of the moon.

I was a little mean in making Denny the Duke of Cleverness. Eddie is the Duke of the Sea of the Edge because of the types of sports that he loves.

Mary, the Duchess of Tycho, is titled after the most brilliant feature on the moon's surface.

Our first child would be the Duke or Duchess of the Lunar Kingdom and the Solar Reaches. Later children would be Dukes or Duchesses of the gas giant planets.

Grandchildren would be titled after the many moons of Jupiter.

May-ling informed me that we wouldn't be using all the available names...

My parents declined titles, so it got me out of having to give titles to my cousins, aunts, and uncles. I would have named Uncle Wally the Duke of Worthless.

It wasn't made public, but the Dukedoms came with a land grant on the moon and a hefty life pension.

The wedding was in high gear. The wedding was reported as a major event by the world's media. The fact that it was to be in three weeks caused considerable speculation.

I had to admire Denny and Janet. In an interview, they informed the world about her pregnancy. That created a storm of controversy. It proved to be a tempest in a teacup and soon was over.

The only major question was would the bride wear white. I loved it when Janet told the female reporter that she would wear blue. In deference to May-ling, she wouldn't wear a Chinese funeral color.

What a riot that caused in the world of fashion! I pity the makers of wedding dresses. While all that noise was going on, I had the job of arranging the venue.

Since I owned the joint, there was no problem with having the Commons on the date in question. The Commons was just a large empty field at this time.

I had to come up with seating for over a thousand people and a stage. I took the easy way out and bought an existing setup from Earth.

There is a 1940s-style bandstand sitting empty outside of Chicago. A group of investors thought they could use it for concerts. They didn't understand that today's bands wanted an indoor setup.

The existing stage was covered by a huge half-clamshell protecting it. The clamshell also collects sound and pushes it out toward the audience. The drawback was that only the band was protected from the elements.

Today's sound systems negated the need for the clamshell. So, the expensive stage and movie-style seats sat empty.

I purchased all but the land it was sitting on. Trying to be fair, I had my staff offer the investors what they had paid for it.

They countered with an outlandish price. They wanted their investment back plus the profits from the next ten years.

My reply to that through my staff was, "Thanks for talking to us. Good luck."

Two days later, they were back asking if the original offer still stood. It did.

A GC barge for transportation made moving the whole shebang to the moon simple. During the move, there was a camera crew recording the whole enterprise.

Since I didn't know why they were there, I asked. That was when I discovered that Denny and Janet were being paid a small fortune by one of the major networks for exclusive broadcast rights to the wedding preparations and the wedding itself.

I wasn't wild about that, but I did have to appreciate the couple's business acumen. It was no big deal, so I let it stand. We would have to have a family conference and decide how we would proceed in the future.

May-ling and I had to maintain a high standard in such matters. Then again, we had money.

In the days before the wedding, security raised a serious flag. A terrorist group had been smuggled to the Lunar colony and planned a suicide bombing during the wedding.

They were a Palestinian group who had come up as crew members of cargo shuttles. They had stayed behind when their shuttles departed.

They didn't know that a strict headcount was kept for the arrival and departure of every shuttle. Not only that but pictures were taken of everyone arriving and departing. We knew there were five unauthorized visitors and had pictures of them.

They thought they were hidden in a building in the warehouse district. My security people not only identified them but their inside people. Once we had all the people involved, the warehouse was raided, and all were taken into custody.

It wasn't a very sophisticated group. They had crude pipe bombs to blow up as many people as possible. Why they chose this event is beyond me, other than the wide publicity they would achieve.

Their trial was held two days before the wedding. Denny and Janet weren't told about it as it would have only upset them.

I presided over the trial. I don't know where the terrorists thought they were. One of them arrogantly told me that they would accept their life imprisonment gladly and give interviews to the reporters of the world to help their cause.

The trial was held in-camera, so the world didn't know anything about them. The terrorists kept insisting they would shout out their message even as I opened the airlock to vacuum. The news would be released well after the wedding.

This incident highlighted a continuing problem. I thought that the entangling of military alliances would prevent wars. They did, to a point.

Palestine wasn't a country, and the terrorists weren't declaring war on the moon, so they didn't fall under any of the alliance's provisions.

In Ireland, the IRA didn't claim to be part of the Irish Republic, but they kept attacking the Protestants.

Tribes in Africa claimed no country but cheerfully kept killing each other.

In the Middle East, the different Islamic sects kept attacking each other.

All these paled to the weirdest one of all. Iran's and Iraq's armies were engaged in heavy fighting. Both sides stated they were not at war with anyone. Yes, some rebel units were engaged in warfare but neither claimed protection under the alliance!

At the UN, their ambassadors hugged each other to demonstrate the friendship between the two countries. I decided a pox on all their houses and let them go to it. When I realized they were killing civilians with poison gas, I asked the demolition company to flatten the ground at their common border.

When the leaders of Iran and Iraq protested the loss of their armies, I apologized for giving the wrong coordinates to the demolition company. I had intended to level part of the Sahara desert.

My bad.

No one asked why I wanted to level the Sahara.

While major wars were prevented, civil wars and evil dictators could still do as they will. I thought it would take an outside threat to unite mankind. Where was an alien invasion when you needed it?

I told this to May-ling, and she was horrified. She was convinced that an invasion would now happen at any minute.

The day of the wedding finally arrived. The powerful, the rich, and the famous all attended. While I was Denny's best man, I spent as little time in public as possible.

Select world leaders were invited to a pre-wedding cocktail party at the palace. Deals were being made in every corner of the room. The only one that bothered me was the corner where Mum, Queen Elizabeth, Janet's mother, Anna Romanov, and May-ling were talking with laughter. I knew no good could come of that. At least Mary wasn't there.

Maybe her not being there wasn't good. Mary's age would have led to some restraint.

The wedding itself went off without a hitch. Mary even behaved herself as the flower bearer. I feared she would get it into her head to streak the event.

I thought Mary would have an escort her age at the wedding reception. Instead, she finagled that Professor Einstein would be her escort. That led to many strange looks from those who didn't know them.

All guests were invited to the reception, but the immediate families and the wedding party were kept in a roped-off area. Most people took this in good part. Of course, my Uncle Wally had to make an ass of himself for not being allowed in with us.

I don't know what Dad said to him, but he left the reception without a backward glance and fewer snide comments.

Mary and the professor were in a corner, writing equations on a white tablecloth. I suspected that the tablecloth would end up in some museum.

Chapter 42

The reception was a lot of fun. Fun in the sense of good conversation with good people. The president of Germany thanked me for helping him.

That puzzled me as I didn't remember doing anything specific for Germany. When I quizzed him, he laughed.

"King Richard, my press has accused me of being too heavy-handed in how I do things. You have taken my place as the boogie man. They call you The Tyrant."

Oh, Great. Several other world leaders standing nearby agreed with him.

I'm not certain how I felt about this. I was protecting my people by executing those terrorists and sending a message about war to the Iranians and Iraqis. They wouldn't make a mockery of our alliance.

If that made me a tyrant, so be it. At least I was The Tyrant. I was competitive enough to want first place. At the same time, I was sensitive to the fact that being considered a tyrant didn't usually end well for the tyrant.

Besides being accompanied by bodyguards, even here, there were staffers nearby.

I signaled one who was standing close enough to hear the conversation.

"Betty, send someone to the common area and see what our people say about me. Specifically, have the staffer bring up the tyrant title. I need to know how our people view me, not the German press.

I schmoozed with the world leaders for another hour. They were all in favor of my actions but agreed that their people would never have let them get away with what I had done.

Not all of their people would disagree, but enough of them to get the leader kicked out of office. It is a good thing no one gets to vote on the king.

Betty came back with Jim, another staffer. He reported that the citizens of the moon were all in favor of my actions. I was protecting them, and they were all in favor of that. If I was a tyrant, then I was their tyrant!

It seems we were a bloodthirsty bunch on the moon.

I wondered if I should be bothered by the world calling me a tyrant. Somehow it was hard to get excited about it.

The world leaders all were trying to get some concession from me. The most common way was to provide them with GC craft or evantonium to allow the GC effect. I had already released how it was done, but they had no access to evantonium, and I wasn't about to allow them to have it.

I was under no illusions that they were my friends. They would do anything necessary to get their hands on the ability to make the working craft.

Once they had some, they would find or manufacture an excuse to take over the source of evantonium "for the good of the world. He's a tyrant, you know."

So far, there was no evidence that the location of the asteroid bearing evantonium had been found. It would only be a matter of time before someone gave out its location.

Once they could obtain the evantonium, my colony on the moon would be done for. I may be vain, but I think I have done a lot of good for the world.

Yes, there were still small conflicts around the world, but no possibility of a world war. On top of that, I was moving the world from an oil-based economy to one of fusion-powered electricity. This change to electricity would be cheaper and cleaner than fossil fuels.

Some people said I was saving the world from a nuclear winter. I don't know if I would go that far.

Another plus for me was how I was investing the fortune in gold from the Australian gold discovery.

The many workers that would have been displaced were being transitioned into new technology-supporting jobs. My support of displaced workers was preventing a worldwide depression. In fact, it was the foundation of a worldwide economic boom.

I opened up the solar system. Granted, I was keeping a close hold on the system-wide investigation. I didn't think any Earth-bound government could have handled the Eels on Jupiter better than I had.

My thoughts were probably hubris, but all I could do was do my best and keep moving along.

My major concern wasn't my actions at all. The fear that I had was how my child would turn out. My and May-ling's heir would be the emperor or empress of China, the world's largest nation. Add to that the power of the Lunar Kingdom and Solar Reaches created the possibility of a true tyrant arising.

These thoughts and others kept running through my mind as I talked to the various world leaders. I finally tried to shut this line of thinking off, as there was nothing I could do at this point.

One request was to allow colonies or space stations to be built around the many planets and moons. There was no problem with this as long as I maintained control of travel to them.

Without telling the requesters, I would have every shipment examined so an armed force couldn't be put in place. There would be no colonies on the moon within a thousand miles of mine.

There was always the danger that a Space Lady in command of one of our ships could be bribed or her family taken hostage. Good pay and working conditions should prevent bribery from being effective, but there was always the greedy one.

I had been encouraging them to settle their immediate families on the moon. We hadn't done one thing: find out if any Space Lady had relatives or serious friends, not immediate family, who could be held hostage.

I took my staffer aside and explained my concern and that a review of all the Space Ladies was to begin at once. No one would be fired. I needed to ensure that they and theirs were safe.

While I thought the reception was a waste of my time, it allowed me to think seriously and take action.

Chapter 43

Several days after the reception, I had to go down to Washington, DC. I had been roped into attending a conference on setting up a police patrol for the GC craft. Since we allowed other nations and private companies to rent them, there were some real yahoos.

The U.S. was chairing the effort, but they had requested my presence for the inaugural meeting as I was the only provider of the GC Craft.

Since it was my staff's recommendation in the first place, I couldn't say no. These meetings would be our first step toward a solar government. I didn't express that thought to avoid the nationalists' kickback, but it was the first step.

An agenda had been set for the meeting. If I had read it beforehand, I would have weaseled out.

It covered subjects such as the organization's name and what color lane markings should be used.

The first item was the organization's name. There had been many names submitted for consideration prior to the meeting. Most of them reflected the name of the submitting country's highway patrol.

The Canadians loved their Royal Canadian Mounted Police. How that would fit in space, I didn't know. I knew I wouldn't have to shoot it down from the attendees' groans. I must say I loved the Canadian Mountie's red jackets and hats. They provided a picture of one of their Mounties on road patrol. Their uniforms were boring.

Belgian put forward the *Wegpolitie*. I have no idea what that meant, but as it was met with dead silence, it was a no-go. I believe no one else knew either and didn't want to ask.

From Argentina, we had the *Gendamerie*. The French wouldn't accept it as they spelled it wrong. I kept my mouth shut. I knew better than to argue with a Frenchman over language.

The U.S. had some competing names. DPS came from Texas, and CHIPS from California. People recognized CHIPS from the TV show but objected to the C for Chips. DPS meant nothing.

One of the U.S. representatives stated that the C was for Celestial, not California. It still didn't get any traction.

Another U.S. representative, obviously from Texas, by his accent, informed us the DPS was the Texas High Patrol. The DPS also included the famous Texas Rangers.

The Rangers' name got instant recognition and became a strong contender.

Highway Patrol was put forward and laughed down. There were no highways in space.

Then why was lane marking on the agenda?

I brought up my favorite. I hadn't submitted it in advance but wasn't too sensitive to the committee's requirements.

I'm a tyrant, after all.

That began a debate on what the mission of the Space Patrol would be. Fight pirates or direct traffic.

I informed them that I would be the pirate fighter and they could handle the traffic. This statement proved an instant downer as they collectively remembered how I handled pirates.

I went on to explain I saw the mission of the Space Patrol to literally direct traffic on the rare occasions it was needed; in addition, investigate accidents in space, and give basic help to broken spaceships until a tow truck showed up.

These comments redirected the conversation about whether there would be a separate ambulance service and who would provide space tow trucks.

I had to chuckle at how the name Space Patrol was adopted without any debate. In a way, it was a shame, as I would have been happy with Space Rangers. I hoped they weren't going along with me out of fear.

Being the elephant resource provider in the room is a good reason, fear, not so much.

Some further debate brought about a reasonable mission statement.

It said the Space Patrol would be enforcing the rules of the road and fining infractions. They would have the power to detain and arrest criminal acts, including drunken spaceship driving. They would also assist the general public with accidents and breakdowns.

It was brought up that a schedule of fines and punishments needed to be developed. Some wanted to do it right then, but saner voices suggested that a subcommittee be formed.

Great, another bureaucracy. Who would incarcerate the guilty, collect the fines, and receive them? I wanted nothing to do with any of this.

The next agenda item was lane markings. Now I would find out what they had in mind.

What they had in mind had nothing to do with the realities of space travel. They wanted physical lanes marked out for travel between all the major planets and their moons.

I tried to picture billions of miles of concrete being poured. It would consume the entire planet Earth.

Fortunately, a British representative who must have been in their navy had a reasonable solution.

With adjustments, the rules of the road used on the seas and oceans of the earth would do the trick. Each craft was to have the traditional red and green lights for port and starboard.

There would also have to be lights for above and below. The old salt stopped when he realized there were no obscure nautical terms for above and below.

I wa certain the navies of the world would come up with something.

The meeting went on and on. I had gotten up twice for coffee. My habit of choosing a seat near the door and coffee pot was good. It also may have saved my life.

I had just poured my second cup of coffee when the door crashed open, and a man with a submachine gun burst in and opened fire.

It wasn't aimed fire. It was what was called spray and pray. The gunman sprayed his shots more than prayed. He missed the first shots, and then the sub-gun barrel rose. He killed the hell out of the ceiling.

I was standing at the coffee pot to the right of the door. I had the coffee pot in hand. I hit the gunman up the side of his head with it. The pot broke, spreading hot coffee over both of us. He started to fall.

As he was falling, another gunman came through the door. This one was turning his weapon on me. I caught the first gunman before he hit the floor and threw him at the second guy.

The second guy fired his weapon, killing his companion. Luckily, the bullets didn't exit the body and hit me. I followed the body of the second gunman and bowled him over.

A glance showed there were only the two of them.

That would be the last time I attended a committee meeting held in the conference room of a public hotel.

Sorry, Mr. Hilton.

Chapter 44

I sat on the second guy to hold him down. He tried to wrestle from under me, but I outweighed him by fifty pounds. He did pull a knife out of his jacket pocket.

I took the knife away, probably breaking his wrist in the process. This was not a time for gentleness or fair play.

Hotel security was there almost immediately. I found out later that they had followed the two guys but had no reason to stop them. Their coats were long enough to conceal the submachine guns.

I didn't recognize the weapons. Later I found out they were Uzis made in Israel, which was ironic as the gunmen were Arabs.

The hotel cops cuffed the guy and covered the other with a fire blanket from a closet.

The other people in the room with me were in total panic and disarray. Some ducked out and left the premises. Others stayed and demanded in loud voices why this was allowed to happen. Didn't the guards know they were important people?

In a few minutes, the DC cops made an entrance. They were as loud and demanding as the committee members. This was going to be a long night.

I told one of my aides who was present to let May-ling know that I would be detained for a while. She was in our suite in this hotel.

When the aide tried to leave, he was pushed back into the room. That is when I got on my high horse and identified myself.

Sometimes having the reputation of a tyrant is helpful. He was allowed to call our suite from a house phone. I knew this would set things in motion.

The police did police things like taking names. They were professional after things quieted down. They didn't have all the names recorded when the FBI and Secret Service showed up.

The U.S. State Department closely followed them.

As expected, a jurisdiction war broke out. The FBI won the investigative rights, and the Secret Service was to protect us. The State Department was to fetch coffee.

The DC Police cordoned off the premises. The way this all went down, I think they'd had this battle many times before.

Each person present was taken to separate areas to write out our statements and be questioned.

When it was my turn, the first question was, "Why did you have to be so rough on them?"

That question was so asinine that I didn't bother to answer. The agent asked me a second time, and I remained mute.

On the third iteration, I'd had it.

"Anyone who tries to commit violence on me or mine will die. I let the second one live for questioning. I will be extraditing him to the moon for execution."

"You mean trial and execution."

"No. Execution. I caught him in the act. He is guilty and will be executed."

At that point, I realized how much harder I had become.

The FBI agent was trying to be hard. I was harder. This posturing would get us nowhere.

"What do you need to know?"

"What happened?"

You could call it a draw, and we were both ready to move on. I gave the agent the story from my point of view as well as I could remember.

I had given so many statements in the last five years I had learned that what we thought had happened and what actually happened could be two different things; depending on how traumatic the event was, the more discrepancies.

This incident wasn't traumatic, at least to me, so my version agreed with most of the witnesses.

It took another hour, but I was finally allowed to go back to my suite. There I had to walk May-ling through it step by step.

Neither of us knew who could be behind this or who the actual target was.

The next day a very senior FBI official called upon us. He had information to share. The FBI didn't like to release information while an investigation was underway, but he had been given a direct presidential order.

I learned about something I had never heard of before. A fatwa had been issued against me. According to the fanatical Muslim cleric who had issued it, all good Muslims should try to kill me.

The fatwa was issued in retaliation to the execution of the attempted bombers on the moon. I had interfered with the attempt to blow up a bunch of world leaders.

It seems I'm now at war with the entire Muslim world. When I brought that up to the FBI assistant director, he told me that wasn't true.

The fatwa only had to be carried out by the followers of that particular cleric. There is no overriding hierarchy in the Muslim religion, so each cleric can do as he will.

That was like saying every priest, minister, or rabbi could issue their commands, including death sentences.

I thought I was a tyrant.

I asked the FBI guy what I could do about it.

"His fatwa is only in effect while he is alive, so you could have him killed. If you do that, you may upset other clerics, who then would issue their personal fatwas."

"That sounds like a no-win."

"From our experience, it is."

"So, I keep on letting these guys try to kill me?"

"They will run out of soldiers eventually, or the cleric will have lost influence, and no one will carry out his orders."

"That isn't proactive."

"We can't tell you what to do, only advise you of what you are up against."

"How have these people survived for so long?"

"The vast majority of Muslims aren't violent people. They have extremists like every major religion."

After the agent left, May-ling and I had a long discussion about how to handle this. We couldn't come to any conclusion. We would have to wait and see what happened next.

We instructed our two staffers to put together reports on Islam in general and the cleric's specific group.

She wanted to know the status of the religion in China, and I was interested in my kingdom.

Chapter 45

The next day started one of my and May-ling's life's most important events. Her water broke.

There were plans in place for this event. The baby was to be born in China as she would be the heir to the throne.

A list of people to be notified had been generated. The list started with family but also included heads of state. This birth would reshape the world.

A secondary release was planned for an hour later to all news organizations. We wanted to be ahead of the curve and control the story. There would be no stories of two-headed babies.

Being able to control the story was a staff fantasy. If the scandal sheets wanted a two-headed baby, they would concoct a story. My real-world experience with the media outweighed their textbook dreams.

We took a GC craft from Washington, DC, to the Forbidden Palace. The palace had a hospital on-site with a newly built maternity ward. It had features that most hospitals only dreamed of. The features centered around medical care but also had luxury suites.

The security around the ward was incredible. It started with the beefed-up crowd control outside the palace. There were several security checkpoints to allow off-site staff access. That was for the day-to-day workers.

Getting into the maternity ward was an ordeal. Only those precleared were allowed in. A second security checkpoint gave this access. The outer guards were for public consumption and didn't display weapons openly.

The guards at the maternity ward gate made no bones about it. Then there was the empress's suite. It had its own set of guards and access requirements. It was a wonder that they let May-ling and me in.

Once inside, it was beyond first class in comfort and service. The working staff and my parents were the only people allowed in this area.

The trip to China took seventy-five minutes, from boarding the craft to entering the maternity suite. During this time, May-ling had her first contraction. It wasn't that bad from the look on her face, so I thought we were home free.

May-ling had been having Braxton-Hicks contractions for the last week, but these were different. These hurt.

Normally a woman was advised to go to the hospital when the contractions last forty-five to sixty seconds every three to five minutes.

Since her water had broken and we were halfway around the earth from the hospital, we left immediately.

I wondered if we would get pulled over for speeding on the flight there. You could tell I wasn't nervous at all.

After May-ling was settled into her bed in the maternity ward, I sat with her holding her hand. The labor went on for years. It was seventeen hours, I found out later.

We had a decent conversation about nothing and everything until the fifteenth hour. First, May-ling decided she hated all men. Then it was specifically me for doing this to her.

At that point, I was removed from the room, and Mum took over. As I went out the door, I heard Mum agree with May-ling that all men were pigs, especially those who got innocent young ladies pregnant.

Thanks a lot, Mum.

Seventeen hours after her labor began, May-ling Empress of China delivered a baby girl. At seven and a half pounds, she was of normal weight. Her twenty-three-inch length made her longer than average. I took credit for that.

Ping Mary Ann Elizabeth Jackson was perfect in all ways, from her tiny fingernails to her dark head of hair.

When I first held her, I felt like never before. Filled with love and wonder, I would protect, guide, and die for this child if needed. I was already looking forward to her first steps.

May-ling was gracious enough to tell me that she forgave me. I wasn't quite sure what she meant, and I wasn't going to ask. I said, "Thank you," and let it go.

New Mum and baby were ready for a nap, and so was I. I felt like I had walked miles in the past hours. Dad confirmed that my pacing easily put in ten miles.

The only thing that wasn't planned and arranged for were cigars. I did have something better to hand out. A commemorative coin had been struck in the baby's name. There were two of them, one for a boy and one for a girl.

Those for the boy were melted down immediately, with only one copy kept for the mint's museum. It would be the rarest coin in the world.

I thanked all the doctors, midwives, nurses, orderlies, and other maternity ward staff and guards. I gave each of them one of the commemorative coins that had been struck.

Coins would be sent to all world leaders, and then released into general circulation. These would be of all denominations. One yuan, 1-2-5 Jiao, and 1-2-5 fen. These would be in copper and nickel-clad silver. The ones I was handing out and sending to world leaders were one yuan in pure silver.

They would end up as treasured family items or in the hands of collectors.

One of the difficult decisions we had to make was what to call our new daughter. She was to have a bunch of names, which is typical in royal families.

Ping was her Chinese last name, always listed first by custom. Then Mary for my grandmother, Ann for May-ling's mother, Elizabeth because it frequently appeared on both sides of my family, and Jackson as my last name.

Any boys would have London, John, or Richard from my Dad's side and Ernest or David from Mum. Chia-Hao or Chun-Chin for May-ling's father and brother.

Halloran was never considered.

Though she had several names, one of them had to be picked for normal use. I had a sister Mary; Ann, though spelled differently, was a major princess, and Elizabeth is a queen or The Queen in the eyes of the world.

We decided on Beth. No one would dare call Queen Elizabeth Beth. Her reign name would be the kid's problem when assuming her throne. I was hoping to be dead and buried by then.

Chapter 46

The news that a girl child was born in excellent health was announced worldwide that day. In China, it was a day of rejoicing. There was cannon fire, fireworks, and general jubilation.

I knew May-ling was a popular ruler, but this drove the point home. On the moon, the news was taken more sedately. That is, rockets filled with gunpowder were launched. They were so large the show could be seen from Earth with the naked eye.

Congratulations poured in from all over the world. The press was clamoring for pictures of the newborn. One picture was released with May-ling holding the baby. The official photographs would be released later.

There was only one sour note. The Chinese CIA had been watching the cleric who had issued the fatwa on me. He now issued one for Beth.

When told this, I almost went berserk. After breaking a few things in our suite, no Ming vases, I thought it through.

I put my idea to May-ling, and she agreed.

The fatwa and its sources were included in a news release. We asked that all good Muslims repudiate it. Within twenty-four hours, we had our answer. Not one Muslim cleric repudiated the fatwa.

Our people theorized that no cleric would repudiate it because it would allow someone to repudiate any fatwa they issued. They didn't want to surrender power.

Some Islamic interfaith groups put out statements, but even those were weasel-worded.

This information was released to the Chinese people. We thought it would put pressure on the clerics.

It did more than put pressure on them. Within another day, there was not one Islamic structure standing within China.

There were many incidents where citizens were killed because of their religion. May-ling had to make a plea from her hospital bed to stop the slaughter.

The destruction of mosques worldwide followed. Fortunately, only a few people were killed. Again, a plea was made that major mosques serving as museums be spared.

I made that announcement during a press conference. As a follow-up, I was asked if the cleric who issued the fatwa should be spared.

My reply became famous everywhere.

"As Allah wills."

Later that day, he was stoned to death by his villagers in fear for their own lives.

I thought that would settle everything down. I was wrong. The same day a suicide bomber exploded himself and the outer security station. Before the dust settled, a large group poured onto the grounds of the Forbidden Palace.

Another suicide bomber blew himself up at the main entrance to the palace. This time they could not progress into the main body of the complex as hidden machine guns opened fire.

They were mowed down to a man.

May-ling and I called our advisors together after this incident. What could be done? No one had an answer. The only way to stop the radical Islamists was to destroy Islam itself.

To destroy Islam would require stamping out their entire education system, where young men were radicalized. Then those already radicalized would have to be hunted down and cut down root and branch.

Millions would have to die. Wholesale slaughter was not the answer we were looking for. Ninety-nine percent of Muslims were truly peaceful. Although they were hesitant to speak out, it was hard to think they supported the radicals.

One advisor suggested we hold some major clerics as hostages against aggression. Hostages wouldn't work as the radicals had no problem killing innocent children and claiming them to be martyrs.

Dad asked, "What if we held their major shrines in Mecca and Medina as hostages?"

A list included the Masjid-al Haram, the Quba Mosque, the cave at Hiram, al-Masjid an-Nabawi, and finally, the Kaaba and Black Stone.

A carefully worded statement was released, which said these items would be destroyed one at a time if any further attacks were made on the royal families of China or the Lunar Kingdom and the Solar Reaches.

If any attacks were successful, all the listed structures would be destroyed.

A cleric from the Grand Mosque in Mecca declared that Allah would protect them. That resulted in a GC craft settling on one of the outer walls of the Grand Mosque and flattening it.

When asked about it, I used what had become my standard answer, "As Allah wills."

That stopped all attacks. Another good thing about being known as a tyrant, it was known I would follow through on my threats.

Attacks against us that is, the Shi'ites and Sunnis continued their slaughter of each other. The Kurds also managed to weigh in occasionally, but we ignored it since it wasn't national warfare.

A question was raised. What would Beth's religion be? May-ling had been raised to follow Confucianism, entwined with Taoism and Buddhism. I was nominally a Christian.

We answered that she would be raised with all those religions' combined common and good concepts. Boy, did that set the cat amongst the pigeons?

Theologians worldwide love a good religious argument. Overnight symposiums and congresses were set up to debate what the common and good concepts from the religions would be. This debate promised to last hundreds of years.

This debate was fine with us as it took the monkey off our backs. We were surprised when Hindu, Muslim, and Jewish scholars asked to be included. They wanted the good in their religions to be recognized. This debate could turn out to be a good thing.

A common religion based on kindness to others was a dream, but oh, what a dream. A small first step, but it was a step in the right direction.

In the meantime, without any fanfare, we moved to the moon. We had better control of our security there. No one was getting near my daughter!

When I say we moved to the moon, I mean our whole entourage. There were enough doctors, nurses, and general help to provide 24/7 coverage for mother and child.

It was two weeks before I was allowed to change a diaper. It would be much longer before I asked for a second opportunity.

Chapter 47

When we moved to the moon, it was like a military operation. There were over three hundred people between Beth's caretakers, May-ling's staff, and mine.

First, advance security ensured everything was in place and safe. Then we moved up, followed by the rear guard.

Baby presents were arriving at the Forbidden Palace. These were from all over. Many were from world leaders and rich celebrities or the simply rich or celebrities.

These gifts had value, some enough for a normal family to live for a year. These gifts were attempts to gain influence.

The ones we appreciated the most were given by the "common" people. These were simple things like hand-embroidered blankets, stuffed toys, or baby rattles. The best of these were chosen for Beth's use.

All of the gifts were scanned for problems. I wish I could say none were found. Some of them were found to have poison in them. There were several bombs.

Security had kept track of the origin of each gift. Some of the dangerous ones were traceable. The senders were tracked down and held. Others weren't traceable and of the most concern.

The ones that were caught had one characteristic in common. They were all raving mad and were locked up for life by their respective countries.

The ones we could track had files created with all the known information and shared with the major police forces of the world. Any future attempts would be compared with the existing files to see if a pattern could be developed.

Our staff sent out thank you notes to each sender. May-ling or I signed world leader notes.

An office in the Forbidden Palace had taken on the task of keeping track of all of this. They also merged with my staff from Jackson Enterprises to maintain files on each person who crossed our lives. Birthday cards, etc., were sent in our names.

More important life events required our signature. There were so many events nowadays from so many people it almost took a gold medal in the Olympics to get a handwritten note from either of us.

We still spent two hours a week on that exercise. A tyrant's job is never done.

Then there were the ribbon cutting ceremonies. Our colony or country was growing like crazy. It was like the Wild West, without the wild. I had to help open a new business almost every day of the week.

I thought at least I would get Sundays off. No such luck. Sunday was a day off for most people, so new stores would want to open then to attract the largest crowds.

The first openings attracted people because I was there. Once people had seen me in public several times, I was no longer the draw. That was good for me but disappointing for the new businesses.

I was able to turn that around temporarily by bringing Beth along. By that, I mean Beth and her entourage. I thought that would wear off quickly, but it became apparent that the public wanted to watch Beth grow up.

May-ling would accompany us to hold Beth. I soon realized that my presence wasn't necessary, but when I mentioned it, I was told to "Suck it up, Buttercup."

May-ling was hanging around my mum too much.

May-ling as empress was above appearing at business openings in China. She soon learned from public opinion polls that the Chinese people wanted to see Beth as much as our Loonies.

Rather than go commercial in her public appearance, she started appearing at award ceremonies. Heroics, educational, and sports events were all attended. All with baby Beth along.

The public never got near the baby. Attendees would see her on CCTV or large screens. Some of the events were live broadcasts. May-ling soon realized that by doing these presentations, her popularity was also rising.

May-ling's and my ratings were extremely high for any world leader, more than eighty-five percent. Beth could do no wrong.

She got positive numbers when she scrunched her face on the screen to poop. I don't know what would happen if I tried that. Revolution in the streets is my best guess.

When Beth is older, we will have to withdraw her from public life. She will need to have as normal a childhood as possible. She would have to be around other children to socialize, but we had to be very careful about who was allowed near.

There would be many attempts to surround her with sycophants, and we had to forestall that as much as possible.

We made a joint public announcement that if anything happened to us, my parents would be her regents. That may have put a target on their backs, but they both knew and agreed to raise her if needed.

There would be no council of regents to despoil our daughter for their ends. Both Russia and China had horror stories about that.

Ivan the Terrible wasn't born that way; such a group created him. When he came to power, they paid for it. It illustrated the saying, "Be careful of what you wish for. You may get it."

What wasn't made public was an agreement that the king or queen of England would step in if my parents couldn't. Not the British government, but the Crown.

If anything, that family had experience in raising royals. Even their track record could be better, but at least they knew the basics of royalty.

The more I thought about the changes in my life, the more I realized that I had come of age. It had crept up on me. I still felt like that kid from Bellefontaine.

I tried to picture myself in high school running a country. It didn't compute. I wondered how much more I would change.

Chapter 48

My life had changed. It had snuck up on me. I had been reacting to events for so long that I didn't think about it as I kept moving.

I am the ruler of a country, on the moon, no less. I blame that on my sister Mary. I wouldn't be in this position if she hadn't come up with the equations that allowed gravity control.

I'm married with a child. I have no complaints about the wife or the child. That started with the lady in the dry cleaners. Who knew where that would end up?

Those two events led to me being a major world leader, if not the world leader. Between May-ling and me, we were The Superpower.

Strangely enough, these weren't the changes that bothered me. It was the little things, like my wardrobe.

Harold, my valet, still controlled it all. It was way past the time that I could have duplicate wardrobes on a GC craft with me. To accomplish that would have taken one of the super barges, as they were now called.

Casual clothes, military uniforms, and formal wear were what I used to wear. Now it was suits, suits, and more suits.

Each of my suits was now custom-made. Nothing off the rack for the King of the Lunar Kingdom and Solar Reaches.

I never knew they made suits where the buttons on the sleeves worked. There were two pairs of pants with each suit because of uneven wear. Each pair of pants had an internal silk liner that fell to the knees, like Bermuda shorts, for comfort and to minimize the wrinkling of the trouser legs.

There was a hidden pocket for your wallet, which I didn't even carry anymore. There was a vest with each suit. My full name was stitched inside the jacket. Each suit cost as much as our first house. It was insane.

Then there were the ties, hundreds of them, Belts, only by the dozen. I always thought it was an affectation for men to wear a handkerchief in their suit breast pockets. Now it was an everyday occurrence.

My shoes were made from my personal last. Any scuff would have a pair relegated to charity. I must have one of the largest expensive watch collections in the world. Cuff links beyond counting.

I only got to wear what I described as California casual: a sports coat and slacks with a polo shirt at Jackson House California. That was when I wasn't going out. Going out meant a suit every time.

I wasn't even surprised when I learned I had a personal jeweler who made the cuff links and tie clasps.

I never wore the same suit twice in the same month.

I complained about all this to Harold one day as he helped me dress.

"Sir, the queen has a whole floor of Buckingham Palace for her wardrobe."

"Yeah, but she's a woman."

"She's a queen, and you are a king. More is expected of you."

Then I made a comment that couldn't be unmade no matter how much I tried.

"At least I don't have a personal perfume."

"Sir, I have been meaning to bring that up. Not a perfume but an aftershave and cologne."

Why me, lord? Some battles shouldn't even be fought.

"Obtain samples and pass them by May-ling. What she approves is what I will wear."

"Sound thinking, sir. We will also make certain they don't offend the princess."

I wonder if I could hitchhike back to Ohio.

My valet has more control over my life than I do.

Another change was my body. Not long ago, I could run daily and do a morning workout. I still could work in pushups and sit-ups, but the morning run was a thing of the past. My day didn't have enough hours.

I hadn't gained any weight but thought I could detect some flab. May-ling calls it love handles. I called it fat.

The only reason I didn't gain weight was that I had no control over my food. Cooks and waiters took care of everything. No grabbing a donut when passing through the kitchen. I wasn't even certain where the kitchen was in my ever-expanding palace on the moon.

Dietitians and my wife strictly controlled what I ate. Even when attending a state dinner elsewhere, it was circumvented if I tried to slip in an extra dessert. After the first time it happened, my wife informed me that it was unseemly for a king to pout.

I replied that it was my kingdom and that I would pout if I wanted to. I have been listening to Lesley Gore lately. It cut no ice with my wife. Since we were in China then, it was her empire, and she would bonk me on the head if she wanted to.

My life was now meeting after meeting, if not cutting a ribbon, on one of the many new businesses coming to the moon.

Then there were the press conferences. You would think the press would fear someone they described as a tyrant. If so, they didn't show it.

The kingdom's government now had a press office with a secretary to answer questions and deliver announcements. I still had to appear once a month for a live grilling.

Last month the questions were my thoughts on the religious conference that broke out in fist fights. While some religious leaders found citations in their religious works to support the good things about their religion, others went over other religions to find bad things.

The fight broke out over the Koran statement about deceiving unbelievers. The point was made that no statement by a Muslim could be trusted. The fight was on.

For once, I didn't let my mouth run away with me.

"I don't get involved in religious arguments."

"This wasn't an argument; it was a fight."

"I'm certain that must be clarified in some holy book."

That set off a worldwide hunt to find justification for a fistfight in all the holy books. I think a U.S. Marine's question was best.

"Why would you need justification for a fistfight?"

Chapter 49

I was the father of the most perfect daughter ever born. I held her as much as I could. It was a fight between my mum, wife, and me for the privilege.

The winners most often were the nursemaids, who always seemed to have an excuse to hold her.

I did get on my high horse a couple of times and demanded my fatherly rights. To have her tiny hands grasp my finger was a delight. She even smiled at me.

My downer of a Mum told me it was just gas. What would she know? Oh, yeah, she did have four children. Maybe it is gas.

It was still a joy. It was fun when she let out a lady-like little fart. Once, she ripped one so loud it scared her into crying. You would think the world was coming to an end when she screamed.

Nursemaids, grandmother, and mother all came rushing to see what terrible thing I had done.

As they surrounded me, little Beth gave an innocent little smile. Like she was saying, "What fart?"

I made a mistake once of burping her without a cloth on my shoulder. Harold was very disappointed in me for ruining a suit. I told him no big deal and sent it to the dry cleaner.

We only had one dry cleaner on the moon then, and Harold wasn't satisfied with their work, so he sent the suit to a preferred dry cleaner in London.

That reminded me of the Gold Rush 49ers sending their laundry to Hawaii.

Beth had fine features, her nose shaped perfectly. It reflected the Normans in her ancestry. Her eyes hinted at the Chinese fold, telling of the other side of her heritage.

She had more hair than many adults, all a shiny jet black. All the women assured me that she would be heartbreakingly beautiful.

I didn't say a word. She still looked like a wrinkled red baby to me. I valued my life enough not to voice that thought.

Our family would be leaving for Stockholm, Sweden, for Nobel week, where Mary and Professor Einstein would receive the prize in physics.

It would be an awkward week for the Nobel people. They hated me and my actions. I think they might have a liberal bent. They denied me the Peace Prize. Adding insult to injury, they asked me not to attend any presentations. This demand was despite Mary's presentation being in Stockholm while theirs was in Oslo.

As though I wouldn't go when my sister was receiving the award. It would be even worse than they thought when I showed up. Mary and Einstein would be handed the award by the king of Sweden.

It would be impossible for the king of Sweden not to recognize and greet a fellow king. I loved it. These circumstances would be more fun than the prize itself. So, sue me. I'm not that old.

When we got there, the king of Sweden, Oscar Fredrik Wilhelm Olaf Gustaf Adolf or Gustaf VI Adolf, was cannier than I thought. He invited our immediate family and Professor Einstein to a private dinner the night before the ceremony.

The king and the professor were old acquaintances from a previous award and spent some time talking about the old days.

He, May-ling, and I spent several hours bemoaning the trials and tribulations of being a ruler. At least my wife and I had more power in our respective countries. Hers was absolute.

Oscar was jealous of her. He would have beheaded half of the ministers in his government if he had his way.

He used this to segue into a request.

"Richard, I cannot recognize you during the ceremony tomorrow because of political considerations. I hope this will not give offense."

"Not at all. Tomorrow is about my sister Mary and Professor Einstein's contribution to physics. I don't want to take away from that. At the same time, I do want to be present. I will not speak to the press before or afterward."

"I thank you from all of my heart. I have verbally let the committee know of my displeasure in no uncertain terms. Also, they are used to having the finest suites at the palace. They are now in servants' quarters."

"They will hate me even more."

At that, all three of us burst out laughing. The committee's hate had little that could affect our lives. It only made them look small.

Cooler heads had me back off having motorized forces on GC barges surrounding the city.

The next day the presentation was in the Blue Hall of the Stockholm City Hall. It was the only place in town to seat the thirteen hundred guests. World leaders and anyone who pretended to be anyone were present.

Our family had prominent seating as Mary's family. Reporters tried to get comments out of me about the Peace Prize not going to me. I ignored them.

One of the reporters was so obnoxious and insistent that the police removed him from the hall. That set off a new round of questions. Why had I let the police take away an honest reporter trying to do his job?

I continued to ignore them. I was having a problem figuring out who the honest reporter was. Not any names, but who among them might be innocent?

I had learned to dislike most reporters. There were a few, like Walter Cronkite, who was trustworthy and professional, but very few.

It seemed like most of them had the story written before they asked the first question. They wanted a statement that would confirm their bias. Some would not even ask questions but twist words to support their story.

Reporters aside, the ceremony proceeded. My sister Mary and Professor Einstein were presented with their awards from the King of Sweden. Mary looked cute in her blue dress as she curtseyed to the king.

At last night's dinner, he had treated her as his granddaughter, so Mary was on her best behavior. I dreaded what her sorority might have suggested. Mum's threats far outweighed any of their ideas.

The gold medal had Alfred Nobel's profile on both sides, with his birth and death dates. The story was he created the prizes to improve his image.

His brother had been erroneously mistaken for him in one obituary. It called him "The Merchant of Death."

I was cynical enough to wonder if this was a marketing ploy.

The two awardees split the money. They received 880,000 SEK, whatever that may be worth. Mary was worth millions, so the money wasn't important. Well, maybe to the animals she was saving. I think she was working on elephants now.

The certificate was fancy-looking with its gold leaf, many ribbons, and wax seals.

The Peace Prize people were there. Since they were sitting behind me, I could feel their glares in the back of my head. I wouldn't be going to Oslo for their ceremony, so I don't know why their panties were in a twist.

I had to chuckle when it came out that the physics committee would have to recognize Mary, the professor, and myself with another prize next year.

Chapter 50

After Mary's presentation, we returned to Jackson House, California, as a group. To say we were cramped with our entourage is an understatement.

Jackson House had been our family seat for some years. Now we had outgrown it. My parents would either choose a new residence or give up entertaining May-ling and me.

May-ling and I, along with Beth, had a traveling group of fifty people. Jackson House could entertain twenty guests at most. It was alleviated somewhat by having Beth's caretakers stay with us while the rest of the staff stayed in temporary quarters at the Forest Ranger hotel facility.

The Forest Ranger camp at one time was considered a hardship post. Now it was a preferred location and was bursting at its seams, so it wasn't a long-term solution.

We were only at Jackson House for two days when we had to fly to Washington, DC for a dinner held in Mary's honor by the United States government.

While Mary is a princess of the Lunar Kingdom and Solar Reaches, she is still considered a citizen of the United States. She still attended school in the U.S., and her companies and charities were headquartered there. The government enjoyed her popularity and didn't want to lose her to those upstarts on the moon.

This desire was true of both political parties. No one had bothered to ask the little capitalist what form of government she preferred. Since she is only ten years old, there is no way she could have an opinion.

Mary was canny enough not to express an opinion. It kept them all dancing to her tune.

She was presented with the Presidential Freedom Medal for her contributions to society. It was amazing to see the politicians extoll her intelligence and, on the other hand, act as though she knew nothing of politics and government.

I thought I knew my feelings on politics, but I asked her directly.

"Mary, what policies do you favor for the United States government?"

I framed my question on policy rather than political party or personality. I didn't want to start a war.

"Rick, I'm all for free enterprise. The less government interference, the better. If you want to refine it more, I'm an adherent of Adam Smith."

Yep, the politicians were right. She was too young to have any opinions of politics.

"One of these days, you will be asked your preferences, which will open one set of doors and close another."

"I presume you will give me refuge on the moon as I'm a princess."

"Always."

"Good, I may need it soon."

"Now what?"

"I have agreed to appear on the Awful Show with John Thomas."

"Why on earth would you do that?"

"He was his normal nasty self with one of my sorority sisters."

John Thomas, advertised as John the Terrible, specialized in belittling his guests. That went well with a certain segment of society. He may have bitten off more than he could chew with Mary.

Bursting the bubble of an adult male was one thing. Attacking a blond-haired, blue-eyed, intelligent national sweetheart, another.

I wouldn't be surprised if his show with Mary would be the last time he was ever on the air. His funeral.

I was surprised Mum and Dad would allow her to do this. When I asked Mary how she got permission, I found out she hadn't. I was to be a party to this attack on the poor unsuspecting TV host.

I refused, but Mary had the big guns lined up. My wife was on her side. So, on the late afternoon of the taping of the show, I found myself off stage watching Mary walk onto the set to her apparent doom.

I had been briefly introduced to Mr. Thomas before the show. I found him to be worse in person than on the air. I no longer regretted being part of this.

The producers of the show had to know something was up. Half the audience was comprised of ten-year-old girls.

I even asked a junior person if they knew why the show had been set up like this.

"His ratings are way down; this is a make-it or break-it event."

I smirked at that. I knew how this would go. Not the details but the end result.

It started as predicted. Thomas was on the attack from the onset.

"You would have the world believe that you are a great scientist while making a personal fortune with your clothing company. Isn't it true that the Jackson Enterprise Research group has made those discoveries?"

Mary replies, "So you are calling Professor Einstein and the U.S. Patent office liars?"

"Not at all. I think you have the patent office, and Einstein fooled with the help of your family."

At that, Mary pulled out the most terrible weapon in her arsenal. She burst into tears and ran from the stage.

Thomas thought he had won the day and told the audience that he had shown her to be a worthless little brat.

I was about to let him have it when a smiling Mary ran up to me. "It worked!"

I was going to ask what worked when I saw it in action. I hadn't paid attention to the front row of the live audience. It was filled with familiar faces, Mary's sorority sisters.

They were there in force and armed with rotten tomatoes. Thomas was a mess after they let fly. In the meantime, all those little girls were shouting boo.

It was almost as if a teleprompter told them to do so. A quick look showed the word "Boo" to be flashing continuously. The network and the show staff seemed tired of Mr. Thomas and his antics.

The next day the network publicly fired Thomas for his picking on such a sweet little girl who had almost single-handedly energized the world economy and expansion into space.

It wouldn't have hurt them to give me a little credit.

A side effect of all this was the creation of a new rating system. Rotten tomatoes rated bad shows. The more given, the worse the show. None ever surpassed the number thrown at Thomas.

I knew Mary could do tears on demand, but she had given a world-class performance. I was so moved that I even bailed out her sorority sisters for their part in this.

Mum and Dad weren't happy campers, but nevertheless let Mary return to the university even though they were a bad influence. They had even threatened to have her return to the fourth grade but decided it wouldn't be fair to the teachers.

Chapter 51

After the hoopla about Mary becoming a Nobel Laureate died, I released information on our findings in space. I delayed it to not take away from Mary's award.

My staff and I worked overtime to come up with a professional presentation. The presentation started with finding small amounts of evantonium around the solar system.

Next was a dog and pony show of our experiments with AC and DC. This demonstration explained how gravity control was achieved.

Next was the building of the GC craft and their use in exploring the solar system. We were careful to explain that Earth had the most gold. The explorers had found little silver or gold.

I emphasized that so that the price of the metals wouldn't collapse.

Next was the discovery of the evantonium moon by the Robinson Family and my purchase of it. They were now one of the richest families in space with their royalties. They were living in space to avoid any Earth taxes. Mr. Robinson hated the idea of taxes so much that if the United States government figured out how to tax him, he would become lost in space.

Then there was the finding of the inner caverns on the evantonium moon. We made it a little more dramatic than it actually was with the various discoveries: First, the control room, the equipment room. The streaming message on how to operate the equipment. We spent a lot of time on the translation across the various dynasties.

We gave all credit where due. Doctor Cyril Aldred was going to become world-famous for his work. Thanks were given to the Queen of England for directing us to him. Mr. Norman wanted to remain in the background. I was beginning to suspect he had been in the background for a long time.

Then there was the ability to move a small model in the control room and have it occur life-sized on Earth.

This discovery brought in quantum entanglement, explained by Mary and Professor Einstein. Their paper on this would lead to Nobel Prize number three for the pair. I wondered if there was a limit on how many times you could be awarded it.

Being able to cause actions at a distance allowed me to announce that we would be leasing GC craft to organizations and private individuals but none to any military except the Lunar Kingdom and Solar Reaches, and the Chinese Empire.

When asked later why the Chinese, I explained it was hard to say no to your wife.

We could now disable from a distance any GC craft found to be breaking the law. The establishment of the Space Patrol would be the enforcement arm.

This announcement opened the solar system to all nations and companies.

The presentation was offered to all networks. As a courtesy, world leaders were sent an advance copy.

As expected, the announcement caused a worldwide furor. The aliens are coming to kill, eat, enslave, save, lead, educate, or watch us. Take your choice; they were all out there.

My statement that we had no evidence of why the aliens left or if they were coming back was ignored. Those thoughts would be a waste of headline space.

The only discovery that was held back was the planet Vulcan. It raised more questions than answers. Besides, Mary had come up with an interesting thought.

She had several equations that led one to believe that an Alcubierre drive could be created. A bubble would surround the ship in an area of space-time compressed in front of it and expand behind it.

It would need a large mass or a lot of energy to do this. The mass would be the size of a planet, so it was a no-go. Energy could be converted to mass, but we currently have no way to create that much energy.

I say we currently have no way to create the energy needed, but we have a clue from a recent breakthrough at Jackson Research. Someone had the bright idea of trying to power a fusion engine with vulcanite.

It is a wonder we didn't lose Southern California. Luckily, a safeguard was built in for excess energy production. This time the safety kicked in at one percent of the fusion process. We might have lost most of North America if it had run unchecked.

Fusion is safe to a point. It won't go critical and create an explosion. An explosion wouldn't be required if that much energy was unchecked.

All experiments in this process were moved to a small moon of Jupiter. Suppose we lost it. No big deal. Jupiter could afford to lose a moon or two. No people were on the station when the reactor started, as we knew we would lose the first reactor.

Lose it, we did. Also, a good portion of the moon. While enormous by any previous standard, the energy release wasn't enough to create an Alcubierre bubble.

It was eighty percent of the way there, so we had hopes for the future.

Once a bubble was created, space-time inside the bubble would be completely flat, so travelers wouldn't notice any relativistic effects. The ship's speed reading would remain the same as in real space, but the bubble would be hurled across the universe.

How fast it would hurl across the universe was anyone's guess at this time. Also, the bubble's speed could be increased with the amount of energy expended.

The engineers had taken to calling it a warp drive. Warp one would be cruising speed. Warp fifteen appeared to be an upper limit. More energy used than that could potentially destroy a star.

With the new information, it was proposed to try a mixture of evantonium and vulcanite to see what happens. The scientist saw no problems doing this. I saw one hundred million dollars going down the tube every time the energy escaped a reactor.

Then there was the little detail of harnessing the energy once we could create it to form a bubble.

When I asked Mary about harnessing the energy, she shrugged her shoulders.

"Rick, my equations say it can be done; the rest is engineering."

It would probably take most of my lifetime and fortune to succeed in interstellar travel. That didn't matter. We had taken the first steps to the stars. What would be waiting for us?

Chapter 52

I had been instrumental in taking man beyond the moon. Did I have to take mankind to the stars? No, at least not out of my pocket. The more I thought about it, the more I was inclined to release all my secrets.

I just thought there was a furor when it became known that aliens had been at work on the evantonium moon. The news that they had hidden an entire planet composed of a previously unknown element set off a firestorm.

I was castigated by every end of the political spectrum. Even the middle of the political spectrum wasn't kind to me.

Who was I to keep such secrets? There were calls to seize all my assets, including the colony on the moon.

Fortunately, wiser heads prevailed. After a week of increasing abuse, it became apparent that those generating all the talk were not in power. Those in power were content to allow things to remain the same.

I further cooled things down by turning over the entire interstellar program to the Alliance. All the nations on Earth could chip in on developing interstellar travel.

By turning it over to committees, May-ling and I figured the program would be set back many years. That might not be a bad thing.

I already had enough adventure in my life. I wasn't interested in writing a Hitchhikers Guide to the Galaxy. My only goal was to settle down with my wife and raise our newborn daughter, Beth.

After serious discussions with my family, staff, and many advisors, May-ling and I decided that we would become constitutional monarchs. We would surrender power to elected governments.

I was close to that now. May-ling's announcement was a real bombshell. The Chinese people weren't certain they wanted to give up their empress.

A Constitutional Convention was set up. As they progressed, it looked possible that Beth's grandchildren might have to give up their power.

The one thing accomplished by these actions was that it made it harder to accuse May-ling and me of being power-hungry.

Mum's comment was, "Sod'em all."

I spent a lot of time wondering how a fourteen-year-old boy from Bellefontaine, Ohio, could end up like this.

In my mind, I was still that person. However, the more I thought about it, I knew this wasn't true.

I had become the richest person on earth. Arguably the most powerful. I was married and a father. These things had to have changed me.

It had been an exciting trip, that was for certain. It was a wonder that I lived through it. I was twenty-one years old and unofficial biographers were writing about me.

Some of them were cut from whole cloth, such as the one done by that blonde that Mary spilled chocolate on. I couldn't remember her name.

Mr. Monroe from Warner Brothers at least had the courtesy of notifying me of a movie that was purporting to be of my life in the offing.

Did everyone think this was the end for me? I hoped not. I did have one curious note from Mr. Norman.

He requested that I stop by when I had a chance. He wanted to talk about continuity. That gave me some unsettling thoughts.

A bigger question was, what would I do now? Go back to school? Whatever for? Explore the solar system? There were plenty of people doing that right now.

I hated to think that I had achieved everything in life that I was going to. That from here to the grave would be one step after another.

I was growing more morose as days went by. If this was coming of age, I wanted no part of it. I wished something dramatic would happen, like a message from aliens saying that they were on their way.

Or better yet, they landed on the moon demanding people to take them to their leader. My luck, they would quickly escort them to May-ling.

None of this happened. What did happen was my daughter started to recognize me and smile. This smile was more exciting than most of my life.

Maybe I was growing up. My saga would now take a different direction. My new direction would be ensuring that Beth and her siblings were prepared for their adventures.

Money and power all paled beside family. I'm not knocking money and power; they help soften the blows.

Golf was okay, but I had proven everything there. Maybe I'll take up tennis.

And we had taken the first steps to the stars.

The End

I hope you enjoyed Rick's adventures. The ending is very much a soft landing. Rick's adventures are done for now. No promises for the future.

Ed Nelson

Sun City Center, Fl

October 29, 2022

P.S. I am starting a new series. A serious engineer is cast to an alternate universe in about 6th century Cornwall. Here is an excerpt:

Cast in Time
Chapter 1

On my deathbed, I thought of my life. Not the rapid review of it passing by my eyes but the slow, systematic review by an engineer.

I was born James Douglas Fletcher on May 28, 1918, in Logan County, Ohio, to Paul Douglas Fletcher, Junior and Janet Elizabeth Fletcher nee Rupert. Math never worked out for the marriage and birth dates, but there was a war.

I was an only child. Complications in childbirth prevented any other children.

Growing up on a small farm in Ohio gave me a taste of hard work and learning to be responsible for my actions. It took several painful trips to the woodshed, but by the time I was fourteen, I was past that.

I still don't think it was my fault the explosion was that large when I lit off the methane gas in the pile of cow manure.

Not that I didn't do rebellious things, I just didn't get caught. I smoked an entire cigarette before deciding the taste was terrible and wanted no part of it. When I inhaled deeply, the smoke liked to tear my lungs apart.

If that were what it took to look older and more worldly, I would look young and naïve.

Now beer was a different story. I loved the taste of it. I also quickly learned the price to be paid for drinking too much. Savoring the taste was better than chugging a bottle and having a hangover. One hangover was enough.

By the time I was sixteen, I had learned my way around a bra strap and other things. The great mystery of life still evaded me.

My father, Paul, had served in the Great War and returned home as a major. While doing well in the army, he had no desire to make it a career. Any career would have been limited because he wasn't in the regular army but a Plattsburg callup.

Still, he always had kind memories of the army, at least when he wasn't in the trenches. Those times weren't talked about.

My grandfather Paul Douglas Fletcher, Senior had been with Colonel Roosevelt and the Rough Riders going up Kettle Hill. That day was his only real battle in the war. He would recount the events at the drop of a hat. I could recite the story along with him.

All in all, the experiences of my father and grandfather left me with a desire to be in the army. I told my parents of my wish when I was in the ninth grade.

Dad told me if I was going to be in the army, it was best to be an officer. To achieve that, I should go to West Point. To go to West Point, I would have to have good grades, participate in school extracurricular activities, and have political backing.

Later I learned my parents, in private conversation, thought this was a phase and that I would never meet all those goals.

High school is where I demonstrated a strength of character that I held for my entire life.

I went out for football and later track and field, making both teams. Making these teams wasn't that impressive, considering the size of my rural high school.

I also joined the Chess Club because I truly loved to play, though I never got beyond expert ranking in my play.

I tried out for several school plays but wasn't an actor. My lines came across as wooden at best. When not acting, I was considered a well-spoken young man and viewed as sincere by my peers. At least, that is how I interpreted it.

Academically, I had an advantage that began to show in the ninth grade when classes became more difficult. I had what is called a photographic memory. The advantage it gave me was that every test was an open-book test.

The disadvantage was that it was like leafing through a textbook. It took time. I couldn't take a test of one hundred and fifty questions and look them all up. I still had to pay attention and learn as much as I could.

Then in a test, I would only have to look up a few items. If there was enough time when I finished, I could go back and "look up" the correct answer if I was in doubt.

One would have thought I would have gotten 100%, but human memory is funny. I would be certain I had the right answer and not look it up. Because of this, I only got 98% correct consistently, which still impressed my teachers.

I had to spend time on my work to understand it. Just because I could remember what the book said didn't mean I got it. I was considered an excellent student but not a genius.

Then there was the fact my mind was frequently on the next bra strap.

Besides my family's military background, my American History teacher was a graduate of West Point. My teacher spoke of his experiences occasionally, so I felt free to share my desires. In return, I learned that my local Congressman made the appointments in our area.

Politics became the only bone of contention between Dad and me. Dad was a staunch Wilson Democrat and the Congressman, a Republican.

I signed onto the Congressman's campaigns, knocked on doors, waved signs at street corners, and helped set up rooms for fundraisers. By doing this, I became known to the Congressman.

As with all campaign events, there were fallow periods where I had a chance to explain my desire to attend West Point. Working his campaign made it easy for the Congressman to award me the political appointment.

The upshot was that I received an appointment to attend the Military Academy at West Point upon graduation from high school. Assuming I succeeded in school, I would be in the graduating class of 1939.

While not the smartest person in the room, I was probably the hardest worker. The material I had to learn didn't need a genius. It just needed someone willing to do the work.

Work was what I was good at. I was like a bulldog in my studies. I wouldn't let go until I had mastered the material and completed my assignments.

My major was mechanical engineering. These courses started me on my lifelong love of engineering in all its forms.

While doing this, I wasn't a recluse. I made friends with my classmates, and when I was made a team leader on projects or field assignments, they followed me willingly.

One report by an instructor stated, "Students follow Cadet Fletcher because they know he will put in the work to complete the mission while taking care of his people."

I graduated seventh in my class of 960 cadets. Like many high-ranking students, I chose the Army Corps of Engineers as my first assignment. In doing this, I followed in the footsteps of such famous graduates as Robert E. Lee.

It would be best if you didn't think I was nothing but a grind in school. I gained fame when I won a bet that I could keep a pet in our barracks for one month without getting caught.

I had noticed a light bulb burned out in a closet. It was enclosed in a globe. I turned the globe into a fish tank. The goldfish lived for six weeks before I had to flush it down. I was lucky that I didn't get a nickname from that event.

Instead, they called me Slim Jim. At five foot eleven inches and one hundred and forty pounds, I did come across as skinny. You would never guess what my favorite snack was.

By the time I was a first lieutenant, I was in North Africa, building tank traps and fortifications. I received my first Bronze Star and Purple Heart there.

By the war's end, I was a major through battlefield promotions with two Bronze Stars and a Silver Star. Three Purple Hearts and the various campaign medals made me look like a serious soldier or like somebody had tossed a bowl of fruit salad my way and scored a hit. As I put it, I forgot to duck a lot but kept working anyway.

It did stick in my craw that we combat engineers couldn't wear the CIB.

After the war, I met a young lady stationed at Fort Leonard Wood. After dating for a year, I married Doris Davidson in 1948. It was the beginning of a partnership that lasted over fifty years. Our one regret was that we never had any children.

After World War II, I continued my engineering education, adding a degree in civil engineering. When Korea came along, I was back on the front lines.

This time I destroyed many bridges and then built them back up. Being a major, I didn't spend as much time at the front under fire. At least that is what I told my wife in letters home.

It still had its moments. Enough moments to receive a second Silver Star, a Distinguished Service Cross, and another Purple Heart. How was I to know that the units I was supporting bugged out and the only thing holding the North Koreans back was my unit?

It was touch and go, but an artillery barrage saved the day. That didn't happen until I had my unit dug in—handy things bulldozers. I then proceeded to round up four hundred troops, a short battalion.

I dug them in and created a salient that stopped the North Korean advance long enough for troops to be brought back into line.

I was awarded the Distinguished Service Cross for my actions during the bug-out and another battlefield promotion to lieutenant colonel.

Unlike Patton, I wasn't observed when I decked the officer leading the bug out. That was later in a bar in Seoul. I chose my moment well when a bar fight had already started.

After Korea, I spent time with the civil engineering side of the Corps of Engineers. My units built dams and levees up and down the Mississippi for the most part. I continued my education in engineering.

My wife Dory was the perfect military wife. She took the enlisted men's wives under her wing and helped with their problems, mostly by counseling and sometimes by direct intervention. Woe unto the soldier who mistreated his wife.

As I rose in rank, she grew in her poise. Now it was caring for wives of philandering captains. Those who didn't learn quickly fell by the wayside. She could chew out a major and have tea with a general's wife equally at ease.

In 1959 I was promoted to full colonel since I now had enough Time in Grade and Time in Service.

When Vietnam came along, I was given my first star. I oversaw all engineering projects in Vietnam. Now I was constructing airstrips, firebases, bridges, digging wells, and anything else the Brass could think of.

I didn't get out into the field very much anymore and didn't care. I was getting too old for that shit. Also, the troops in this war differed from the other two I had been in. There were few volunteers. Most were draftees, and many were resentful.

There was no real sense of purpose. On the occasions I got out in the field and talked to the people on the sharp end, it seemed like the Brass back in Saigon had no idea what was happening.

It was good that the army had sent me to General Officer Training, or as they called it, "Charm School". Its purpose was to teach me how to deal diplomatically with foreign governments and their military, congress, and high-ranking officers of sister services.

As I privately thought, it taught me how to say nothing, lie my ass off, and smile while doing it.

In 1970 I was promoted to Lieutenant General and Commanding Officer of the U.S. Army Corps of Engineers and given the traditional set of "Gold Castle" insignia passed down from General Douglas MacArthur.

I surrendered them in turn when I retired as I reached the forced retirement age of fifty-five in 1973.

Since I was in a specialized branch of the army, I was never under consideration for a fourth star. That was fine by me. Getting my third took more political posturing than I had the stomach for.

The only regret I had about all the awards I had been given was that I wasn't eligible for the Combat Infantry Badge. I had been under direct fire for days in three different wars. If they were shooting at you and you were shooting back should be enough to earn the award.

During my tenure in the army, I never quit my schooling. I had a Ph.D. in Mechanical Engineering and a Masters in Civil. I had so many minors I had to make a list.

I was now about to start another phase of my life, a life-changing phase.

Chapter 2

Upon retirement, we moved to Florida and started the retirement lifestyle. Golf outings, fishing, movies, and dinner with new friends.

That lasted for about six months. We both hated it. We were used to doing things. Doing nothing wasn't for us. I realized that we weren't being fair in our thinking to those who were happy with that life, but it just wasn't us.

Finances weren't a problem. My army retirement, plus our savings and stock investments, left us comfortable.

I had bought stock in technology companies like IBM and Western Electric. My wife likes what she calls people companies such as Coca-Cola and that new hamburger chain, McDonald's.

We hemmed and hawed around for months, checking things out. We finally decided to join the Peace Corps.

The initial training was interesting. It covered various technical, linguistic, cross-cultural, health, and safety, including security areas.

As far as technical, health, and safety, plus security, they immediately wanted me to stay in the U.S. as an instructor.

We wanted to go out into the field, so I declined. Linguistic training was a slog, but I got through it. Dory flew through it. What surprised me the most was the cross-cultural training.

It wasn't the African culture that gave me a problem. The program was based on comparing African ways with American ways.

I didn't have a problem with the African ways. After serving on three continents and many countries, I expected them to be different. It was what I learned about American culture that was amazing.

The culture of the American military is different than that of mainstream America. I had been in the military since I was seventeen years old.

It turned out that I had visited America but hadn't lived in it. First of all, the army is a male culture. Yes, there are women in the army, but don't kid yourself; it is a male culture. It is a physically fit culture. We cull the weaklings.

It is a culture of order and slow change. As an officer, I was used to giving orders and not having to coax people.

When I needed resources for a job, I requisitioned them. I decided in what order the requisitions would be filled at my retirement rank.

In this position, I was expected to beg, borrow, or steal what was needed.

When we finally got in-country after our three-month training, we had more lessons to learn. The Peace Corps expected us to live with our host families. In some cases, this meant sleeping on the couch.

Since we had private funds, we rented a grass shack of our own. We would eat meals with our hosts or even invite them to our place for dinner.

There were other Peace Corps Volunteers (PCV) in our area. We were by far the oldest. Most were in their early twenties.

Dory soon became the den-mother. I was treated as a senior officer, which was like our old life. It was the locals that drove me nuts.

I would work on a project to improve their farming methods, and they would sit under a tree all day long. They knew that free food would be shipped to them by the many non-governmental organizations, so why bother to work?

I couldn't convince them that the NGOs might not be around forever or that PCV people like me wouldn't be available to teach in the future.

Dory and her cadre of female PCV workers were more successful with cleanliness and sanitation. The idea of not losing so many babies appealed to the local women. The men didn't seem to care. They could always make more.

So instead of improving farming methods, we worked on a clean water supply and a sanitation system.

I'm not talking about running water in the house or an indoor privy. We ran PVC pipe from a fast-running stream to a filtration bed, then pumped it to a water tank by hand. From the tank, water could be obtained from one of several water faucets installed below the tank.

This setup gave a reliable water supply to the small village. Previously the village women would haul buckets of water from the nearest stream. The easiest place at the stream was downstream from where their few cattle grazed. The cows would go into the stream to cool off and, of course, would poop in the water.

I even saw a couple of the boys herding the cows do it the same way.

It worked fine until the water tank was empty. No one wanted to spend time or energy pumping it.

While this project was ongoing, we also built a communal privy with separate men's and women's sides.

It required a lot of digging by the PCV and pipe laying, but we had water from above the water supply running through the privy and returning it to the fast-running stream far below the water supply.

It worked fine until it stopped up. It seemed the privy was a good place to dump any unwanted items.

We had made it possible through a small door to go down and unblock it. After my third trip, I refused to go anymore. Other PCVs felt the same.

To obtain the building materials, we had to trade and barter. The Peace Corps only lent people. The local government and NGOs had to come up with money or the materials needed.

The NGOs were mostly church groups, and I finally got tired of having to attend their services in trade for the materials. Near the end, they even required me to bring so many locals to their events so they could try to convert them.

The few locals I could convince to come were teenage boys who wanted to ogle the white girls there. I didn't care about the race issue. It was the cultural differences that could cause problems.

I finally just started paying for the materials out of pocket. After two years of backbreaking labor, we had a water system that wasn't used because no one wanted to pump water and a blocked-up sewer system.

Despite requests and even a little pressure, Dory and I decided the Peace Corps wasn't for us. When we got home, I made another discovery.

The Peace Corps would occasionally send camera crews around to film our work-in-progress. Most pictures were staged with other volunteers directing smiling natives.

The natives were smiling because the Peace Corps paid them an extortionate rate to work that day.

I saw the result one evening of a PSA being run on late-night TV. They were recruiting for the Peace Corps and using retired Lt. General James Fletcher as a role model.

To say I was upset would be putting it mildly.

When interviewed on a local TV station, I was asked about my African experience.

"I learned that the saying, 'You can lead a horse to water, but can't make him drink,' is absolutely true."

"If you are disillusioned with your Peace Corps work, why are you allowing them to use you in their ads?"

"I was never asked. I hadn't read my contract close enough to know the corps didn't need my permission."

"So, will you and your wife be going back?"

"We are done. It isn't the Peace Corps people who are the problem. It is those who won't help themselves."

The Peace Corps had been trying to get me to sign for another two years. After that interview, they quit calling.

Now Dory and I were back to where we had started. We were both fifty-eight years old and had to figure out what to do.

While waiting for something to come up, I went back for some more engineering courses at a local college. I was halfway through my first semester when it hit me.

I would become a professional student. Why not spend my time doing something I loved? I applied to several of the major engineering schools. All of them accepted me.

I chose MIT, where I would be a student for the next thirty years. We bought a house within walking distance of campus. Dory joined several women's groups and was always on the go.

I earned Ph.D.s in Mechanical, Civil, and Geo-Technical and Masters in Chemical and Electrical Engineering.

I had majors in Manufacturing, Material Science, Transport, Optical, and Mining Metallurgical.

I had minors in Aerospace, Thermal, Paper, Agricultural Processes, Structural, Water Resources, Architecture, Power, Electrical, Petroleum, Geological, and Ceramics.

That sounds like a lot but considering how many prerequisite courses I didn't have to repeat, it wasn't a heavy load, just consistent yearly.

I was written up in many journals as the most educated engineer in the world. I tried to remind everyone that I had practical experience in the army, but I should be considered a new grad for everything else. Full of book learning but no use until I gained field experience.

I enjoyed learning for the sake of learning. It was much better than having some son of a bitch trying to kill you. The young reporters didn't get that either.

By the time I was eighty-eight, I had enough trouble getting around that I quit going to school. MIT surprised me by throwing a going-away party. They also presented me with an honorary degree with a Ph.D. in Professional Studenting.

All in good fun. I was sad as I knew this was my last run in life.

Dory's health had deteriorated, and she had to be put in a nursing home. I visited her every day for two years until I showed up one morning, and they told me she had passed an hour before.

Soon after my health went downhill. I blamed it on a broken heart. I was admitted to a facility and lived there for the past two years.

One evening I relived my life almost scene by scene. I realized it was time.

As I faded away, my last thought was, "So much wonderful knowledge wasted, never to be used."

Back Matter

Visit my webpage at http://enelsonauthorcom

If you want information on having Janet E. Rupert edit your fiction project, email:

janeteditorrupert@gmail.com[1]

Other books by Ed Nelson **The Richard Jackson Saga**

Book 1 The Beginning

Book 2 Schooldays

Book 3 Hollywood

Book 4 In the Movies

Book 5 Star to Deckhand

Book 6 Surfing Dude

Book 7 Third Time is a Charm

Book 8 Oxford University

Book 9 Cold War

Book 10 Taking Care of Business

Book 11 Interesting Times

Book 12 Escape from Siberia

Book 13 Regicide

Book 14 What's Under, Down Under?

Book 15 The Lunar Kingdom

Book 16 First Steps

In the Richard Jackson World

Mary, Mary

Stand-Alone Story

Ever and Always

Cast in Time Series

Book 1: Baron

Book 2: Baron of the Middle Counties

Book 3: Count

Book 4: Earl

Book 5: Earl of the Marches

Did you love *First Steps*? Then you should read *Baron* by Ed Nelson!

An engineer finds himself in an alternate reality, Cornwall in the year 715 A.D. A retired lieutenant general, former head of the Army Corp of Engineers, has led a full life as a decorated veteran of World War II, Korea, and Viet Nam. His love of engineering has him taking university courses his entire life. When his health falters, and he can no longer continue his education, MIT awards him an honorary Ph.D. in Professional Studenting. After a long illness, he lies dying. His last thought is, "What a waste of such wonderful knowledge." As he fades to black, the fun begins. He awakens in the body of a young Baron. He is to build a modern civilization without being burned as a witch!

www.ingramcontent.com/pod-product-compliance
Lightning Source LLC
Chambersburg PA
CBHW070308260626
47160CB00003B/772